VILLIANOUS

LOU WILHAM

Midnight Tide
PUBLISHING

ALSO BY LOU WILHAM

The people who make mistakes. The people learning who they are one day at a time. The constantly evolving.

This one is to you.

AUTHOR'S NOTE

Please note that this book contains issues of misgendering, ableism, discrimination, and violence. Please take care of yourself.

A VILLAINOUS HEROICS BOOK

VILLAINOUS

LOU WILHAM

CHAPTER ONE

AFTER WEEKS OF TRACKING THE VILLAIN ALL OVER THE CITY, IT had finally come down to this—the last big chase.

Below, drenched in a dense summer rain, the city splashed on as if nothing at all had changed. As if Jericho wasn't on the verge of the biggest break her career had ever seen. Above, the sky lit in another harsh crack of lightning, flashing over the rooftops and setting everything into sharp relief. Jericho could see her breath as it turned to steam in the air. It had been an hour. An hour of waiting. An hour of crouching there on that damned rooftop, just watching.

Her sources said the villain would be here tonight. That he'd decided to break into a data bank before the company moved their servers in the morning. Whatever the villain was looking for, it would be here, and tonight was the last night he'd be able to get to it before it disappeared into an undisclosed location that would no doubt take months to track down again. Now was his last chance, and he would come. Jericho knew it. All she needed to do was wait.

So wait she did. Until the soft thud of a door being opened outward against its building perked up her well-trained ears. Looking down, her green eyes narrowed on a lone figure, and a soft growl curled her lips over elongated canines.

"Well, well, well. Come all alone, have we?" Jericho murmured to herself.

At his quick glance to see if anyone was around, the villain's dark hair fell in stark contrast across his pale fox mask. His shoulders seemed to loosen when he saw that no one had stopped to pay him any mind. The cars still buzzed along the street. A couple walked by on the opposite side-walk, oblivious. And otherwise, the city of Mythikos moved on as if nothing were amiss.

"That's it. Relax. No one's looking," Jericho cooed softly. Her legs ached from being in place for so long, muscles twitching to run, to chase, to hunt the moment the villain made his move. As if he'd heard her, the villain looked up. Jericho froze. If she didn't know any better, she'd say he'd seen her. But . . . how could he? She'd perched herself all the way across the street, in the shadow of a taller building. Even with her gleaming armor, she was hidden. Still, the curling smile of that white mask seemed to widen. Then, in a flash, the villain ducked into the alley alongside the data bank and disappeared. "Shit."

Gloved hands deftly grabbed one of the glass flasks at her hip. Uncorking it, she took a quick swig. Her eyes glowed brighter, vision sharpening in the dim light of the city to home in on the figure in the dank alley. The villain climbed up a fire escape, only just visible because of the white mask. A smirk twitched on her lips. No one could outpace her on the rooftops.

The villain stepped onto the roof, giving Jericho a better view of his long coat and well-pressed suit. The eyes of the mask, their outlines gleaming red in the light, trained on Jericho once more. He lifted one darkly gloved hand—

Jericho jerked back, hackles rising in defense—and waved cheerfully at her.

"Cheeky little fucker," Jericho snarled, but her inner wolf rumbled low, amused at the obvious challenge.

Then the chase was on. The villain turned to take off across the closely cropped rooftops of Mythikos. Jericho raced after him, her feet quiet and breaths even as she kept pace. The rain made things harder but not impossible.

"Gotcha," Jericho muttered when her eyes fell on one of the footbridges that connected two buildings. Boots landed softly on the roof, only skidding a little as she ran across, her sights set on the villain the whole time. He was slowing down, almost like he was giving her time to catch up. No. That couldn't be right. He probably just wasn't used to running along slick surfaces.

"No use running!" Jericho shouted after the villain.

The man skittered up a nearby fire escape with ease.

One building led onto the next and then the next, until their wild chase took them out to the city limits. Here the lights were warmer and the buildings lower. Here at least there would be fewer civilians to get in the way. Jericho was thankful for that. The next building was the last for at least a block. A dead end. The villain skidded to a halt at the edge of it, turning to Jericho with not a hair out of place—though his chest heaved with exertion.

"That's right. You're out of places to run. May as well give up now, *Dusk*." Jericho let the moniker curl off her tongue as if it were a dirty word. She'd thought it was a stupid name for a villain when she'd first heard it, and that opinion hadn't changed. She pulled a pair of cuffs from her belt—*Wait*. One glittering eye, tucked behind the mask, closed and reopened. "Did you just fucking *wink* at me?" she asked, incredulous. "Who the fuck does that?"

Dusk lifted his hands.

Jericho fell into a defensive position, already twitching for the two long katana strapped to her back.

"Easy," Dusk said, holding up his gloved hands in a placating motion. Then he pulled off the crisp white fox mask to reveal brown skin littered with freckles that covered a pert nose and high aristocratic cheekbones.

"Sol?" Jericho's arms fell limply at her sides. *How could—?* No. Sol was gone. He'd died. Years ago. *This . . . this can't be—*

"Oh, Lettie." His fingers moved, forming the words in gestures that Jericho recognized immediately—sign language. A smile split that face, showing off buck teeth and a dimple on the right cheek. Just like Sol. So much like Sol it ached. Jericho's fingers twitched to reach out to him, but she forced them to stay at her side. "You're telling me you've been chasing me for the better part of a month and didn't realize it was me all along? Honestly, I'm offended. Did our games of tag mean nothing to you?" His hands moved gracefully, dancing around the words. A strand of teal-striped hair slipped into his dark eyes, just as it always had since the day Sol had gotten his hair cut short. The color was the telltale sign of a banshee.

"What the fuck?" Jericho signed back, fingers moving in jerky, unpracticed movements. It'd been too long. She felt clumsy.

A soft chortle left Dusk—Sol? "Ah, as well spoken as ever," Sol said along with the movement of his fingers. "Now, are you going to take me in or what? Because if not, I've got other stuff I could be doing." He gestured over his shoulder as if he had someplace to be.

There was a brief, silly, impetuous moment where Jericho considered not cuffing the idiot and just letting him go. She'd tell him to skip town and never come back. But she squashed the thought as soon as it came. She was a hero, and Sol was an Unseelie causing trouble. A villain. With a flick of her hand, the cuffs latched onto Sol's wrists, and Jericho twisted her hand in the long chain that connected them to herself to keep Sol from jerking them away.

"You're not going to like what comes next," she warned.

Sol shrugged.

Jericho tapped the spot where her jaw met her ear, activating a little communicator on the lobe. "Hey. Colette Jericho here. I've got Dusk. I need a car at . . . " She looked around for street signs and huffed when she saw none.

"We're almost to the intersection of Forest and Gold," Sol supplied helpfully. His tone was tinted with an amused smile.

"Forest and Gold," Jericho repeated, then tapped her jaw again to end the communication. "You keep your mouth shut."

Sol rolled his eyes. "If I wanted to use my Voice, I'd have used it by now," he signed with small, half-formed motions, words cut short by the cuffs on his wrists. But he kept his lips pressed firmly together.

Jericho didn't respond. She wasn't afraid of Sol, but she knew the damage he could do with his Voice if he decided to. She'd seen more than once what was left when a banshee wailed: rubble.

A car sped up the street, sirens blaring and lights reflecting off the darkness of closed shop windows. Jericho jerked the chain in her hand, dragging Sol—no, Dusk along behind her. If he wanted to act like a villain, she'd use his moniker. Off to their right, a door that looked to lead down into the building waited. She pulled a charm from her belt, waving it in front of the knob, and the door sprung open to reveal barely lit steps.

"Go." Jericho shoved Dusk down, not caring if he couldn't see in the dark as well as she could. He stumbled forward but made no complaint.

The car hummed lightly on the curb, waiting for them.

Jericho opened the door and pushed her hostage into the back seat before climbing into the front. Without waiting for instructions from Jericho, the car pulled itself back out onto the street and buzzed its way toward Spring Hill Hold.

●

No words passed between them. And when they arrived at Spring Hill Hold, two extra-large robotic K.N.I.G.H.T. units came to the car and escorted Dusk inside and away from Jericho. Which was fine with her. She had paperwork to do anyway, and a debrief to handle. She didn't have time to see Dusk through processing, and Jericho didn't owe him that.

It was a while later—after Jericho had stripped off her hero armor to don a more masculine, loose-fitting black T-shirt, and signed "Colette Jericho" over and over and over—when the soft tap of something landed on Jericho's desk. His eyes, which up to that point had been trained on the screen in front of him, flicked to a little device no bigger than his thumbnail. "What's that?"

The K.N.I.G.H.T. stared at him for a moment with blank, backlit eyes as it processed his question before answering, "Miss Jeri—"

"Mister," Jericho corrected. "Or just 'Jericho' would be better." And it would be; it was easier that way. Mister, Miss —they were titles that just got people confused when he suddenly didn't feel like one or the other anymore. "Jericho" worked best. Especially for the androids, who didn't under-stand gender to begin with and sure as fuck didn't under-stand it when someone was fluid about it. "I thought I'd had that programmed into all of you by now, but we must have missed one. Or maybe there was a patch." He drummed his fingers on his desk thoughtfully.

"Jericho," the bot amended. "This is what the suspect was stealing."

"Okay. But what is it?" Agitation laced Jericho's tone. His fingers twitched toward the device, assuming it was safe. The K.N.I.G.H.T. units had been programmed to protect people, like the knights of old once had. It was unlikely that one of them would drop a dangerous device onto Jericho's desk. At least not without warning him of its danger first.

"It's a thumb drive," a chirping voice answered. A two-toned head poked out from around the monstrosity of an android. "Old bit of tech, really. I don't even think we have the means to plug it into anything anymore."

"Plug it in?" Jericho asked blankly. What the hell did that even mean?

"Yeah." Ildri nodded, patting the android on the shoulder with a soft metal *tink*. "You can head back to your post, Ratcher."

The robot didn't even bother nodding. It just spun on its wheel and headed back the way it had come.

"You're not supposed to name them." Jericho scowled, his eyes still trained on the—what had Ildri called it? Thumb drive?

Ildri shrugged, a strand of garishly blue hair flopping into her face as her wings twitched behind her. "There's no rule that says that."

"But the captain asked you not to."

Ildri blinked at Jericho, unbothered.

"Right." Jericho sighed and decided to just move on with things. It'd be easier. He could talk in circles around Ildri's logic all day and get absolutely nowhere. He was too tired for it tonight. "What *is* it?"

"Old school information storage." Ildri smiled. "The humans invented them back in the day, before everything went into the cloud. I haven't seen one in . . . " She tapped a spindly finger against her cheek thoughtfully. "Oh, a couple hundred years or so. They were quite the thing when I was at university."

"You went to—Wait. Never mind. I don't care." Jericho shook his head. "Just tell me how to find out what he put on it."

Ildri pouted, lips turning down at the corners as she brushed a neon strand of pink hair back from her face. She'd clearly been gearing up to regale him with some story of the dark ages of technology, and he'd spoiled her fun. Too bad. "We don't."

"We don't."

"No. We don't. USB ports are a thing of the past, my friend. Have been for at least a hundred years. They went the way of princes and princesses. I doubt we even have anything in the basement that has a port left on it. And even if we did, by some miracle, it probably wouldn't boot up. So, yeah, no, we don't. But isn't it cool?! I mean, who even knew these things still existed!" Ildri's words left her at a mile a minute, hammering at Jericho's ears in a disgustingly cheerful manner. It built like pressure behind his eyes.

"Then how the fuck did he get information *onto* it?" Jericho rubbed at his temples, taking a deep breath to hold the headache at bay.

"Magic."

"Magic?"

"Magic."

"Can we use magic to get the information off of it?" Jericho pressed hopefully.

"Nope!" Ildri chirped.

Jericho ground his teeth together to keep from screaming at the tiny pixie. He took a deep breath. In through his nose, out through his teeth. Calm. "Why not?"

"Oh. Because it's encrypted, of course. Unless we know

what spell he used to encrypt it, we won't be able to decrypt it without corrupting the data to the point of it being unusable." She sounded far too delighted with this fact.

"So . . . What do I do?" Jericho glared at the slick black device, and it seemed to wink back at him—just as its owner had.

"I guess you get the spell from him. We'll only get one shot at this. If I try to break it myself, that thing will probably melt."

"Fuck," Jericho said, more to himself than to the pixie, who was bouncing on the balls of her feet. "I need to go down to interrogation."

He rubbed at the bridge of his nose. He'd thought perhaps he could just let Dusk rot down there and not have to bother with him ever again. Jericho could pretend he hadn't just dragged his ex-best friend—ex-boyfriend? Whatever they'd been before Soliel had thrown away his chances on the hero exam all those years ago—down to the hold. He could forget the guilt that had lingered in the back of his mind for years now, spoiling all his other relationships and closing him off to the world around him. He could . . . He could move on.

"You better hurry up. They're about to move him to Evening Isle."

"What?" Jericho jerked up, chair clattering into the desk behind him. "What do you mean they're about to move him?"

Ildri shrugged. "Captain said he's too dangerous to keep around here."

Jericho took quick steps around his desk.

"Wait. Where are you going?"

"I'm going to stop his transfer."

"Good luck with that," Ildri called after him.

●

SOMEHOW, by sheer force of will—and his loud mouth, prob-ably—Jericho had stopped Dusk's transfer to Evening Isle. He'd spent days calling in favors, making a nuisance of himself, and refusing to take no for an answer until the order for transfer had been halted.

Although he'd known it was what he wanted to do —*needed* to do—the question remained: Why? It wasn't out of some misplaced sense of loyalty, or the feeling that Jericho owed his . . . whatever Soliel was to him, anything. But what exactly the reason was, he didn't know. He supposed maybe it was the idea of Soliel locked away in a damp, dark cell without windows and left there to wither into nothing that had spurred him on. The image of Sol's glittering brown eyes fading into a dull, lifeless gray, sucked dry by the dark-magic-lined walls of the island prison that housed only the most damning of Mythikos' villains sent a shiver down Jeri-cho's spine. The only way to stay warm was to fight.

"He's not talking to anyone," a voice drifted up from the desk behind Jericho. Erling, the lone Griffin on Mythikos' Erahil hero division.

"Who?" Jericho asked, continuing to type away at his report, studiously ignoring the thumb drive that was still where Ildri had left it days ago.

"Dusk. They've had him down in interrogation since you stopped his transfer, but he won't talk to anyone."

"He'll talk eventually. They all do."

"I dunno. He seems pretty tight-lipped. Hasn't even asked for representation."

"Have they brought down a translator?" The words slipped from Jericho's lips before he could stop them. Before he could remind himself that what happened to Dusk now that Jericho had saved him from the Isle was no longer his business. He didn't care. Dusk was a villain, and he'd get what he deserved.

"A what?"

Jericho jerked around in his seat to frown at the white-haired man behind him. "A translator. Dusk is a banshee."

"So?"

"So, he's deaf." Erling's eyes widened in sudden understanding. "Oh, for fuck's sake. Do I have to do everything around here?" Jericho swiveled back around, pressing a few buttons on his keyboard till a video chat popped up on the screen.

"What is it, Jericho?" the captain asked gruffly.

"Bring in a sign language translator for Dusk. That might get him talking."

The captain snorted, rolling his eyes. "I'll see what I can do." Then he hung up.

"Asshole," Jericho muttered under his breath. He grabbed the leather jacket from the back of his chair as he stood.

"Where are you going?"

Jericho didn't bother to answer. He was not going to the interrogation cells. He was *not*. He had done enough for Dusk as it was, called in favors he'd been saving, burned bridges he'd never get back. And then Jericho had unofficially taken himself off the case because a not-so-small part of him hated Dusk for who he'd become. For the side he'd chosen. Let Dusk sit down there until he decided to talk. Jericho breathed deeply when the cool evening air hit his skin. He inhaled the smells of the city.

The moon shone brightly against the tops of the buildings, waxing gibbous. Jericho rolled his eyes at the scrambling of his inner wolf, itching for a fight, for a run, anything. If he wasn't careful, that beastie would take him exactly where he didn't want to go—to Dusk. He heeded the call to run instead and headed home.

CHAPTER TWO

FOR A WEEK, JERICHO HAD AVOIDED THIS. SHE'D WALKED PAST the stairs that led down to the interrogation cells and didn't make eye contact with them. She'd ignored the looks from her coworkers as she became steadily more agitated. A week with no new information meant her report sat half-finished, and *that* bothered her far more than any other part of this fucked-up situation.

So, here she was, doing the thing she told herself she wouldn't do. Boots trod softly on the stairs as Jericho made her way down to the interrogation cells.

A young man slumped against the wall outside the interrogation room, fidgeting with his phone.

Jericho could have been kind. She could have cleared her throat to alert the guard to her presence. But instead, she just narrowed her eyes on him.

"Bracken, what are you doing?" she asked, voice sharp.

"Jericho!" Bracken jerked his head up, dropping his phone with a harsh clatter. He crouched quickly to pick up the device, tucking it into his back pocket with a guilty expression.

Jericho shook her head. "Just don't let the captain catch you at it."

"What are—" Bracken cleared his throat when his words came out too high and nervous. "What are you doing down here, sir?"

"I'm going to talk to the prisoner. Isn't that obvious?"

"You can't—" Bracken rushed, reaching to stop Jericho before she could touch the scanner just outside the door. Jericho saw Dusk perk up on the other side of the glass, his eyes narrowing in interest as he took in the scene. "Sir."

"Why not?" Jericho tilted her head, not taking her eyes off Dusk's assessing dark gaze. They had certainly piqued Dusk's interest. Jericho could see that dimple on his freckled cheek growing the longer the exchange went on, amusement dancing across his face.

"The captain said all interrogations were to cease until a translator can be procured."

Ah. That was why no new information had come to Jericho's desk. The captain was keeping people away until he could find someone willing to translate for a banshee. Jericho knew well enough that it wouldn't be hard to find someone who could sign amongst their ranks; there was more than one species of fae who wound up deaf or mute from their abilities. The issue was that Dusk was a banshee, and they were, by nature, terrifying, with screams capable of leveling entire city blocks and making one's brain melt out through their ears. Far scarier than any siren who could wiggle their way into one's subconscious.

"Everyone is too scared he'll attack them," Jericho murmured.

Bracken wilted. A look of shame flickered over his own face, but he didn't argue.

"Well, I don't need a fucking translator. I can sign just

fine." Jericho's fingers moved in quick, deft motions along to her words.

"Good to see your pronunciation is still sloppy at best!" Dusk shouted from inside the room, a slow smile splitting his lips.

Jericho lifted one hand to flick him off.

"Ah, but that one never did give you trouble. Did it?" Dusk laughed, eyes glittering in delight.

"Banshees can hear all right if you don't scream at them. It's mostly the higher volumes and pitches he has trouble with. And he was always pretty good at lipreading. Honestly, it's like they don't teach basic fae physiology in schools anymore." Jericho scoffed, then turned back to Bracken. "They took his hearing aids?"

Bracken merely nodded before adding, "We weren't—"

He was cut off by another delighted shout from inside the room. "Awww. You're no fun, Lettie! I had a good thing going there."

Lettie. It'd been so long since someone had used that name. Dusk had said it the other night too, but Jericho had been too caught up in everything to notice. Once, that name had made her laugh and smile. Once, it had made her feel warm and cared for. She wasn't sure how she felt about it anymore. Jericho's eyes jerked back to Dusk, who was slumped back in his chair, arms stretched across the table in front of him lazily, his lower lip poking out in a pout. *Little shit.*

"They were worried about a communication device," Jericho finished for Bracken with a scoff. "I know all that, it came across my desk. Now let me in there."

"Yes, sir." Bracken hurried to press his palm to the scanner, and the door opened with a soft whoosh. "And sir, be careful. Without the glass between you, you'll have nothing to protect yourself from his Voice."

"Worry about yourself, Bracken. If he's going to attack anyone, it's going to be the guy standing outside his room."

Bracken's face paled, and he backed away from the open door. Jericho didn't spare him another glance before entering. The door shut behind her softly.

"Soliel." Jericho spoke softly as she approached, sitting in the acrylic chair across from the villain. She arranged the long sweater she'd thrown on over her leggings that morning in a motion that was distinctly *not* a fidget. Her eyes flicked over the man across the table from her, taking in the way the muddy-gray jumpsuit fit Dusk a little too tightly in places.

Dusk smiled softly at the name, as if perhaps he hadn't heard it in a long time.

"What happened to you?" Jericho continued to keep her volume low but her words clear so that Dusk could hear her. If they were going to get anywhere, they had to be able to understand one another.

A roll of the eyes told Jericho that Dusk wasn't going to make this as easy as she'd hoped. Some stupid, sentimental part of herself had thought she could fall back on their old relationship to get everything she wanted from him. But this wasn't Sol. Not anymore. He was Dusk now, and he had a list of crimes as long as Jericho's arm.

Dusk didn't wait to start on his diatribe. "Every hero needs a villain, right?" The words fell from his lips, accompanied by his fingers as he spoke. He kept his own voice low, matching Jericho's volume. "Isn't that what you used to say? Remember? You always made me play the bad guy, or the damsel in distress. I was never allowed to be the hero; that was your job. Well, here I am, Lettie. Your self-made villain."

Lettie. It didn't feel as uncomfortable as Jericho thought it might for her to hear that name again. Dusk had been the only one she'd ever allowed to call her that. A sign of their friendship, their closeness, when Jericho couldn't express her emotions any other way. But now there was no closeness. Still, the name left her feeling . . . nostalgic. For a life that was long gone, back when things had seemed simpler. When her parents had been there to patch her up every time she fell on the playground. Before . . . Before . . . Before the guilt had settled in and broken everything.

Jericho stared at Dusk for a long time, her eyebrow twitching in irritation and disbelief. "Seriously? That's what you're going with? My best friend never let me play hero when we were little, so I decided to become a villain? That's the most cliché shit I've ever heard."

Dusk held the look for a moment longer before snickering, as if they were both in on some age-old joke. Maybe they were. But it didn't feel like it would have all those years ago. This felt brittle, strained. "Nah."

"Then what?" Jericho blew out a breath, rustling the loose blond strands fluttering around the opposite side of her undercut.

Dusk made a noncommittal noise in the back of this throat. His fingers moved over the cool acrylic tabletop he was chained to. They'd left him enough chain to move his hands in the familiar intricate patterns but not enough to stand. How long had he been sitting there?

"What's on the thumb drive?" Jericho pressed on, vowing not to think further about what Dusk had gotten himself into. That was his problem, not hers.

Dusk lifted his eyes, a smile unlike any Jericho had ever seen on his face before—cold, calculating—curling his lips. Suddenly, that dimple on his cheek didn't look quite so charming. Despite the smile, he remained silent, lips and fingers unmoving.

"Damn it, Sol! Tell me!" Jericho growled, jaw clenching around the words as her anger flared.

"What's that? Can't hear you." Dusk leaned forward so he could hold a hand up to his ear.

With a deep inhale, Jericho lowered her voice again, although she couldn't keep the heat out of her tone. "You should be thanking me, you know. If it weren't for me, you'd have been shipped off to Evening Isle already. Locked away and forgotten until the day you died."

Dusk snorted, the manacles on his wrist jingling as his fingers started moving again. He let his fingers do the talking, moving in slow, sarcastic motions that Jericho recognized all too well. "Ah yes, ever the hero. Just had to prove that one more time, didn't you? Well, thank you, Lettie, for everything. Thank you for leaving me behind when you went off to be a hero. For forgetting about me. For locking me in a cage where the only sun I see is through a two-by-two-foot window. But hey . . . at least I'm not withering away on an island somewhere, right? You're a real sport."

"Hey!" Jericho shouted, her own fingers working along to her angry words to make sure Dusk would understand her. "Don't get shitty with me. You did this to yourself. This was your choice. Actions have consequences, Sol."

"Yeah, they do. But I guess Seelie don't have to think about that, do they?" Dusk asked, fingers moving slowly, as if he wanted every word to hurt. To chip away at something inside of Jericho.

It didn't work. Jericho held firm. "What's that supposed to mean?"

"Why don't you ask your captain? I'm sure they'd be more than happy to enlighten you on all of the 'choices' I've made that led me here. They probably have a file on me somewhere," Dusk signed, still refusing to speak to Jericho with his voice, and shrugged. "And while you're at it, take a trip down memory lane. Try to think of how your actions have affected others."

"What?" Jericho spat.

"Actions have consequences, hero." With that, Dusk lowered his hands to the table and looked away from her.

Jericho was being dismissed. She didn't appreciate the connotation that Dusk was the one in charge, but she didn't have the patience to sit there any longer.

"I'll be back."

Dusk didn't look away from the window, but he did speak. "Whatever tickles your fancy, hero."

Jericho didn't bother hiding her irritation as she stormed out of the room. Nor did she pay any mind to Bracken when the young man called after her. No. She didn't stop until she was outside the captain's door, hand poised to knock. She and the captain had never been friends, or even on good terms. That tended to happen when someone got promoted simply because of their lineage. And Bim Oakfur had most certainly risen through the ranks as quickly as he had because he'd been the previous captain's snot-nosed brat.

Even still, he was Jericho's superior. So, she took a moment to compose herself, swallowing the rage that threatened to take over and force a shift into the wolf. It wouldn't do to wolf out right there in the middle of the bullpen. Not after all those anger management seminars she'd been forced to attend. After a quick count to ten, Jericho rapped her knuckles on the door.

"Enter," the nasally voice of the leprechaun called. The door opened with a soft creak, and there behind the desk sat Bim Oakfur, looking for all the world like a petty king ruling his kingdom, chin tilted back and upturned nose in the air as he looked down it at Jericho. Jericho swallowed down an annoyed snarl.

"Captain." She bowed her head in a respectful nod.

"What can I do for you, Jericho?" Oakfur spoke in a tone

that sounded benevolent, like anything he did would be a favor.

Jericho ground her teeth to keep from saying something she might regret. Her plan was to request Soliel's file and get some answers on what had happened to her friend over the years. She wasn't going to get personal, because this wasn't personal, this was her job. Jericho was going to remain completely professional.

But what came out of her mouth was, "Why isn't Dusk wearing his binder?"

"She's on suicide watch."

That was it. The rage returned full force, gripping Jericho's insides and making her nails grow long and sharp against her palms. "First off, Dusk is a *he*—"

"He," Oakfur amended. Although he didn't sound apologetic. His dull brown eyes flicked over Jericho's twitching features with interest. The sick bastard was getting off on pushing Jericho to see what her feelings were about this whole thing. She was being tested, and she didn't like it. Fuck. "Never formally filed a change of gender form. In the eyes of the law, Soliel Tsuki is female."

"I don't give a flying fuck what the law says. Sol is now, and always has been, male. When you talk about him, when anyone talks about him, they will do so correctly. Or do we want the Prisoner Rights people involved in this?" Jericho hissed, a knowing look in her eyes. It was a low blow, a threat that she'd probably pay for later, but she didn't care. "We all know what a pain in the ass they can be."

Oakfur's eyes narrowed in annoyance, and for a moment, Jericho thought perhaps there would be some kind of retaliation, but then he blinked and moved on. "Very well. His binder will be returned to him. Was there something else you needed, Jericho?"

"Yes. I want his full file. I need everything we have on

Soliel Tsuki and his alias Dusk, from birth till his recent capture. If I'm going to be interrogating him, I need to know his mental state."

Oakfur raised a brow in question but nodded. "It will be on your desk by this afternoon. And since you've taken an interest in him, we want the location of his lab facility. We believe he may have more information stored there, plus whatever harmful tech he's been working on. All of which will need to be recovered and neutralized. I expect results, Jericho."

"Yes, captain," Jericho muttered through a clenched jaw. Then she turned on her heel to head back to her desk. She'd worry about the ways Oakfur would punish her for her outburst later. For now, she had more important things to do.

Like tracking down Mrs. Tsuki.

CHAPTER THREE

TRACKING DOWN ADELIA TSUKI, DUSK'S MOTHER, TOOK Jericho a trip on two separate train lines—the Opal and the Ruby—downtown to their old neighborhood.

Ilygroth wasn't so different from how he remembered it. Perhaps things were a little more dilapidated than when he'd been sixteen, but some of that might have been the rose-colored glasses through which all adults remembered their childhood home. It was good that his parents had gotten out when they had, moving far from Mythikos to a small town in the country where they could rest and allow their wolf instincts freer rein. Even if their leaving had been because of the distance already present between himself and them.

Would Mrs. Tsuki have done the same? She was human, but humans moved too. Especially after Soliel had "died," what would have been left for her in Ilygroth?

Jericho's feet moved without thought—he'd walked this path hundreds of times—from the train station to his house, then to Soliel's. He could make it there with his eyes closed. Which left his mind plenty of time to wander back to when things had been simpler. When life had been easy.

.   .   .

"*RACE YOU TO YOUR HOUSE!*" *Soliel shouted, fingers moving along to the words. His tiny light-up sneakers pounded against the pavement, sparkling in the fading summer light.*

"First one there gets all the pudding!" Jericho let out a whoop of excitement, his own shoes padding along more lightly as he ran after his friend.

"No cheating." Sol's breath came in harder pants as he pushed himself to run faster, trying to keep up with Jericho.

Jericho rolled his eyes but didn't argue. Instead, he picked up his pace, pulling away from Soliel.

"You heard me! No cheating!" Sol scowled at him, freckled face twisting up into unhappiness. "Don't use your wolf."

"I heard you, damn it! I'll be fair," Jericho promised. He was always fair, at least with Soliel. The other children he couldn't care less about, but Sol was his best and only friend. And one day, they'd be a part of the Hero Alliance together. They were a team. They would always be a team.

ONLY . . .

Only that had never happened. Ten years later, they'd both applied to apprentice with heroes, and it had been Jericho who had received an acceptance letter, and Soliel who was rejected.

Jericho's gut twisted in guilt. But that hadn't been how he'd felt at the time, had it? Not guilty. No. He'd been—*shit*—he'd felt justified. Like he really was better than Soliel, despite all the promises they'd made as children. And he'd been ashamed of himself for the things he'd felt for Soliel. For . . . for loving Soliel as he had when Soliel was a failure. A nothing. A nobody.

Jericho's steps fell heavily on the stairs of an old apartment building. They were badly in need of repair, creaking with every shift in his weight. And then he was faced with that thin plywood door. Apartment number 403—the gilded numbers had tarnished through the years, and the three hung upside down from a single nail—but the door was still the same. The memory of it, of the last time he'd knocked on this door, stung deep under the skin where he couldn't rub it away.

"SOL! Sol! Sol! Damn it, Soliel! Open up!" Jericho's fist hammered on the flimsy wooden door of the Tsuki residence in time with every word. His heart was pounding in his chest, rabbit fast. "Don't make me break this doo—"

The door flung open to reveal Mrs. Tsuki, all dark hair and eyes, just like her son. The only things she was missing were Soliel's freckles and a strip of teal hair hanging in her eyes. Jericho had always assumed the freckles had come from Soliel's father, but neither of them ever found out if that was true since Sol's father had died before he was born, and Mrs. Tsuki hadn't kept any pictures.

"Sorry, J, Soliel isn't really up to playing right now," Mrs. Tsuki said softly.

"But I got my letter!" Jericho shouted, pressing past her even as she tried to stop him from heading into the living room. "I got it, and I want to show—" Jericho's words died in his throat when he caught sight of Soliel's hunched form on the couch. A blanket was wrapped tightly around him, his long hair limp over his ears and hanging in his eyes. But it wasn't that that stopped Jericho dead. No. It was the shreds of cream paper scattered on the old coffee table. In spite of Soliel's best efforts, the gold embossed seal of the Hero Alliance still glittered ominously in the light—intact. "Sol?"

Soliel didn't lift his head to look at Jericho, he just remained focused on the rough shapes of torn paper. "You got in, didn't you?"

he asked. Dead. His voice was dead. It lacked the richness and warmth of Soliel's deep well of emotion that seemed to color everything he did.

"You didn't," was Jericho's answer. He didn't have to ask; he knew. And he felt something in himself being shredded to little bits just like that damn letter. But it didn't hurt. Not yet. Maybe it would have been better if it had. Maybe then Soliel's next words wouldn't have sliced through him.

"They don't allow Unseelie into the Alliance, you know that." Soliel's words were condescending, and Jericho felt them settle like a weight on his chest, pressing all the air from his lungs. "You should know better, Lettie. I'm evil."

Evil. The word slapped Jericho in the face, tore at his heart, and he did the first thing he always did when he was hurt: he lashed out. "Or maybe you're just weak," he spat.

Soliel didn't say anything. He didn't even flinch. He just remained staring at those scraps of paper. Like if he stared long enough, the ink on them would shift to read something else.

"You didn't try hard enough," Jericho accused. Because that had to be it. There was no other reason Soliel wouldn't have gotten in. He was strong. He was good. He was kind! All he'd ever wanted was to help people. He'd make the perfect hero. And they'd make the perfect team. Always there for each other. Always having each other's backs. Who would have Jericho's back now? No one. "You slacked off."

They were silent for a long time, and when Soliel finally spoke, it wasn't with his voice, it was with his fingers.

"Get out," he signed tiredly.

Jericho didn't have to be told twice. He turned and left, slamming the door on his way out.

THE NEXT DAY, Soliel's shoes and backpack were found beside one of the bridges that crossed the river, connecting

Ilygroth to the next neighborhood over. Everyone assumed the worst, but the body never surfaced. And while the neighborhood around him mourned, Jericho packed his backpack and left for his apprenticeship. He was angry with Soliel for being weak and selfish. For leaving them all behind to grieve just because *he* couldn't face what had happened. Over the years, that anger and resentment had sustained him and kept him from feeling the hole Soliel had left behind. It also kept him from trying to fill the hole, because he couldn't fill what he didn't notice.

But now, standing before the home of Soliel Tsuki again, Jericho felt it seep into his bones. It tugged away at the age-old rage and morphed it into something else. He couldn't identify it, not yet, and he didn't have time to try before the door opened to reveal a blue-haired young woman with wide brown eyes.

"Can I help you?" she asked.

"Uh, yes. Is Mrs. Tsuki in residence?" Jericho pulled his badge from his back pocket, offering the little sun shield to her as if that would explain everything.

"No one by that name lives here."

A frown tugged his lips down. "How long have you lived here, ma'am?"

"Oh, I don't know." She scratched her cheek in thought. "I guess eight years or so?"

"And how did you come to own the property?"

"In an auction. It was a foreclosure."

Jericho nodded. "Thank you for your time, ma'am."

"Of course." She smiled and shut the door as he headed back down the stairs.

He sighed, pulling out his phone and dialing.

"Talk to me," the voice of Ildri chirped from the speaker distractedly. "And make it quick, I'm about two seconds from blowing the lid off this—" The sound of an explosion cut off her words. "Ah, shit." She coughed away from the device for a moment before regaining her breath. "All right, what is it?"

Jericho clicked his tongue. "Did you just blow up the hold?"

"No, I did not. Now what do you want, Jericho? I'm a little busy here."

"I need you to track someone down for—"

"You know that's not my jam, J," Ildri interrupted him. "We've got a whole squad of Huntsmen in charge of tracking people. Why not ask one of them?"

Jericho huffed. She was going to make him beg, wasn't she? "Because I need this quick. Like, before tomorrow. And the proper channels will take a fucking month to get back to me what with all the paperwork. Can't you just do me this favor, Ildri?"

The line was silent for a long moment, and if not for the sound of her breathing, Jericho would have thought she'd hung up. "Fine. But you owe me."

"I am in your debt," Jericho murmured, sufficiently binding himself to the promise of doing one favor of indeterminate size for Ildri. Promising such things to fairy of any kind was a dangerous game to be playing, but Jericho really didn't have time to worry about that shit right now.

"Good. Now, give me as much information as you have on this person."

As Jericho boarded the train back to Erahil, he gave Ildri everything he knew about Mrs. Tsuki. Her full name, last known address, physical description, species, and known relations. It wasn't a lot. An identification number would have worked better. But it would have to do—Ildri said as much before they hung up.

●

THE TRAIN RIDE home was uneventful, leaving Jericho alone with his thoughts. Normally it would have calmed him, but with everything he'd learned over the last week, all it did was make him more nervous. It felt like he was caught in the calm before a storm—the moment right before everything would blow up in his face and his world would go to shit. Maybe he should have kept out of this whole Dusk business, listened to his initial instincts, and stayed away. What Dusk had gotten himself into was none of Jericho's business after all. Jericho had been without Dusk for years, and he'd been fine. Honestly. Things probably should have stayed that way. It was clear after that blow up that they were on separate paths. But he was in it now, and there was no getting out.

Jericho shook himself, vowing not to think any more of Dusk and Soliel and Ilygroth that night. He pressed his palm to the pad outside of his apartment, and the door clicked open. Once inside, he discarded his boots and leather jacket at the door.

Jericho dropped his phone onto the counter to charge, then turned to dig through the refrigerator for something to eat. He knew he should make something healthy, but it'd been a long day, so instead, he heated up a frozen dinner.

"Music on," he muttered, and the gentle sound of jazz floated through the speakers as the microwave hummed.

A loud buzzing drew his attention to his phone, and Jericho frowned at the picture that popped up.

"Thanks, but no thanks, Mom." He sent the call to voice-mail with a quick tap. The microwave dinged, and Jericho pulled the steaming tray from it, his eyes narrowing on the phone when it buzzed again to indicate she'd left a voicemail. Rolling his eyes, he tapped on the screen, opening the voice-mail app, and turned it on speaker to listen.

"Colette." Jericho huffed at the use of his first name. His parents were the only ones he'd let get away with it, but it still felt oddly formal. He supposed that was fitting with how little they'd spoken over the last few years. Since Soliel had . . . not died? "It's Mom. Not that you don't know that already, but whatever. Look. The summer solstice is coming up, and your dad and I want you to come out to the lake to celebrate. It's supposed to be a full moon, you know. And we haven't seen you in—" Her voice faded as she either thought about how long it had been or checked with his father. "Whatever. It's been a long fucking time. Your dad misses you. *I* miss you. You can't just bury yourself in work like this. You have to have something else in your life. It's not healthy. You have to—" She stopped again, and Jericho could hear her take a deep breath. He could imagine her shaking her head as if to dismiss a thought before she pressed on. She had been about to tell him to move on again. Jericho had heard it at least a hundred times in the last eight years, but the thing was that, until recently, he'd thought he *had* moved on. Even still, she knew a lecture wasn't going to change anything. "Please. It'd be nice to see you."

The message ended with a soft click, and Jericho reached over to delete it just as his phone rang again. One glance told him that it was Ildri, so he grabbed it, balancing the device on his shoulder as he ate.

"What is it?" he mumbled around a mouth full of plastic macaroni.

"Jeez, you're in a pissy mood. No 'hello'? No 'how are you'? Just 'what the fuck do you want, pixie'?" Ildri grumbled on the other side of the line.

"I didn't say that, did I?" Jericho asked, stuffing another too-big bite of whatever meat was in the frozen dinner into his mouth. It tasted like fucking cardboard, and his wolf chattered its teeth, craving something fresher. "What is it, Ildri?"

The pixie huffed, and he could practically hear her rolling her eyes. "I finished my search."

"And?"

"And she's gone."

"What?" Jericho dropped his fork onto the tray so he could hold his phone closer to his ear. "What do you mean she's gone?"

"I mean, Adelia Tsuki disappeared after her son jumped off that bridge. She quit her job. Her house was foreclosed on. She fell off the map. The woman's a ghost. No bills. No forwarding address. No employment record. No death certificate. She's just gone."

"That's not—that can't be possible. We keep records of people. Unless they—" He stopped himself from saying "unless they fake their death," setting his half-eaten dinner on the counter so he could grip the cold granite to steady himself. "Unless they die, there is no way to just disappear."

"There shouldn't be," Ildri agreed. "But she managed it. It looks like she worked some menial job at a tech company— Efsenor Industries. From what it says in her files, all they had her doing was data entry, but—"

"But she's human, so of course they would give her a low-level job," Jericho finished for her, taking a breath. He'd never known what Mrs. Tsuki did for a living, but he knew it had something to do with technology. He remembered once when he'd dropped his phone, and everything had glitched out. He'd been crying, swearing his mother was going to kill him for breaking it. It was brand new! Mrs. Tsuki had grabbed it, locked herself in her bedroom for about half an hour, and returned with the device in 'like new' condition.

"Well, that combined with the fact that she'd sired an Unseelie child," Ildri added. That thought struck Jericho in a way he hadn't thought it would. He knew about the way the Unseelie were treated, but Mrs. Tsuki was human. She was neither Unseelie nor Seelie. The fact that she'd sired a banshee wouldn't have affected anything. Would it? He shook himself. "Either way, she's a ghost. I don't think I could find her even if I scoured the footage from the whole damn city dating back to the day Soliel Tsuki supposedly died, which I won't do. She—" Ildri breathed in awe. "The woman was clearly a genius. If it weren't for Soliel's birth records, they would have had no means to track her at all. Before then, it was like she didn't exist, and then suddenly she did, and then she was gone again when he died. It's amazing."

"You sound like you've got a crush."

"Maybe I do." Ildri giggled. "Looking at her, this woman would be exactly my type."

Jericho grunted in annoyance. "Let me know if anything comes up."

"Yeah. I will. But, J, you aren't going to find this woman, trust me. If she doesn't want to be found, she won't be. Which makes me wonder . . . " Her voice drifted off thoughtfully, and he could hear the tapping of keys in the background.

"What?" Jericho pushed his food around on the tray. It'd gone room temperature by now and would probably taste even worse. He dumped it into the bin instead of trying to salvage it.

"Well. It's just," Ildri said, tone hushed as if she were speaking to herself. "If Adelia Tsuki is this good, how did we find Dusk? If she's this smart, then he could have stayed under the radar for the rest of his arguably immortal life if he wanted to. But instead, he let us track him. I mean, the captain sent me his records—"

"Send them over to me. Now."

"Right," Ildri mumbled, still only half paying attention. He heard her typing again, and then felt the buzz of a notification pop up on his phone. "Anyways, like I was saying, if Dusk faked his death and fell off the map, he could have stayed off the map just like his mother did. But he didn't."

"Why not?"

"That's what I'm trying to tell you! I don't know. It doesn't make sense. Just . . . Look at the file. It's weird, J."

"Yeah, I'll look at it." Jericho pinched the bridge of his nose and hung up. Green eyes flicked to the empty marble tiles of his living room, devoid of any furnishings or personal touches. It wasn't like he had anything else to do.

He found himself shortly thereafter leaning against his headboard, flipping through the pages of the file on his tablet. Ildri was right. It was weird. After Soliel's presumed suicide, he'd gone dormant for a year or two before he was arrested on charges of obstructing traffic. He was released and arrested a week later for assaulting a hero. This time after he was released, he disappeared again for several years. Until about six months ago, when Dusk appeared on the scene. Where had he been all that time? And how had that time changed him?

Jericho rubbed at his tired eyes, shut off the tablet, and rolled over. Tomorrow, he'd have all of his questions answered. He wouldn't stop talking to Dusk until he knew what had happened to Soliel.

And maybe, *maybe*, Jericho would even convince Dusk to give up whatever moronic crusade he'd gotten into his head and return to civilian life. Jericho owed him that much after all these years.

CHAPTER FOUR

BEFORE JERICHO COULD SEE SOLIEL AGAIN, THERE WERE SOME things that needed to happen. The first of which was putting on the armor that made her into the woman, the hero, who could take on anything. She hoped it would make her ready for the conversation ahead. Jericho always felt stronger with the cold metal weighing on her shoulders, and that's what she needed right now as she went to see Captain Oakfur again.

She didn't bother knocking, just pushed the door open.

"What is it, Jericho?" the red-haired man asked, looking up from his computer screen. "Something else not to your liking?"

"Has Dusk been released into the general population?"

"What?"

"Last I saw him, he hadn't been allowed to leave the inter-rogation cell. It didn't even look like he'd showered. If we want information out of him, he needs to be comfortable." Her words were simple, concise, logical. It was true: if they were going to entice Dusk over to their side, they needed him to see that they wanted to help him.

Oakfur's eyes narrowed on Jericho. "That was done for the safety of the other prisoners and guards alike. We can't risk him using his Voice on anyone."

"What if I can talk him into wearing a blocker collar?" Jericho wasn't sure how she'd get Dusk to agree to that, but she was willing to try. If Dusk wanted to be able to leave the cell, then this might be the only way. It would protect the other inhabitants of the hold and put the captain's mind at ease. Surely that would be enough to convince Dusk.

The captain's eyes lingered on her for a long moment before he nodded. "Very well. You get him to wear a collar, and we'll move him in with the rest of the prisoners."

Jericho nodded, then made her way to the equipment locker.

Checking out a voice collar only took a few minutes, and then she found herself outside the interrogation cell again. Tugging on the cream-colored armor to settle it against her shoulders, she took a deep breath. Her gloved hands brushed over the gold sun emblazoned on her chest. She could do this.

"Now or never, J."

The cell door opened to reveal a delighted Dusk, whose wide smile crinkled his eyes into crescents.

"Lettie! How good to see you again," he signed, his expression open and earnest. Maybe Dusk *was* genuinely happy to see her, or maybe he'd just gotten better at lying in the years since they'd been teenagers. "I have to say, this look suits you." He paused, probably for dramatic effect. "Get it? Suits you. Because it's a suit of armor." His fingers danced over the words.

Or maybe he wasn't actually happy to see her, just happy to have someone to mock.

"Hilarious," Jericho muttered.

"I heard you yelled at your captain until he gave me back

my binder. And then told him I had to be called 'he.'" Dusk's hands were moving in languid motions, long broad strokes of thin fingers, to form the words he was saying.

"Yeah. So?"

"Awww. Lettie, you do care." Dusk cooed, his voice dipping lower, and one side of his lips curled upward. Jericho couldn't tell if it was an act or if Dusk was genuinely touched by the sentiment. It didn't matter, she decided. "Watch it. You keep defending my honor like that and you'll wind up in here with me."

Jericho rolled her eyes and flopped down across from him, dropping the collar onto the table between them with a sharp clatter.

Dusk's smile fell, and for a moment, Jericho saw the scared little boy she'd known so many years ago. That image was quickly replaced by the fury of a villain, eyes hardening and lips pressing into a thin line. "You can't possibly be serious. I'm not putting that on."

"You are."

"I'm not. I refused to wear one during school, and I'll be damned if I'm about to wear one now."

Jericho's jaw twitched at the mention of school. She'd never known it'd been suggested that Soliel wear a voice collar to school, but now was not the time to go soft on him. "If you want to be released into the general population and allowed to do normal things—like shower—you have to wear this. That was the deal I struck."

Dusk eyed the collar with a stony expression, his fingers twitching in distress as they tapped against the table.

"Fine," he said at length.

"Once it's on, a guard will come to take you to a proper cell with a bed." Jericho glanced around the room, frowning deeply. The interrogation cells weren't meant for long-term use. It was outfitted with a toilet but nothing else. If Dusk had been sleeping—which he hadn't been, gauging by the bags under his eyes—it had been sitting at the table.

"I've slept in worse conditions," Dusk signed, fingers dragging indifferently.

Words pressed at her teeth, but Jericho kept her jaw clamped shut, grinding them together to keep the questions from escaping. Pity would do neither of them any good. She rose and locked the collar firmly around Dusk's throat, then waved for a K.N.I.G.H.T. unit to enter and see Dusk off to his new accommodations.

"I'll be back to continue our discussion soon."

"I look forward to it," Dusk signed, a hint of dry amusement in his eyes. Then he followed the droid willingly out of the room.

●

WHEN JERICHO RETURNED to her desk, she found a file waiting on her tablet. Another case, something to take her mind away from Dusk. The thought of walking away from unanswered questions, even if it were just for the time being, didn't sit right, but this was the job. So, she'd headed out to chase down the lead. They went by the name Chaos, and they'd left a trail of destruction in their wake that didn't take a werewolf to follow. It had been a troll, simply intent on causing as much property damage as possible. Nothing nearly as interesting as the mystery waiting for Jericho back at the hold.

Still, it took three long days to catch Chaos, even after they'd spent a few figuring out where he was hiding. And when she returned to the hold, she had a dark bruise forming along her jaw that ached when she pulled her armor over her head.

"Why don't you take the rest of the night off?" Erling

offered from where he was changing at his locker. "I'll handle the paperwork, and you can go have a nice dinner with some friends."

Jericho clenched her jaw to keep herself from retorting, *What friends?* Instead, she shook her head. "Nah. I'm sure your wife is waiting for you. I've got it."

"Are you sure? I really don—"

"I said I'll handle it." Jericho frowned, staring into her locker instead of looking at Erling. "Go home, Erling. You have people waiting for you."

She said nothing else, just pushed past the griffin and went to settle behind her desk to work up the report.

Which is precisely where she was when she got the alert. Her feet padded quickly and silently through the hold toward the section of the building where they kept prisoners. It was relatively small, meant to only be a temporary stopover for them while they provided the Hero Alliance with information before being shipped off to one of the larger prisons.

Although she hadn't been there before, it was easy to find Dusk's cell. Especially with two extra-large K.N.I.G.H.T.s standing outside it. The two androids stared ahead blankly but made no motion to stop her when Jericho opened the door and entered the cell. She leaned back against the bars, arms crossed over her chest. Dusk was laying out on his cot, completely unbothered by the sudden intrusion. His eyes flicked to Jericho, interest crossing his features before he closed them off again.

"You assaulted a guard," Jericho offered blandly. It wasn't a question or an accusation. It was a statement of fact. The fucking idiot had gone and attacked one of the non-android guards on staff and would likely lose all the privileges he'd only just gotten for it. Not even Jericho could blame the warden for that decision.

"Good evening to you too, Lettie." Dusk sat up slowly. He was sporting a bruise on his temple, likely from where someone had hit him with a baton to try to get him under control.

Jericho sighed, scratching at the soft, white-blond hair near her ear where it'd been buzzed close to create an undercut with an intricate pattern of swirls.

"You assaulted a guard."

"In all fairness, Lettie," Dusk started, signing again.

Jericho wondered if the collar was hurting his throat but brushed the thought aside. Dusk had made his choice. He would have to deal with the consequences.

"You're the one who taught me that if someone hits me first, I have the right to hit them back."

It was reasonable, and Jericho would definitely be taking it up with whoever was in charge that someone had hit Dusk. But that wasn't the point.

"This isn't elementary school anymore, Sol!" She signed along with her shout to be sure she got the point across.

Dusk shrugged.

"They're threatening to put you in solitary."

Another shrug.

"I won't be able to visit you there." Jericho's fingers made the motions of the words as small as her voice would have left her had she spoken them. Whisper-quiet so no one else could hear or see.

Dusk eyed her skeptically, one dark brow rising as if to ask, *So?*

Which. Fair. Because Jericho was beginning to ask herself the same thing. So what if Dusk lost his privileges? So what if she wasn't able to visit him in solitary? But the reasoning was simple.

"I need answers. I can't get them if I can't interrogate

you." Honesty. Dusk had always appreciated that before; maybe it would work now.

Dusk stared at her in silence.

"That's my fucking job."

"Is it?" Dusk sat up further, his lips pressing into a sharp line. "Is it your fucking job?"

"Don't start."

"Don't start *what*?!" Dusk shouted, voice rasping around the collar, his eyes turning a lighter shade of brown. He couldn't use his Voice, but that wouldn't stop him from drawing on his power to frighten anyone in his vicinity. Too bad for him, Jericho knew better. Jericho heard one of the bots behind her turn to inspect the threat, but she held up a hand to keep it from entering the cell.

"Acting like a spoiled brat," Jericho bit out. "Now, behave yourself or go to fucking solitary, your choice. But let me warn you, if you go to solitary and I can't close this case, fuck whatever we had as kids, I'm sending you to the Isle. And you can die there for all I give a fuck."

Dusk rolled his eyes and flopped back against the bed, making it squeak. "Fine. Whatever. I'll behave."

Jericho nodded, slumping against the bars. Fuck. When had she gotten so tired?

"Go home. Get some sleep. I'll see you in the morning, Lettie," Dusk ordered, flicking his hand at Jericho in a shooing motion.

"You don't get to fucking tell me what to do." Jericho's jaw ticked where it clenched too tightly. Then she spun and stormed off.

And . . . did just what Dusk had said. She dragged herself back to her empty apartment and crawled into bed without even bothering to change.

●

ANOTHER DAY, another dimpled smile from Dusk. He grinned at Jericho every time they met, as if they were just meeting to play a game in the park or to see a movie together. As if nothing had changed between them. But everything had changed. That was evident by the collar locked securely around what was once Jericho's best friend's throat. And by the way Dusk's shoulders remained rigid, as if he were always ready for a fight, even when he was smiling.

"A little bird told me you went back to Ilygroth the other day to see my mom," Dusk offered. A sneaky smile split his lips that spoke of 'I know something you don't know.' He was trying to set Jericho on edge, and he'd succeeded.

Jericho clenched a fist at his side, keeping his face carefully neutral as he sat at the table in the interrogation room once more. A soft, hollow sound filled the silence as he set the tablet on the table before him, open to Dusk's file.

"You won't find her, you know. She's gone."

"Gone?" Jericho repeated.

Dusk hummed nonchalantly, head turning to look out the window. "She died a few months back. Cancer. All the magic and technology in the world can't cure that, especially not in a human. It moves too fast. Not that we've tried much." The last bit was said under his breath, as if he didn't mean for anyone to hear the bitterness in his tone. Jericho did.

Jericho nodded slowly.

"It's funny, you know," Dusk continued at length.

"What?" Jericho frowned. He didn't know what was funny about Mrs. Tsuki dying of cancer. Nothing, it seemed to him. Even without having seen her for nearly a decade, it ached to know that she was well and truly gone. Jericho would have to deal with that later.

"That you think you're on the side of the good guys, when they're the ones hurting people." When Dusk's eyes flicked away from the window, his gaze was sharper, clearer than it should have been if he were truly mourning the loss of his mother.

The hair on the back of Jericho's neck rose as a thought struck him. Maybe Dusk wasn't mourning her at all. Maybe he didn't fucking care. How cold had Dusk gotten in the years since they'd been sixteen and stupid? Cold enough to not miss his mother?

Jericho didn't answer, and eventually Dusk continued. "When we live in a world where a child can be deemed evil before they can even feed themselves or even know what the word really means. Put on a list in some dingy basement somewhere so they can be watched and monitored, all because of something they were born with."

Jericho snorted. He'd heard this particular speech before, back when they'd been in high school, but Dusk had never had any proof of his being on a watch list. But then, the Tsukis had been a little poorer than everyone else in Ilygroth, especially with Mrs. Tsuki working at an elite tech company like Efsenor Industries. He shook himself. That was a rabbit hole he couldn't afford to go down. Not now. Not ever.

"This again?"

"Check for yourself." Dusk reached over to the tablet and flipped through the file while reading the words upside down. When he got to a particular page, he pointed. "I've been on a watch list since I was two, when I used my Voice on a dog that bit me."

It was hard to disbelieve something that was right there, set into pixels as much as the old records had once been set in ink. The file recorded the event and made mention of "further monitoring."

"What?"

"The dog was fine. I just startled it," Dusk offered conversationally, as if that made what he was saying all better. It didn't. He continued on as if Jericho hadn't spoken. "But me?

I wasn't allowed off this list unless I underwent surgery to have my vocal cords altered. I'd have been mute."

"You're full of shit. They don't do those kinds of surgeries on kids. They're for dangerous Unseelie."

Dusk shook his head, a lock of dark hair falling into his eyes. "No? Well, check for yourself. I believe the project was called 'Tongue-Tied.' Cheeky name, isn't it?" He laughed. But the sound was hollow and cold.

Jericho frowned, chewing on the inside of his cheek. He had other more important things to deal with right now. Dusk's bullshit was low on the list. But he couldn't help the chill that had settled into his bones at that laugh. It sounded . . . It didn't sound anything like the boy he'd known.

"I'll be back," was all Jericho said before he exited the room. He needed space to sort out which of Dusk's words were a manipulation and which were true. Space away from the eerily familiar smile that was also so unfamiliar, space to think.

●

WHEN HE RETURNED around lunch time, he decided to cut straight to the point. Jericho wasn't going to let Dusk continue to dictate the conversation. This was an interrogation. He was an officer of the Hero Alliance. They were no longer friends or anything else.

Dusk looked up from where he'd been tapping his fingers on the table to smile at Jericho again. Why did he have to look so fucking happy to see Jericho all the time? Jericho guessed it was part of this persona he'd crafted. The person sitting at the table wasn't Soliel. He wasn't the little boy who had bandaged Jericho's scraped knees and cried when the dog died in their favorite movie and given Jericho his first kiss. No. This was Dusk. A villain. Someone who would, and was, using the facts to manipulate Jericho. To warp his sense of what was right and wrong. And Jericho was fucking done with the games. It didn't matter if Dusk had been telling the truth about Tongue-Tied.

Jericho sat across from him again, the tablet on the table. "Your file says you spent six months in a minimum-security facility aft—"

"Have you been checking up on me, Lettie?" Dusk leaned forward, pressing into Jericho's space. "Naughty, naughty, hero. If you have questions, ask me. Don't read their propaganda."

Jericho didn't even blink, he just continued on. "That's after spending a month in the same facility for—"

"Obstructing traffic." Dusk curled his legs into his chair so he could shift onto his toes, bracing himself heavily on the table to invade more of Jericho's bubble. "I was at a protest for Unseelie rights. Funny thing, that."

"What?" Jericho rolled his eyes in exasperation. How had they gotten to where Dusk was dictating the conversation again? Well . . . Jericho supposed as long as he kept Dusk talking, eventually he'd slip up. They always did.

"Unseelie rights. I mean Unseelie, Seelie. Fae is fae, right? We're all magical in the end, aren't we? Who gets to decide which races are Unseelie and which are Seelie?" There was a hint of mania in Dusk's tone, his eyes growing wide and wild. Jericho wanted nothing more than to back away from him. To put distance between himself and the man who no longer resembled his childhood friend at all.

"Our ancestors," Jericho said as if he were reciting it straight from a textbook. Maybe he was. Who knew where these facts came from once they'd been in someone's head for so long? "The Seelie sided with the humans when the Unseelie rose up and tried to obliterate them in the war."

Dusk choked out a laugh, his fingers moving to sign again

as he tried to hold back his soft snickers. "Banshee sided against the humans. But my ancestors were human. I'm only fae at all due to an accident of birth. Because my father died, and my mother mourned with all of her heart, and her grief turned me into this. But then, you knew that."

Jericho stopped, his breath stuttering for a moment. Those glittering eyes, the ones he'd once known so well, watched him closely as they fell into a heavy silence. He'd . . . never thought about it that way. That banshee didn't have banshee ancestors. They had human ones. Just like vampires, and even some werewolves. Why did they have to suffer for the actions of the fae who had come before them?

"Do you know what happens to people like me in those places?" Dusk signed, not willing to break the silence as every word sunk into Jericho's mind like lead weights. "People who aren't evil or bad, just Unseelie by some weird twist of fate? Let me tell you: prison is not kind to us. But worse than that is the loneliness."

"Loneliness?" Jericho choked on the word and forced his fingers into motion to be sure he was heard. Something ached at the thought of Dusk being lonely. The boy who had once been so bright and happy should never be lonely. Jericho couldn't line the two images up, the little boy and Dusk. It was the boy he ached for now, not the man in front of him.

Dusk shrugged, his feet thumping on the floor as he sat back in his chair. "What's for lunch?"

"What?" Jericho blinked, head still spinning with nostalgia and images of light-up sneakers.

"It's lunchtime. What's on the menu?"

"I'll . . . I'll go find out," Jericho stuttered, rising mechanically from the chair and turning to leave the room.

He didn't though. He left Dusk there, escaping to the courtyard at the center of the hold to catch his breath and try to make sense of all of the things he'd learned about Dusk over the last week. None of it made sense. Soliel had been a sweet-natured, good child. But just as Dusk had said, he'd always been considered Unseelie, evil, no matter what. Jericho just hadn't understood fully what that meant. It couldn't be as bad as Dusk said—there was no way. The only explanation was that Dusk was twisting the facts, using them to get a reaction out of Jericho.

"Jericho," a small K.N.I.G.H.T. squeaked at him from the ground, looking up from about knee-height.

"Yeah?"

"Captain Oakfur wants to see you in his office immediately." The tiny droid skittered off to continue its other duties before Jericho could give it an answer. Jericho took a deep inhale of the fresh, warm air, then headed back inside.

Oakfur was waiting for him when he reached the office. The small man was leaning against his desk, arms crossed over his chest. Trying to look imposing, Jericho supposed. Jericho dropped down into one of the chairs.

"You haven't gotten any information out of Dusk yet."

Jericho's shoulders tensed, but he forced his face to remain impassive. "We're building a rapport."

"That so?" Oakfur eyed him dubiously.

Jericho nodded.

"Well, step it up," the captain ordered.

"And how would you suggest I do that . . . sir?" The "sir" was added belatedly as if that could make Jericho's insolent tone sound more respectful. It didn't work, they both knew that, but it seemed Oakfur had decided long ago it was easier not to pick a fight with the volatile werewolf. Especially when Jericho had a track record of getting results.

"Ask him what he wants in trade. The council is willing to cut him a deal if he cooperates. But we need the location of his lab and the information off that device."

"Yes, sir." Jericho rose from the chair and went back to his desk. After some digging through one of the bottom drawers, he procured a legal pad and pen, then headed back down to the interrogation room. Dusk was waiting for him with yet another dimpled smile and a tray of food in front of him.

"What's this?" Dusk asked, eyes flicking to the yellow pad as Jericho dropped it onto the table with a soft *clap*.

"The council wants a list of demands. They're willing to meet them, provided they're reasonable, in exchange for the location of your lab and the information from the thumb drive."

As he lifted a brow, a slow, sly smile crept up Dusk's lips. "Well. That didn't take long," he signed.

Jericho tilted his head in question, but Dusk didn't say anything else. He reached over to grab the paper and got to writing.

"They won't like them," Dusk said when he was finished, sliding the pad back over to Jericho.

Jericho's eyes flicked over the words, brows creasing. "You want a complete purge of council seats and a revote."

"I said they weren't going to like them." Dusk smiled darkly, his eyes twinkling with wry amusement.

"And for Bill 219 to be passed. What's Bill 219?"

Dusk rolled his eyes. "Of course, you haven't kept up on politics. You never did. Look it up."

"Or you could just fucking tell me."

"Oh, Lettie, never wanting to work for your answers. See, this is why I always got the better scores. And yet you got accepted into the apprenticeship program, and I didn't." Dusk leaned back in his chair, looking smug.

"Fuck you."

"Do your own research for once. I'm not going to hold your hand in this." Dusk propped his feet up on the table, crossing one ankle over the other.

"Whatever." Jericho clicked his tongue. "And if they say no?"

"Then I guess I'll rot in here, won't I?"

"You don't mean that." Because how could anyone mean that? Least of all someone like Dusk, who had just admitted how lonely prison could be.

"And why don't I? You're willing to die for your cause, right? You put your life on the line every day that you go out there fighting quote-unquote 'evil.' Why can't I die for mine?" Dusk's arms moved to rest behind his head, relaxed.

"It doesn't have to be like that."

"No?"

"No!"

"I don't see how it doesn't."

Jericho shook his head, silently seething, and forced himself to leave. There wasn't time for a deeply philosophical discussion about right and wrong. He considered not delivering the list in person, not particularly wanting to hear Oakfur's rattling laugh as he read the things Dusk wanted. But Jericho knew not delivering it himself would just put Oakfur in an even worse mood. He steeled himself and knocked on the captain's door.

"That was fast," Oakfur muttered, looking up from his tablet.

"Soliel has always been very decisive." The pad made a soft clapping sound as Jericho dropped it onto the desk. "Though I don't know that the council is going to be up for any of this."

Oakfur spent about thirty seconds looking over the demands and then laughed loudly. "Well, this is just stupid."

"Which part?" Jericho asked, settling once more into the chair on the other side of the desk. It looked like he was in for the long haul; may as well get comfortable.

"He wants to force the anti-discrimination act through.

Has he lost his mind? Everyone knows that's Unseelie propaganda. They have equal rights already."

"I can't see where it could—"

"It'll never go through. And even if it did, the matter still stands. The humans might have short memories, but the history books aren't going to let anyone forget when the Unseelie tried to wipe them out." Oakfur fell silent, fingers tapping on the pad in thought. "No. The council has a better idea."

Jericho officially did not like the sound of that.

"What's that, sir?" he asked anyway.

"We release him into the rehab program. We don't have any real proof that he's done anything worse than stealing information, and even *that* we aren't sure about because we can't access the information itself. The best we can get him on is breaking and entering. We wouldn't be able to hold him for more than a year, tops. But if we put him into the program, maybe he'll lead us to the lab."

Jericho blinked slowly, taking his time to process the words. And once he had, he scowled. "He's not that stupid. If we send him home with a hero, he'll just bide his time until the program is over and then be on his merry way. No muss. No fuss."

Oakfur smiled, all teeth and narrowed eyes. Jericho didn't like it. "He might let his guard down if we send him home with a hero he knows and maybe trusts."

"Maybe. But we don—" Jericho's scowl cemented onto his face. But they did have someone, didn't they? Someone who Dusk knew intimately. Someone who had known Dusk since he was too young to even write his own name. "No."

"No? Why not? You two were childhood friends, right? You even applied to the hero program together, by his records. Convincing him that you're on his side should be easy."

"'*Were*' is the keyword there, Oakfur. We're not anything anymore. He's a villain, and I'm a hero. We're not friends, and we won't ever *be* friends again."

"How hard could it be for you to—?"

"No."

"Did I ask?" Oakfur's lips pursed. No, Jericho supposed he hadn't. "You've been bugging me for an undercover mission for a year now. Here it is. This is your undercover mission. We'll release Dusk into your custody before the week is out, and you are to get him to trust you enough to lead you to his lab. That is an order, Jericho."

Jericho exhaled heavily. Stress threatened to hunch his shoulders, but he lifted his chin instead. "Yes, sir. I'll schedule a psych eval for tomorrow and start on the paperwork."

"Good. I look forward to your results." Oakfur dropped the pad of paper into the bin beside the desk and returned to his work without another word.

•

DUSK WAS STILL WAITING for him when Jericho returned to the room around dinner time. He had a tray of food before him again, mostly untouched, but a smile still lit his face when his eyes landed on Jericho. Which was . . . fucking annoying.

"Lettie! I was starting to think you weren't coming back!"

"The council has refused all of your demands," Jericho offered, pulling up the paperwork for the rehabilitation program on his tablet.

"Ah well. That's a shame." Dusk pushed back in the chair, sliding the tray of food away from him a little.

"Instead, they've decided to put you into the rehab program under the care of one of the heroes." Jericho kept his tone purposefully distant. This was a business transaction. It was official. It wasn't them running away from home to hide in the playground because Jericho's mother refused to give them a second pudding cup after dinner. Or sneaking out after dark to make out on the swings.

"Wait. So . . . I'm getting out?" Dusk asked suspiciously. He was frowning, implying he didn't understand nor like what was going on. As if he'd been ready and willing to sacrifice himself to a cell for the rest of his life. And all to protect . . . What? His lab? Some information? A fool-hardy ideal? It just didn't make any sense to Jericho. "Who is my hero going to be?"

"Me." Jericho didn't look up from the tablet.

Dusk blinked for a moment before the words registered. "Oh! That's wonderful!" He laughed brightly, eyes lighting with mischief. "Living with Lettie will be so much fun. Just like old times."

"Right. Old times," Jericho grunted, irritated. "Before any of that can happen, I need to file paperwork for it. To do that, I need some more information on your background."

"Of course. Of course." Dusk flapped his hand and sat up straighter in his chair. With his legs crossed neatly at the ankle, he folded his hands in front of him, then forced his face into a look of seriousness. It didn't fit. Not with the Dusk that Jericho had seen so far. But Jericho appreciated the attempt. "Ask away."

"This protest you were arrested at. It was for Unseelie rights."

"Right. What about it?"

"Why?"

Dusk blinked owlishly, his head tilted to the side in confusion. "Why what?"

"They're killers, Dusk." Jericho sighed, frustrated. "It's in their instincts. That's why they're Unseelie."

The mask of the innocent, freckle-faced boy who'd just

gotten mixed up in the wrong thing slipped away. Dusk glared at Jericho. And, oh . . . That must be what he really looked like now. Not this performance he kept putting on of the playfully mischievous, misunderstood young man. But this . . . this hardened person.

"Killers?"

"Yeah. Killers." Jericho refused to lean away from the dark expression being leveled at him.

In his agitation, Dusk's hands shook, signing the next words as if perhaps he couldn't trust his voice to say them. "Do you remember that little old lady with all the cats who baked cookies for us every weekend?" He paused, waiting for Jericho to answer.

Jericho nodded.

"Redcap." He signed the word in quick, concise motions, as if that were answer enough. Maybe it was in his mind.

"Okay. Just because one redcap was nice and gave us cookies, that—"

Dusk's fingers were moving again, stilling the words in Jericho's throat. "How about that little boy with the stutter and the really thick glasses in second grade? The one who shared his PB and J with you after a bully stomped on your lunch?" This time, he didn't even wait for Jericho to nod, he just continued on. "The bully was a hippocampus. One of your Seelie. One of your 'good guys.' That little boy was a kelpie."

"Is there a point you're trying to make here?"

"Yes." Dusk spoke softly, his hands signing along to the slow words. "We cannot continue to judge those around us by the decisions of those who came before them. There is good and evil in all of us. It's all in what wins out."

"So, the Unseelie are the good guys?" Jericho asked flatly.

"No." Dusk rolled his eyes. "Don't be dense. There are no good guys. There are no bad guys. There are just people."

CHAPTER FIVE

Paperwork could be filled out anywhere, Jericho reasoned, which was how she found herself standing in front of the door to Ildri's workshop. A hand-painted—and frankly tacky—sheet of metal hung lopsided from the door, declaring 'Ildri's Inner Sanctum' in big bold letters. Underneath it said 'enter at your own risk' in smaller, haphazard handwriting.

"Cute," Jericho scoffed, knocking on the door. When no answer came, she knocked again, louder.

"Come in." Ildri's voice sounded muffled and far away through the steel, but Jericho's keen ears heard it just fine. Pushing the door open, she peeked around for the bright-colored head of the pixie. Ildri was sitting at a long work bench, feet dangling from a high stool, a pair of protective goggles keeping her hair out of her eyes. She glanced up from the device in her hands and smiled at Jericho. "Hey, J. What's up?"

"I have paperwork to fill out." Jericho held up her tablet by way of explanation. "I thought this would be a quiet place to do it. May I?" She gestured to a stool along the bench, and when Ildri nodded, Jericho slid onto it, rearranging her black skater skirt as she crossed her ankles and settled. She turned to the bench, picking up something that looked like a part of an old printer from the table.

"Don't touch that," Ildri scolded, and Jericho put it back gently.

Jericho reached for a glass screen that seemed to be a piece of a tablet to move that instead.

"Or that." Ildri frowned. "Just . . . Let me clear you a space." Ildri hopped down from her stool and moved to clear a small bit of the surface for Jericho's tablet and coffee cup by removing all the bits and bobs delicately. "There. Sorry. I wasn't expecting company."

"It's all right. I didn't mean to spring this on you. I know your workspace is kind of . . . " She let the words hang, gesturing to the mess that surrounded her.

"Right." Ildri snickered, hopping back onto her stool and getting back to work. They were silent for a few short moments while Ildri settled into her work before she spoke again. "So. Why are you really here?" she asked without lifting her head from the piece of electrical equipment she was working on.

"It's nothing."

"It's something," Ildri insisted. "You don't put on your war paint unless you feel like you need it."

"My war—" Jericho started to ask, confused. Then she caught sight of her reflection in the polished innards of a K.N.I.G.H.T. unit. "Oh, right. The makeup," she muttered, eyeing her reflection. That morning, she'd lined her eyes and thrown on a dark shade of red lipstick. War paint. It was an apt description. Whenever she was feeling particularly vulnerable, this was the look she went with. It became armor just as much as her hero equipment had.

"And the skirt. I don't think I've seen you in a skirt since

Oakfur's promotion party, when he became captain." The device in front of Ildri sparked, and she yelped, jumping back a little and almost falling off her stool. "Shit."

"Maybe you should try wearing your safety goggles, idiot."

Ildri grunted, her blue eyes focused on the thing before her, which was now steaming. Whatever it was, it probably wasn't going to work after this. "Don't get off topic. We were talking about you and that lipstick. Which is, honestly, stunning, but that's beside the point."

"Can't I just want to look pretty for once?" Jericho countered, tugging self-consciously at her skirt. Stunning? No. But she was comfortable. At least for right now.

"I mean. I guess. But that's not your usual getup around here. Usually, we're lucky if your jeans don't have rips in them. So, spill it." Ildri's keen eyes flicked from the thing on her bench to Jericho. There was always something calculating about the pixie's brilliant blue gaze. Like she could pick a person apart and know exactly what made them tick, just as much as she could any device she came across.

Jericho shifted, the rubber of her tennis shoes squeaking against the stool. "You've been around a while, right?"

"Yeah. A few centuries. Not long by pixie standards, but hella long by human standards." Ildri ducked her head back over the still smoking device and ignored Jericho's clear discomfort. Which was a relief. Jericho did not want to be psychoanalyzed, thank you. She'd had enough of that through the years. Especially recently with Dusk, who made her feel like he was just playing with his food half the time.

"You were around when the war between the Unseelie and the Seelie happened," Jericho continued, her fingers tapping on her now lukewarm coffee mug.

"I mean, I was pretty young. I think I was maybe . . .

twenty at the time? Still a baby really. What are you getting at?"

Jericho sighed, looking down at the paperwork on her tablet. So far, all she'd been able to do was fill in the basic information: Dusk's name, species, age, and so on. She hadn't been able to fill in the part about why she thought he'd make a good fit for the program. She wasn't really sure that he would. Nor was she really sure she wanted to be the one to rehabilitate him. It seemed like a foolish idea. Still, she had to know if Dusk could be brought back to their side. If he could once again be the person she'd known all those years ago.

"Can Unseelie ever be good? I mean, we always kind of write them off as evil. Like they're all out to hurt humans. But . . . "

Ildri looked up again, eyes flicking over Jericho's face. She looked lost in thought, teeth worrying at her pink lower lip. She shook her head and exhaled, narrow shoulders slumping.

"I don't think anyone should be written off as evil before they're given a chance to prove themselves one way or the other." Then without another word, Ildri turned back to her work, pulling her safety goggles down to her nose.

Jericho nodded, ducking her head back down to her own work. There would be no more discussion, but that was okay. She'd gotten her answer.

●

THE FIRST PSYCH-EVAL was scheduled for two days later. During that time, Jericho thought over everything that he'd heard from Dusk and Ildri, and even what he'd read in Dusk's files. Dusk had the capacity for good and wanted to be good, in Jericho's opinion. He just needed a little help finding his way back to that path. Whether or not Jericho was the right person to provide that help remained to be seen, but Jericho supposed he owed it to that freckled little boy to try. After all, maybe if he hadn't left Dusk behind, things wouldn't have ended up as they had.

"You don't need to be in here," the psychiatrist, an elf with pointed ears and green skin, offered. "I think I can handle him on my own."

"I know. But sometimes he resorts to sign language, and I thought it'd be helpful to have a translator," Jericho reasoned. "Besides, I need to know what I'm getting into when I bring him home."

"Very well."

They entered the interrogation room, and Jericho braced himself in a corner while the woman took the chair across from Dusk.

"Oh, Lettie, you brought a friend," Dusk signed, a wide grin on his face.

"Stop being cheeky and answer the lady's questions," Jericho signed back, rolling his eyes.

Dusk's lips twitched, but he turned his attention to the woman across from him.

"Hello, Dusk. I'm Doctor Rolim," the woman said with a little smile.

Then Doctor Rolim began her questions, keeping them light and easy as she scratched answers onto the tablet in front of her. It went on like that for a while. She'd ask a question, Dusk would answer, and she'd write something down. At some point, Dusk grew bored with the questions and leaned back in his chair, yawning. Jericho couldn't blame him; the whole process was rather tedious.

"And what do you know about your father? Did your mother talk about him?" Doctor Rolim asked.

"Did you know the term 'acceptable loss' was coined by

the good guys?" Dusk asked, willfully ignoring the question about a man he'd never known.

The psychiatrist blinked, dark eyes widening, looking briefly flustered before she regained her composure. "What does that have to do with the current conversation?"

"Nothing. I just find it interesting. Much more interesting than your questions, anyway."

Jericho choked back a laugh and narrowed a glare on the banshee. "Behave yourself, or you'll never get out of here," he signed.

Dusk perked up, lips spreading in a smile, sharp and dangerous. "Oh, but Lettie, I'm right where I want to be. It's just that, as always, you're missing the bigger picture." His fingers drawled lazily over the words, like a cat stretching in a spot of sun.

"What did I say about being cheeky?" Jericho asked out loud.

Dusk waved him off. "Please, do continue, Doctor . . . "

"Rolim," she supplied.

"Right. Doctor Rolim."

The questions continued, albeit without any more discussion of Dusk's father, and eventually they took a break for lunch. When a guard brought in food for Dusk, Doctor Rolim excused herself, gesturing for Jericho to follow her.

"What is it, doc?"

She waited until the door had shut tight behind them, and Jericho tugged her away from the glass so that Dusk couldn't read their lips. He ignored the furious shout he got from Dusk through the glass. Unrest stirred in Jericho's belly, making the wolf rumble uncomfortably in his gut. Was she going to say Dusk couldn't enter the program? Would she insist that he was too dangerous? Jericho wasn't sure which he was more afraid of: Dusk being deemed unfit or taking him home.

"I'm going to recommend him for the program," she said at length.

Jericho nodded, not letting the relief show on his face. "I'm sensing a 'but.'"

"No but. I think you two are a good fit. Your past will help you connect with him and rehabilitate him. I do want to have a private session with him once a week though, to make sure he's on target. I'll have the council provide me with a translator for those sessions."

"That's not necessary. I'd be happy to come and tran—"

"No." Doctor Rolim shook her head. "I need to have him on his own. As you could see in there, he's putting up an act to impress you. I need him without you around."

"Okay." Jericho had to force the word past his tongue, but he managed it. He didn't like the idea of letting this doctor dig into Dusk's mind without Jericho present. He wasn't sure why. "When will he be ready for me to take home?"

"I want to have a private session with him this afternoon, but after that, I think he'll be ready tomorrow. If that's all right with you and your captain."

"I'm sure it'll be fine," Jericho murmured, running over a quick list of the things he'd need to pick up between then and tomorrow.

"Great. Let the captain know if there is anything you need for your guest. The council will be happy to provide you with an allowance for such things, within reason."

"Okay." Jericho pulled his phone from his pocket and started typing up his list.

"And Jericho," Doctor Rolim called, drawing his attention back to her. "Do be careful. I have a feeling he's much more than he seems. I know this is all an act to get information from him, but I can't guarantee he's not dangerous to you, in spite of your shared history."

"Right."

CHAPTER SIX

"IT'S ITCHY," DUSK GRUMBLED AS HE RUBBED THE HEEL OF HIS foot against the tracker strapped tightly around his ankle. He'd been complaining the entire car ride back to Jericho's apartment.

The tracker was itchy.

The air conditioning was too high.

The collar was chafing.

His borrowed hearing aids needed tuning.

The car smelled like old donuts.

And now, here they stood, in the hall with Jericho moving to press his palm to the pad by the door.

"Maybe you should have thought about that when you decided to be a villain," Jericho muttered under his breath.

"It's rude to talk about people behind their backs," Dusk countered primly.

"It's not behind your back. You're standing right beside me."

"But you know." Dusk narrowed his eyes, pressing his lips together into a tight line, and signing the next words in sharp, angry motions. "You know exactly what you just did."

Jericho rolled his eyes. He did know. He knew Dusk couldn't read people's lips when they mumbled, and without properly tuned hearing aids ...

"Whatever. Get inside." He ushered the shorter man in and shut the door behind them.

"Couldn't they have given me my own hearing aids back?" Dusk grumbled, fiddling with the devices in his ears to adjust them again.

"Be thankful they gave you a replacement set at all, and that they gave you back whatever *that* is." Jericho gestured to the outfit Dusk was currently wearing. The neat slacks were wrinkled from being in an evidence bag, and he had his over-coat draped over one arm, but otherwise, the outfit Dusk had been wearing on the night Jericho had brought him in was intact. Right down to the glittering brooches on the lapels of his overcoat—one sun and one crescent moon—that the tech lab had had a field day with while proving they weren't dangerous.

"Oh, this? This is my villain costume. Isn't it awesome?" Dusk gestured to the well-fitting waistcoat and haphazardly rolled-up sleeves of a mussed white dress shirt.

"Right." Jericho kicked off his boots near the door and hung up his leather jacket on the rack. "Shoes off," was all he said before he headed down the hall toward the open kitchen and living room space.

"Of course, Lettie. I remember the rules." Dusk chuckled, toeing off his own shoes and hanging up the overcoat next to Jericho's jacket. Then he followed.

"Make yourself at home." Jericho gestured to the apart-ment in general on his way to the fridge, where he pulled out a water pitcher to pour himself a glass.

Dusk nodded with a smile, but when he turned to face the living space, the expression seemed to freeze on his face. "Umm ... Lettie ... I think you've been robbed."

"What?" A pain was starting to build in the space between Jericho's eyebrows. He rubbed at it, but it didn't go away. Great Merlin, this was going to be a long day.

"It's just . . . Where's your couch?" Dusk whispered, still standing half in the hall and half in the main room as if he were afraid he'd get blamed for the lack of furniture. "And your TV? And your . . . oh, I don't know . . . *everything*?!"

"I don't need any of that shit. I'm hardly ever here," Jericho said, grabbing another glass from the cabinet to pour Dusk some water. Maybe it would get him to shut up for a few seconds so Jericho's headache would go away. "I've got a futon in the spare bedroom for you though."

"By futon, do you mean a couch that folds out into a bed, or do you mean one of those thin floor mat thingies?" Dusk moved to the island to grab the offered glass and took a slow sip.

"Does it really matter?"

"Yeah. It kinda does."

"Look, if you don't like it, you can just give me the location of your lab, and you'll be free to go."

Dusk's expression hardened into something that Jericho hadn't seen since he was fifteen and Sol was gearing up to ask Jericho out for the first time. Sol had always looked like that right before he was about to do something unbearably stupid. Still, Jericho couldn't hold back the fond feeling that warmed his belly at the sight. He'd missed that look.

"Not until my demands are met." Dusk's tone was cut from steel.

"Then I guess you're just gonna have to get used to sleeping on a paper-thin mat thingie," Jericho said. "No skin off my nose."

"Is this part of the whole rehab process?" Dusk leaned forward, his mouth twisting into a wry smile. "Is this that 'tough love' thing they talk so much about?"

Jericho didn't bother answering. He just turned to the sink to pour out the rest of his water. "Bathroom's second door on the left. Go get freshened up. I'm going down to the market to grab some stuff for dinner."

Dusk nodded, turning to head in that direction, then he stopped and turned back to Jericho with a thoughtful frown etched into his brow.

"What is it now?" Jericho heaved a sigh.

"I don't have any clothes. Would you mind lending me something?"

Green eyes narrowed on Dusk for a moment as Jericho considered his options. He could tell Dusk to stuff it and just wear what he'd brought with him. Or he could be a good . . . whatever the fuck they were now and offer him something. He nodded, then headed to his own room, dragging out a pair of jeans that he hadn't been able to fit into in a couple of years and a soft black hoodie. The less Dusk stood out, the better. When he returned to the main room, Dusk had already ducked into the bathroom and shut the door firmly behind him.

"If you'd just tell me where your lab is, you could go back to your own place," Jericho called through the door, each word enunciated precisely so Dusk would be able to understand him.

"What was that?" Dusk asked, opening the door a crack to peek out at him. There was a cheeky grin etched onto his freckled face again, and Jericho saw the flash of his hearing aids still in his ears. Fucker. He'd heard just fine. "Oh, thank you." Dusk snatched the clothes and disappeared into the bathroom again.

•

WITH JERICHO'S CLOTHES ON, Dusk almost looked normal. The jeans covered his tracking anklet, and the high neck of the hoodie made the voice collar almost look like an outdated accessory instead of what it actually was. No one even batted an eye when the pair entered the small grocery store. They were just customers—not hero and villain—a thought that felt strange to Jericho.

"You know, you could always take the collar off," Dusk said conversationally as he picked up a tomato, giving the fruit a light squeeze before replacing it with all the others. "I promise I won't use my Voice on you."

"On me," Jericho repeated with a raised brow, bumping Dusk lightly with the shopping cart. "Like I'm going to take that fucking chance."

"If you want me to trust you enough to show you where my lab is, you need to trust me too, Lettie." Dusk's words were thoughtful as he plucked another tomato from the stack and turned it over and over in his hand, inspecting it for imperfections. "It's gotta be give and take here."

Jericho grunted, not bothering to answer. He knew Dusk was right, that to get the banshee to talk, he'd have to give something of himself too. But he also knew that Dusk would see the trick behind that. The boy he'd known wouldn't expect Jericho to just roll over and play nice. No. He'd be expecting this kind of resistance. It may have seemed counterproductive on the outside, but Jericho was playing the game exactly as he should be.

"Why are you even looking at tomatoes? I don't put them in my curry."

"No, but we got deli meat. I thought they'd be good for sandwiches." Dusk snatched a second from the pile, gave it a soft squeeze, and set both into the cart. "Then I can make Lettie lunch."

"You're not a fucking househusband, you're a convict."

Dusk moved on to the apples, unbothered by the harsh words.

•

THEIR FIRST DINNER together was eaten mostly in silence as they both stood around the island in Jericho's kitchen, enjoying the curry he'd made. Dusk insisted on cleaning the dishes afterwards, then he excused himself to his room.

That night, Jericho lay in bed listening to every movement outside his door with the heightened hearing of one of his Alliance-issue potions and a growing sense of paranoia. He waited for Dusk to try to escape or to go to the kitchen and grab a knife to kill his captor. But when neither of those things happened, and the sun finally peeked through the curtains, he allowed himself a couple hours of sleep.

He awoke to the sound of off-tune humming and the smell of eggs cooking. Rolling out of bed, he padded into the kitchen, running a hand through his long blond hair.

"I don't remember you being a morning person," Jericho muttered, heading straight for the coffeemaker.

"Things change, Lettie. I remember you putting so much sugar into your coffee it couldn't really be called coffee anymore," Dusk teased, sliding a plate of eggs toward him.

Jericho blinked. His hand stopped as he reached for the sugar bowl, and instead, he took a sip of the bitter coffee, letting it sit heavily on his tongue before he forced it down with a hard swallow. *Shit. That was bad.*

"What's this?" Jericho gestured to the plate.

"It's eggs. Scrambled. With cheese. Just like you like them."

"No. Is it supposed to be a peace offering or something? Because I'm not doing that with you. We aren't friends anymore."

Ducking his head, Dusk hid his expression. "No. I suppose we aren't. But . . . we could be again. Right?"

Jericho eyed him thoughtfully for a long moment, taking in the hunched shoulders and the downcast eyes. "No. We can't be. Because I'm a hero, and you're an Unseelie intent on doing . . . whatever you were doing."

A cold laugh left Dusk. Too high. Too reedy. Thin in a way his laughs had never been before. And when he lifted his head again, there was a twisted smile stretching his lips. It didn't touch any other part of his face, as if it'd been pasted there from a picture. Hair stood up on the back of Jericho's neck, a shiver wracking down his spine. Cold. He felt cold. When had his friend gained *that* expression?

"They haven't figured out what was on the drive yet then?" Dusk asked, tone deceptively light.

"Not yet. But I'm sure it's just a matter of time. You'd do well to tell us before they do. Once we have that information, I doubt you'll be able to make a deal," Jericho warned.

Dark bangs fell into Dusk's eyes as he cocked his head, lips pursed, seeming to think about Jericho's words. "I suppose you're right. But then . . . there is the matter of my lab. Isn't there?"

Jericho gulped another mouthful of bitter coffee to give himself a moment to answer, keeping his face carefully neutral. *Don't show your hand, J. You can do this.* "I mean, I guess it depends on what's on there. If it's something really dangerous, you could be put away for a long time. Fuck your lab."

The sly smile was back, dimpling one freckled cheek and lightening Dusk's eyes in dark amusement. He'd read Jericho like an open book. *Fuck.* How had he done that after so many years apart? Was Jericho really so transparent? "I dunno about all that. I mean, do you know why they want my lab?"

"No, I—"

"Oh, would you look at the time? We'd best finish getting ready, or you'll be late for work!" Dusk cut him off with a tone of mock cheerfulness, then he ducked into his own room to change into the clothes Jericho had loaned him.

A car waited for them at the curb, buzzing softly in the early morning hum of the city. Jericho shook himself. He could have sworn they'd been making headway for a moment there. Although Dusk was still being cagey and secretive, he'd felt they were reaching something like an understanding. As if maybe Dusk was starting to see the true danger he was in. But in a flash, all of that was gone.

"Am I just going to sit at your desk and color like when we used to go to your mom's work for 'take your child to work day'?" Dusk asked, skipping along beside Jericho with a little smile as they entered through the heavy metal double doors of Spring Hill Hold.

"Jericho. We are here to escort the villain to the holding cells." A medium-sized K.N.I.G.H.T. unit outstretched its arms to grab ahold of Dusk as soon as they entered the facility.

Dusk yelped at the tight grip, trying to pull himself free. "That's not necessary. I'll be good. Lettie, tell them. I've already been good," he crooned darkly. "Haven't I?"

Jericho sighed, scrubbing at the space between his eyebrows again. The headache was back. "I'll have to talk to Oakfur about it. Just sit tight, and I'll see what I can do."

"Promise?"

"Promise." Not that he was sure why he was bothering. Jericho reasoned it must be because they needed information from Dusk, and he wouldn't exactly provide that from a cell.

"Okay." Dusk nodded easily and held out a shiny black bento box that Jericho didn't remember owning, neatly wrapped in a red scarf that he also didn't remember ever purchasing or being gifted. "Don't forget your lunch."

Jericho reached out to awkwardly take the lunch. He stared down at the parcel as Dusk was carted off to the holding cells, trying to figure out where the man had found the lunchbox. Then Jericho shook himself. It had probably been packed away in one of the boxes in the guest room from when he'd moved in. It looked like something his mother would have bought him.

"That's so cute," Erling cooed from behind him. Jericho spun on his heel to glare at the griffin. Erling's lips twitched in amusement. "How do I get myself a live-in hubby to make my meals?" he teased, nudging Jericho playfully with his elbow.

"You have a live-in wifey," Jericho reminded.

"Yeah, but she doesn't make me box lunches anymore."

"I wonder why that is," Jericho muttered sarcastically. A smile twitched at the corners of his lips as Erling pouted. He continued toward the bullpen with a half-hearted shrug. "Besides, it's probably drugged."

"You aren't going to eat it then?"

"Oh no, I'm going to eat it." The box made a dull thump on his desk, and Jericho smiled a little at it.

"What? That's crazy!" Erling rounded on him, wings rustling in agitation. "You're going to deliberately make yourself sick?"

"Sure. What's a little food poisoning between *friends*?" Jericho offered with a wry smile. He was mostly kidding about it being drugged. Dusk had been locked up in his apartment all evening. Where would he have gotten anything to drug Jericho? But still, he wouldn't put it past the villain. "Besides, I need him to trust me, and to get him to do that, I need to prove I trust him. If that means getting food poisoning, so be it. And hey . . . being taken care of when I'm sick is probably the quickest way to get him to take pity on me."

"That's dedication." An elf at another desk whistled.

Jericho shrugged. "Is Oakfur in yet?"

"Nah, he won't be in till later."

Jericho nodded and settled into his chair to work, studiously ignoring the shining lunchbox on the corner of his desk.

●

MEETING WITH BIM OAKFUR was becoming too much of a regular occurrence for Jericho's liking. She didn't like that every time she needed something for Dusk, she had to clear it with the captain. Still, it was a hero's job to do things the right way—the legal way. So, instead of complaining or going behind the captain's back, Jericho went down to the locker room, lined her eyes in charcoal gray, and put on her Alliance-issue armor. Was it necessary to suit up to see the captain? No. But pulling on the gold-trimmed metal eased Jericho's mind and made her feel more confident. Even with the way the cream-colored breastplate made it hard to sit down.

"What is it *now*, Jericho?" Oakfur asked when he noticed the hero loitering outside his office. "If you have something to talk about, you'd best get your ass in here and say it. I'm in no mood to dawdle."

"Yes, sir." Jericho nodded, heading in to stand behind one of the metal chairs, gloved hands gripping the back of it perhaps a little too hard. "I would like to request that Dusk not be relegated to the holding cells while we are here."

"You what?"

"I want him to be allowed up in the bullpen with me while he's here. He can sit and read a book, or doodle, or something. I don't know. I just don't think he should be down in the holding cells."

Oakfur blinked at Jericho for a long moment, his eyebrow

twitching in what could only be described as barely restrained irritation. "Explain to me why you think letting that—" He swallowed roughly, perhaps narrowly avoiding saying something he shouldn't. After a breath, he continued. "What evidence do you have that he can be trusted with such liberties?"

"None," Jericho offered with a little shrug, her armor riding up around her shoulders. "But if I'm going to get him to trust me, I have to at least pretend like I trust him. This is a good first step."

"And what of all the information he could obtain while sitting there?"

"All the truly dangerous case information is disseminated via the intranet in the bullpen. We don't sit there and chat about our cases generally. And if we do, it's nothing that he could use. I don't think."

"You don't think?!" Oakfur all but yelled, his face turning an interesting shade of red that very nearly matched his hair. "And what about when you're out in the field? Who will be babysitting your pet-villain then?"

"He'll go back to the holding cells when I'm not around to watch him. Sir, you want information, and the best way to get that is by convincing him that I'm in his corner. He won't trust me unless he thinks I want to help him. I can't do that unless I give him certain freedoms. This is one of those freedoms."

"Or. He'll think he can get one over on you and he'll slip up," Erling added from where he stood just outside the open door. "Win-win."

"This was a private meeting," Jericho hissed.

"I know. But you're both being loud. The whole bullpen heard you, and we agree with J. If Dusk really is as dangerous as the council says he is, then we need to get to that lab in a hurry. The best way to do that is by tricking him, like J said.

And I, personally, trust J's judgement. They've never been wrong before. Plus, they know Dusk better than we do." Erling shrugged, his wings rustling.

The twitching had spread from Oakfur's eyebrow to the entire left side of his face as he restrained whatever emotion was vying for control. "Very well then. But you two idiots are responsible for him. If this goes south, it's your necks."

"Yes, sir," the two heroes said in unison, both giving curt nods before they turned to leave Oakfur's office.

"And shut the damn door!"

Jericho huffed and kicked the door shut behind her before heading back to her desk.

"I didn't need your help," Jericho muttered to Erling.

"You didn't. But I agree with you, this is the most efficient route."

"It's logical." Jericho dropped into her chair, scrubbing a hand along the soft peach fuzz on one side of her head.

"It is." Erling propped his feet up on his desk, looking annoyingly smug. "When're you going down to get your pet-villain?"

Jericho rolled her eyes, but she couldn't help the amused smirk at the term. Pet-villain. Apt. She chuckled. "I'm going to get changed into my civvies first. This armor is hell to sit in all day."

"Can't wait to meet him." Erling waved from his spot behind his desk.

●

IT WAS CUTE.

The damn lunch that Dusk had made him was ridiculously adorable. With fruit cut into flowers, and a smiley face carved into the top of the sandwich. It was *disgustingly* adorable.

"Do you like it?" Dusk asked, leaning over to watch him eat with wide, calculating eyes. A scientist watching mold grow. "I got up early to cut the fruit flowers."

"It's fine." Jericho shrugged, lifting the sandwich to take an experimental bite. It didn't taste like it had been drugged, but that didn't mean anything. And he wondered, did Dusk have the guts to poison him in front of the entire squad of heroes in the bullpen? The Soliel he'd known back when they were sixteen wouldn't have, but this wasn't that boy, not anymore. Even if Dusk's record was clear of blood, they didn't know what he'd been up to before he'd appeared on the scene.

"Just fine?" Dusk flopped back into his chair to sulk. "Your mama taught me how to do the fruit. Remember?"

"I remember you almost losing a finger trying to turn a strawberry into a rose," Jericho mumbled around a mouthful of ham and tomato.

"Gross, Lettie. Manners. No one needs to see your half-chewed food!"

Jericho heard the griffin behind him choke on a snicker. "Not. A. Fucking. Word. Erling."

"Wouldn't dream of it . . . Lettie."

Jericho whipped around to glare daggers at the other man, a low snarl pulling back his lip to reveal sharp incisors.

"Oh no. Don't do that," Dusk chided, his bright eyes narrowing on Erling. "No one calls him that but me." There was something dangerous—possessive—in Dusk's tone, but Jericho decided not to look too closely at it. Dusk was right at least; no one was allowed to call him Lettie except Dusk. Because it was Dusk's name. A mark of friendship that Jericho had never really outgrown.

"Right. Sorry." Erling held up his hands in surrender, and Jericho spun back in his chair again.

"What's with that fucking guy?" Dusk signed, his eyes

only barely budging from where he still had Erling fixed with a cold look.

Jericho's fingers twitched to reply, but he kept them still. As friends, this had been common, signing to one another and talking about the people around them in a way most others wouldn't understand. But they weren't friends. And they weren't doing that.

"Sooooo . . . " Dusk rolled his eyes, looking only a little huffy about Jericho refusing to play along, before he grabbed an apple slice from his own lunch and crunched into it. "What am I allowed to do while I'm here? Or am I supposed to just sit here and look pretty?"

"What do you want to do?" Jericho forced his shoulders to relax.

Unsurprisingly, Dusk seemed to have an answer ready. "Could I do some shopping for furniture for your place? We could use a couch, and a TV, and maybe even an armchair. Oh. Oh! And a new shower curtain!"

"We?"

Dusk nodded, the look of excitement not dimmed in the slightest by Jericho's obvious dislike of the term 'we.' Not that Jericho thought he'd be able to dissuade Dusk from using it.

"And how do you propose to do that?"

"On the computer, of course. You'd be amazed by the things you can order online these days. Not that you would know, since it seems like you haven't spent more than five minutes furnishing your place. Or did you just move in? Is that why there isn't anything there?" Dusk tapped his chin as if riddling out the answer.

"Nah. J's been there for going on five years now," Erling called from behind Jericho, and Jericho made a mental note to give him the stale breakroom coffee when he went to grab them refills later. "He also never invites people over."

Jericho clicked his tongue. "I don't have time to worry about interior design or parties. Some of us have jobs to do."

"Yeah, sure, whatever you say." Erling laughed.

Jericho shrugged Erling off. "I'll see Ildri about getting you a tablet that'll keep you out of trouble. Happy?"

"Delighted." Dusk nodded, a smile spreading his lips that dimpled both cheeks.

That was Jericho's first mistake.

CHAPTER SEVEN

THE SECOND MISTAKE WAS DRAGGING DUSK ALONG *WITH* HIM as he headed down to meet with Ildri in her lab about the tablet the next day.

"Oh my goodness, your hair is so cute," Dusk fawned over the little pixie. "Look at it, Lettie. Look at the colors! So bright. Do you dye it? Or is that the natural color?"

Ildri giggled much too loudly for the early hour, shaking her head. "My, my, my, J, you didn't tell me that your new charge was so damned adorable! How could this sweet face be labelled a villain? Look at these freckles." She squished Dusk's brown cheeks between her fingers, her eyes dancing with laughter.

"We didn't come down here for you to . . . whatever this is." Jericho gestured to them with an annoyed huff, kicking at the leg of one long work bench.

"Then why *did* you come down here?" Ildri turned to blink wide eyes at him.

Jericho scowled, his teeth clenching as he thought of how to say what he needed to, but before he could open his mouth, Dusk was talking. "He wants to make sure I'm comfortable in my new home, so he's letting me go shopping. Isn't that sweet?"

"The sweetest," Ildri agreed, eyeing Jericho suspiciously. "You need a device he can shop from that he can't use to access the hold's intranet or get in contact with any of his people."

"Exactly." Dusk nodded, too eager for someone who was being held captive in every sense of the word. Jericho wasn't sure what Dusk was getting out of making friends with Ildri, but he was sure Ildri could handle herself. She was the best tech in the Alliance after all.

Ildri nodded and set to work, but something about what she'd said niggled at Jericho. His *people*. He'd never thought about whether or not Dusk would have more than one person working with him, but it made sense. The things he'd accomplished in six months—breaking into data banks all across the city, leaving the citizens feeling unsafe and as if they couldn't trust their own devices—it spoke of a team. Even so, Jericho still couldn't pinpoint what Dusk had been doing with the data. None of it had been publicly exposed; it seemed all he'd meant to do was spread fear. Which he had.

No. This was bigger than that. Jericho would have to look a little deeper.

●

JERICHO DIDN'T HAVE time to supervise Dusk's furniture selection. The full moon came two days later, and there was too much else to think of. With another person living in his apartment, he had to worry about if his wolf would lash out at Dusk during the mandatory twelve-hour seclusion period. So, for the first time since he'd been a teenager, Jericho resolved to lock himself in his bedroom that night. The wolf wouldn't like it. It'd probably get destructive and destroy the pillows, the mattress, some of Jericho's clothes, anything it could find within reach. But that was a small price to pay.

He stood looking down at the supplies sprawled over his bed.

Extra protein. Check.

Chew supplement. Check.

Sedative . . . Where was the sedative?

Picking up the little tote into which Jericho had loaded everything he needed, he looked on the bed for the little packet of patches. They weren't enough to knock him out— not much was—but they'd take the edge off the change and make his wolf far more docile. They weren't there. They weren't on the dresser or the nightstand either. The only other place would be the kitchen or the bathroom.

"Dusk, have you seen my . . . " Jericho frowned, looking at where Dusk stood behind the island, the packet of patches sitting in front of him.

"You don't need these." Dusk wiggled the packet against the marble with a soft shuffling sound. "You never needed them before. When we were kids, I always helped you."

Jericho jerked up straighter, his eyes narrowing. "We aren't kids now, are we?"

"These things aren't good for you. You know that." Dusk was looking down at the packet with disgust written clearly across his features, not meeting Jericho's eyes. Which may have been for the best, because Jericho was furious, and he wasn't sure what the pacing wolf would do if Dusk looked him in the eye. It would be seen as a challenge, that he did know. "They muddy you up."

"I know what they do, Dusk. I've been on and off them since I was thirteen." He didn't love the foggy feeling that seemed to cling to his senses for days after, but it was the trade-off for being in control. He hadn't been those first few shifts after . . . He shook himself. Now wasn't the time to wallow in the grief his wolf had felt at the loss of Sol. The clock was ticking. He had an hour for the sedatives to kick in, and to load up on carbs before the wolf took over and it was too ravenous to think. He'd gotten this down to a science. The chew supplement, the protein, the sedative, and the carb loading: it all helped to keep the wolf relatively happy and less likely to run off into the night to hunt.

"I could help you again. I could . . . " Dusk trailed off, a fingernail scratching at the cardboard packaging of the patches. "We're friends. It always recognized me as its friend. I calmed it down. I could . . . I could sing for it like I did before."

That. That was too much. The offer to sing like Sol used to, his voice soft and out of tune but oh so comforting and familiar, was too much. Jericho stomped over to the counter and snatched the packet from him.

"It won't recognize you like that anymore," he bit out in a snarl.

Dusk looked up, stricken. "Why not?"

"Because we aren't friends, *Dusk*! I don't know how I can make that any more clear to you!" He spun and went back to his room, slamming the door behind him.

That full moon was the worst he'd had in a long time. Even with the sedative and his regular medicine to alleviate the symptoms of a shift, he felt every change from man to wolf. He felt his bones moving and restructuring. He felt every hair grow thicker. He was hyper-aware of all of it. And when the morning came, the shift back left Jericho panting, sweating, trembling, and weak. This is what he got for not carb loading beforehand. This is what he got for locking himself up. This is what he got for deviating from routine. This is what he got for helping Dusk.

He surveyed the damage with a sigh. There were feathers fucking everywhere.

"Fuck."

●

THE FURNITURE WAS DELIVERED two days after the full moon, and that's when Jericho realized his third mistake: letting Dusk furnish his apartment without any kind of oversight.

"What the fuck is that?" Jericho glared at the overstuffed armchair that was almost the size of a loveseat. It was a glaring shade of green. He hated it.

"It's an armchair," Dusk said in a flat tone as he gestured where the moving men should put it.

Jericho growled, clenching his jaw slightly.

"I can see that it's an armchair, Dusk. I meant, why the fuck did you order it? You got a couch, didn't you?" He gestured pointedly to the matching sofa and coffee table. "We don't have space for three huge pieces of furniture."

"Put the bed in that room over there." Dusk pointed to his door. "And the dresser as well. Thanks guys."

Molar on molar, Jericho felt his teeth creak in protest at the effort it took to keep from screaming.

Dusk blinked over at him and began to move his fingers in soft soothing signs. "Calm down, Lettie. I promise it won't get in the way."

"Whatever," Jericho snarled, stomping off to his room and slamming the door behind him. He didn't know why he was so annoyed with all of it, not when he'd been the one who said Dusk could get whatever he wanted. But it felt like Dusk was entrenching himself in Jericho's life. Carving out a place for himself there where one hadn't been and shouldn't be. They weren't friends.

●

HE WAS LURED out of his hiding place some hours later by the smell of dinner cooking. Jericho would be hard pressed to admit it, but other than the curry he'd made the other night, he hadn't taken the time to enjoy a home cooked meal in . . . Well, he couldn't remember the last time. He knew instant meals weren't the healthiest; they were loaded with unneeded sodium just to make them taste bearable, and freeze-dried meat made his wolf grumpier. But as evidenced by the files loading down his tablet, he spent all of his time either working or thinking about working.

"Look who it is," Dusk teased cheerfully, his hands working diligently to stir whatever was in the pot in front of him. "Decided to come out of your cave, have you?"

Jericho grunted, moving to lean against the island. "Is that arroz con pollo?"

"Just like Mama used to make." Dusk hummed happily.

Jericho's brow rose. Sensing the opening, he asked, "Where did your mom go, anyway? Ildri couldn't find any trace of her after your . . . " The words drifted off into an uncomfortable shrug.

"My attempted suicide," Dusk filled in for him.

Jericho jerked. He'd assumed—but no, he'd been wrong. "What? I thought you—"

"Faked it." Dusk shook his head. "No. I didn't fake it. Mama just didn't let me succeed."

Jericho felt his frown deepen, his body leaning heavily across the island to get closer to Dusk's face as if trying to sniff out a lie. There was no trace of deception. No increased heart rate. No lingering shift in body language. But that didn't mean he wasn't being a manipulative little shit. Perhaps Dusk really was just saying it so Jericho knew. Or perhaps this was meant to sting after their fight during the full moon. It did sting. More than it should have. Because a part of him knew it was his fault.

"Why would you?"

Dusk reached to turn down the heat on the stove, then turned to grab the spices. "I was never going to be a hero, and my best friend hated me. What did I have left?"

It *was* meant to sting. Jericho felt it clench sharp around his insides, and a dull ache that he hadn't noticed before suddenly burned brighter. A gulp permeated the silence, and Jericho realized the sound had come from him.

"Anyway," Dusk continued after letting Jericho stew for a moment. "She found me and dragged my ass out of the water. Great Merlin, you should have heard the screaming." Dusk laughed, shaking his head. "You would have thought *she* was the banshee."

"And then what?"

The pot sizzled as the silence stretched between them. Dusk focused on the food, and Jericho waited. That's all he could do: wait. Let Dusk work through his words or decide which ones he wanted to use. Dusk had never been the type to think much before he spoke, but that was then, and this was now. So Jericho waited.

"And then she tried to teach me there were more ways to save people than by being a hero," he said finally.

Jericho shook his head. There was no better way to save than to be a hero, not in his mind. All he'd ever wanted out of life was to be a part of the Hero Alliance. To protect those around him and make sure no one hurt them. This idea that there was another way felt strange. It didn't line up with what he believed of the world, nor what he knew of Dusk. Dusk, who had been right there with him all along, wanting the same things.

Dusk continued making them dinner, turning to grab bowls from the cabinet behind him, and dishing out healthy portions into each. He slid a bowl across the island toward Jericho, and they both ate quietly. Jericho thought maybe that would be the end of the conversation and he'd get no more answers.

Jericho was halfway through his food when his phone rang from the counter. One glance showed the word "Mom" on the caller ID, and he tapped the screen to silence it.

"Not going to answer?" Dusk asked, his eyes lingering on the phone.

"No."

"Are you and your folks not—?" The question hung for a moment, Dusk's eyes flickering from Jericho to the empty walls of the apartment. No pictures. No mementos. Nothing to show a life lived outside of Jericho's work. "What happened between you and them?"

The answer was complicated and not something he particularly wanted to discuss with Dusk at the moment. Jericho didn't want to tell Dusk how his suicide—attempted as it might have been—had torn Jericho's family apart. How they had all grieved in different ways, and Jericho's way had been through an anger the likes of which his parents just couldn't handle. How the only way to deal with it had been to focus himself solely on his work and nothing else. How that had left things between himself and his mother particularly strained. Jericho shook his head.

"I remember when we were kids, that's all you wanted, to be a hero. Just as much as I did," Jericho said instead, his words distant and soft. His mind drifted back to happier, easier times. Games of tag and heroes and villains on the playground. Long before that hard glint had entered Dusk's eyes.

"And you told me I could. That we'd be a team," Dusk added, his tone almost fond, but Jericho didn't miss the searching look in his brown eyes. Jericho had pushed the topic of his family off for now, but they'd come back to it at some point, that look said. "But we were just kids then, we didn't know any better. And the adults who said we could do that . . . they were lying to us."

Those words held so much weight, and Jericho felt them sink into his shoulders, dragging him down till he was hunching heavily against the marble countertop.

"No," he whispered almost desperately. "You could still be a hero and work with me." Jericho had to believe that. If he didn't, he wasn't sure what he was really trying to achieve by keeping Dusk here anymore.

Dusk snorted. "My definition of hero is drastically different than yours these days, I'm afraid."

"What's that supposed to mean?"

"Ask around. See what kind of heroes the Alliance really are. What kind of heroes the council really wants them to be."

"What?"

When Dusk looked up from his food, that hard light was in his eyes again, and his lips pressed into a firm line.

"Who are they really protecting, Lettie? It's not people like me." With that, Dusk scooped up his bowl and retreated to his bedroom, leaving Jericho to blink at the spot where he'd been a moment before.

●

JERICHO'S fourth mistake (or his fifth; by this point, he'd lost count) was looking into who the Hero Alliance was really protecting. They had a longstanding record of locking up dangerous villains in the name of keeping the streets safe for humans and fae alike. But upon further digging, Jericho found that some of those villains were just ordinary Unseelie who had made mistakes. Just people, like Dusk had said. A kelpie who'd been caught shoplifting. A young goblin who was spray-painting graffiti. Nothing they had done could really label them as villains. Troublemakers, yes, but not the sinister evil the heroes depicted them as. What did that mean for the heroes?

"It just doesn't make sense," Jericho growled, slamming his hands on his desk. Thank Merlin Dusk was down in the lab with Ildri that morning. He didn't need more questions than he had answers at this point.

"What is it?" Erling asked, the wheels on his office chair squeaking loudly as he pushed himself to sit next to Jericho. "What's the problem, J?"

"That last villain we apprehended—what was their crime?"

Erling shrugged, his dark face impassive. "Destruction of public property."

"Right." Jericho nodded, looking back down to the file. "And how much time did they get?"

"I don't really know. They don't tell us that." Erling blinked.

"His records say five years. Does that seem right for something so minor? I mean . . . He didn't hurt anyone." Jericho felt his brows pinching together in the middle.

"No. He didn't."

"What kind of destruction?"

Erling frowned. "The captain didn't say when we went out there to get him. It's not in his file?"

"No, it's not." Jericho wrinkled his nose, sighing. "I just— it feels weird, doesn't it?"

"That's the job, J." Erling rolled back to his desk. "Don't think too hard about it."

"Yeah. That's the job," Jericho agreed softly, tone lacking the conviction it might have held two or three weeks ago.

CHAPTER EIGHT

JERICHO WAS LOSING TIME. THERE WERE BIG GAPS IN HER memory. Dark spots where events should be.

Like after dinner the other day, when she'd planned to work through some of her paperwork and had woken up the next morning not having remembered even going to bed. Or two days ago when there had been a whole hour after they got home from the hold unaccounted for.

She wasn't sure when it had started, not exactly. Had it been with that first packed lunch? Or was it the night Dusk had made her dinner? Or only since the full moon? She didn't know, nor did it matter in the end. The point was, the gaps were littered throughout the last week. At first it had been a half hour here, twenty minutes there. But last night, it had been two whole hours.

She didn't know what Dusk was doing with the time. According to the tracking data, the banshee never left the apartment. Not that that couldn't be faked. But if he was leaving, where was he going? What was he doing? And how could Jericho find out?

That's how Jericho found herself on the floor of her bathroom. The cool tile bruised her knees through the fabric of her pants, and the steam from the shower was choking her. But she needed to get whatever drug Dusk had slipped her out of her system before it took effect.

"You okay in there, Lettie?" Dusk called through the door, maybe worried his captor had passed out in the shower and hit her head.

"M'good," Jericho said, not even having to pretend when her speech slurred. She could feel whatever it was already taking effect. It made the edges of her vision blurry and dark, and if she didn't get it out soon, she really would be passing out on the bathroom floor. She waited a beat, ears trained to Dusk's movements as he stepped away from the door, then finished expelling the contents of her stomach into the toilet.

Ten minutes later, with a raw throat but fresh, clean hair, Jericho emerged. She played into the drowsiness Dusk would expect, keeping her lids heavy and her movements sufficiently slow. She couldn't afford for Dusk to realize that she'd caught on. Not yet.

"M'tired," she slurred, leaning heavily against the doorframe of the bathroom.

"Poor dear." Dusk tutted lightly, moving to Jericho's side and looping her arm over his narrow shoulders. "Let's get you to bed." The pair of them stumbled to Jericho's bedroom, where Jericho flopped facedown on the comforter. "You get some rest, Lettie. I'll be back soon."

Jericho waited until she heard the apartment door close behind Dusk before she scrambled to her feet. Her vision was still a little hazy around the edges, making her reaction time slower, but that was all right. She didn't need to be in top shape to follow Dusk. It took her longer than she would have liked to stuff her feet into her boots and tug on the black leather jacket, but soon enough, she was following Dusk out into the night-drenched city.

It was surprisingly easy to follow him. Jericho would have thought that after spending so long not being caught, Dusk would be harder to track, especially with her own drugged state.

At one point, she stumbled, toe catching on the uneven pavement of an empty, disintegrating sidewalk.

"Shit," Jericho hissed through clenched teeth.

Green eyes widened in panic when she saw Dusk stop. Jericho ducked into the thick shadow of a closed shop, holding her breath and praying Dusk would write it off. A neon sign hummed above the awning, and an electric car buzzed as it passed. Dusk stood for a moment, listening, and then looked back to the darkened street before he seemed to shrug it off and kept walking.

Jericho waited a moment, inhaling a deep breath to steady her nerves. She placed her steps more carefully, taking her time so that her fuzzy mind didn't trip her up again. They were at least five blocks from Jericho's apartment now, and she was about ready to tackle Dusk and drag him back to the hold when he stopped in front of a run-down warehouse. In the yellow glow of the streetlight, Jericho could see an expression of peace cross Dusk's upturned face, and then he entered the building.

With a quick glance down at her watch, Jericho saw it was only 8 p.m. She decided to walk around the building to check that there were no other exits, then settled herself against the building to wait for Dusk to come out. Maybe this was his lab. If it were, she couldn't go barging in; it would be too dangerous. Merlin only knew what traps the villain had in place to keep intruders at bay. Seconds ticked by into minutes, and the next time Jericho checked her watch, it was 9 p.m.

What was Dusk doing in there? Should Jericho call it in? What if it was a false alarm? No. She'd wait it out and see what came of it. If nothing else, she could bring in a squadron once she had Dusk cuffed again.

"Are you going to stand out in the cold all evening, or are you coming in?" Dusk's voice drifted from where he'd pushed the door open a crack on silent hinges. A sliver of light cut its way across the dark sidewalk, illuminating the tips of Jericho's boots. "If you're interested in what I'm up to, get your ass inside."

"It's not cold." Jericho huffed softly, swallowing down the swelling panic threatening to take over. She moved to pull the door open the rest of the way, forcing her hands not to shake. "When did you realize I was following you?"

"When did you realize I was drugging you?" Dusk countered, holding the door to usher Jericho inside.

Jericho's movements stuttered a little, breath growing shallow in her chest. "You admit it."

"I'm not stupid enough to try to deny it now." Dusk sounded so . . . so . . . unbothered by it. It made something hot and furious crawl under Jericho's skin. How fucking dare he. How fucking *dare* he drug her and then try to act like it didn't matter. What kind of fucking psycho did that to someone?

"And you expect me to just, what? Forgive you?"

Dusk cocked his head, his fingers drumming on the doorframe that he was still holding open for Jericho. "No. But I know you. You're pissed. But your curiosity is going to get the better of you."

Jericho tsked, looking away from Dusk and further into the building.

"Suit yourself." Dusk let the door fall from his fingers and turned to head inside. Jericho caught it sharply on her hip, but she ignored the sting in favor of skulking after Dusk.

Through the main door, there was a small lobby tiled in

grungy green flooring and a lightbulb flickering above an abandoned reception desk. "The fuck is this place?"

Dusk didn't answer. Instead, he kept walking to a set of double doors with narrow windows in them. Pushing through, Jericho found herself in an old cafeteria. Round tables were scattered throughout, each with a few too many chairs shoved around it, people pressed shoulder to shoulder as they hunched over their food. Along the back wall was a row of tables with several people standing behind them, dishing out hot meals to a line, all waiting their turn patiently.

Jericho's nose lifted to sniff the air softly. Below the smell of unwashed, stale bodies, she could smell Unseelie magic. The odor clung to every one of the people around her, a sharp metallic smell like rusted wet copper.

"They're all Unseelie," she whispered, eyes narrowing to slits.

"Most of them." Dusk nodded. "But they're also hungry."

"Dusk," one of the men called from the line of people dispensing food. "Is your friend here to help? We could use some extra hands." The man smiled, his inhuman eyes bright and cheerful. *Redcap*, Jericho's brain supplied for her. But even with the shark-like teeth, the man's smile was kind.

"Well, Lettie? Are you gonna help?" Dusk quirked a brow. A challenge.

Little shit. He knew she couldn't just say no. Not when there were people who needed her help. Even if that help was something as simple as dishing out food. He knew!

"Uh. Yeah." Jericho nodded, scurrying over to the food line and taking up a pair of tongs to dish out baked potatoes.

●

JERICHO'S WATCH read 11 p.m. by the time everyone was fed and the heating trays were empty. She stood back, leaning against a wall as she watched Dusk talk to the others who had been on the line.

A soft expression had settled onto Dusk's face, eyes crinkling slightly, mouth relaxed.

"Home?" Dusk asked, tilting his head toward the door.

"Home." Jericho nodded.

The walk back passed in silence. Jericho needed that quiet to process everything she'd just seen. A redcap managing a soup kitchen. It seemed counter to everything he knew of their kind. Redcaps were violent, vicious creatures. But that man had put so much care into each interaction he had with those around him. And it wasn't just Unseelie amongst them; there were humans too. Tucked in amongst the others, and just as at ease as if they weren't sitting shoulder to shoulder with creatures who might kill them before saying hello. It was . . . It didn't fit with the image of the world Jericho had always seen in her mind. Where the Seelie protected the humans against some sinister threat. A threat that, up until a few hours ago, had been more shadow than man.

It had a face now, a freckled face, but it somehow felt less like a threat. Jericho shook herself.

As soon as the apartment door clicked shut, Jericho reached over and smacked Dusk upside the head. Her eyes narrowed, and a dark growl vibrated her throat.

"Okay. Okay. I deserved that." Dusk laughed, holding his hands up in surrender.

"You deserve more than that! You drugged me!"

"I did," Dusk agreed. "Would it help if I said I was sorry?"

"No. It would help if you never fucking pulled that shit again," Jericho spat.

Dusk nodded, offering Jericho a sincere smile. "Of course

not. Now that you know where I'm going, there's no reason to continue drugging you."

"You've rigged your tracker somehow, and you've drugged the hero in charge of your rehab. Tell me why I shouldn't just drag your ass down to the hold right now?" Jericho narrowed her eyes further; she couldn't trust him. The man was, after all, a villain. And he'd proven that he wasn't above doing something shady, underhanded, and dangerous to get his way.

"Because if you do that, you'll never get any information out of me at all." Dusk's lips twitched at one corner. Fucker. He knew he had Jericho there. "Lettie. I swear. I won't do it again."

"I want the stuff you used to drug me. Where is it?"

Dusk frowned a little but ultimately conceded and went to pull a bottle of pills from the back of the spice rack. It rattled softly, and Jericho scowled at the label. "Where the fuck did you get wolfsbane?"

Dusk shrugged. "I've got my ways."

"And how do I know you won't just get more?"

"Pinky promise," Dusk said, holding out his hand with his pinky extended for Jericho to take.

Jericho's hands remained firmly pressed into the counter, one clenched around the bottle hard enough that she could feel the plastic giving beneath her grip. "No."

Dusk pouted, his lower lip poking out, eyes going wide like some kind of kicked puppy. Jericho wasn't fooled and wasn't playing this fucking game with him.

"I said no."

Dusk sighed and dropped his hand to his side.

"And you're not fucking cooking anymore without my supervision." Dusk opened his mouth to protest, but Jericho held up a hand. "I can't trust you."

Dusk nodded.

"Now, why shouldn't I tell the Alliance about your little field trip? I'm sure they'd be interested to know you've been fucking with your tracker."

"Consider what I'm doing community service, all right? I'm helping people, aren't I? That's what they want me to get from this whole rehab process. If you tell them, I'll be locked up again, and that won't help any of us."

"I want the information off the thumb drive." Jericho clenched her jaw tightly. She knew she was pushing it. She knew that any moment now, Dusk would shut down again. But she had to try while she had a reason for Dusk to listen.

There was a twitch at the corner of Dusk's eye. Barely noticeable if Jericho hadn't been looking for it. A sign that Dusk's impassive expression didn't match whatever he was thinking and feeling. "I'll give it to you. Just you. But could I convince you not to turn it over to the council right away?"

Jericho chewed on her response for a moment, her teeth gnawing at the inside of her cheek. She knew, ethically, she needed to turn it over immediately. But the information on that drive was less important than the location of the lab. And in order to find the lab, she needed Dusk to trust her. Maybe this was a way to develop that trust. A way to prove she was worthy of it.

"Well?" Dusk shifted his weight back onto his heels and tucked his hands behind him to hide their fidgeting.

"I will assess it and decide if it is a danger to the public. If it poses a threat, I will release the information to the proper authorities. If not, it can remain between us." Jericho's tone was even, level, fair. This seemed as good a solution as any.

Dusk's eyes narrowed, but he nodded. "I suppose that's fair. But when I open the files, I want them opened on a device controlled by Ildri, in her lab. So there's no possible leak."

"Deal." Jericho held out her hand, and Dusk shook it firmly.

•

As PROMISED, Jericho got in contact with Ildri the next day to set up a time to view the files. Which was how Jericho found himself crammed between Dusk and Ildri as they all sat around an ancient PC, stools pushed so close together their legs were nearly overlapping.

"Are you sure this will work?" Jericho asked. The machine had made a couple false starts in the booting process, fans whirring, then stopping, then whirring again with soft clicks. Jericho wasn't entirely sure where Ildri had even found it, but she had. And strangely enough, it hadn't taken more than a couple of days.

"Eighty-nine point seven percent sure," Ildri said, tapping a couple of keys on the noisy keyboard before she stuffed the thumb drive into a port at the base of the monitor.

"Is that an exact calculation?" Jericho muttered dryly.

Ildri turned to blink at him. "Of course it is."

Dusk snickered to Jericho's right, shaking his head. "Stop grumbling, Lettie. It'll work."

"I'm glad one of you is confident."

"Oh hush, J. Just trust the process." Ildri patted Jericho's head condescendingly.

Jericho hissed, swatting her hand away. "Just get on with it."

"I'm working on it. Jeez, so grumpy. Did you not feed them breakfast this morning, Dusk?"

"Lettie is just Lettie," Dusk said.

At the same time, Jericho said, "He's not allowed to cook anymore."

Ildri blinked between them for a moment, frowning. "I

feel like there is a story there, but you know what? I'm not touching that. Nope." Then she turned back to the computer.

Finally—*finally!*—the screen flickered on to reveal a desktop with a blue background and one tiny folder icon. Ildri jiggled the mouse, making the little arrow wiggle erratically on the screen, before she moved to click the folder and open it. Inside was a stash of pictures from what appeared to be a dating app. That in itself wouldn't have been enough to encourage Dusk to commit such a heist. No, it was the person who was in the pictures. Each photo held one common face, and Jericho recognized it immediately because it was plastered on billboards all over Mythikos.

"Councilman Eldar?" Jericho muttered in disbelief. He saw Dusk's smirk spread in the reflection of the screen just before the man chuckled darkly.

"Yup."

"But this isn't illegal," Ildri argued. She was flipping through the pictures, none of them particularly scandalous. Although it looked like there was more skin further down in the folder, making an uncomfortable shudder crawl up Jericho's spine.

"No, it's not. Provided all of those people are of age, which we have no reason to believe they aren't." Dusk shrugged. "But really, that's not why I wanted them."

"No." Jericho frowned, shaking his head, understanding dawning immediately.

"Then why does it matter?" Ildri asked, enlarging one of the pictures so they could get a better look at the two faces smooshed together in a selfie with what was clearly a motel on the dingier side in the background. A young man, boasting a smattering of scales along his cheeks and neck as some might freckles and a flash of fang that marked him as a basilisk, was in Eldar's lap. He looked all too comfortable there.

"His whole campaign is run on traditional Elven family values. If his husband ever found out . . . " Jericho's voice drifted off.

"He'd be ruined," Dusk finished for him in a coldly gleeful tone. "I'd like to see him condemn Unseelie when there is so much proof he doesn't mind sinking to using them for a quickie."

Jericho felt his shoulders hunch a little.

"So, what say you, Lettie? Is this a danger to the public? Am I a menace?"

"You are a menace." Jericho huffed. "But this isn't a threat. I'll keep your secret. For now."

"As will I," Ildri added without having to be asked.

Jericho frowned at that, not understanding why Ildri would be on board with keeping information like this secret. But he supposed Dusk and she had built a strange comradery over the last week. Whatever they did during the day down in Ildri's lab together must have left an impression. He'd have to keep an eye on that.

"Right then. Welcome to Team Eventide," Dusk muttered with a soft chuckle. The sound was closer to a cackle, really, and it sent a shiver up Jericho's spine. Dusk would drug his childhood best friend and steal information to blackmail a councilman all while running a soup kitchen?

What was his end game?

CHAPTER NINE

OAKFUR HAD INSISTED THAT JERICHO START TAKING WEEKENDS off—like a normal person. He said having more time outside the office to spend with Dusk would move their "relationship" along more quickly.

Jericho hated it.

For years, she'd been putting in extra hours to avoid spending time on her own on the weekends. The fact of the matter was that, when she'd left Soliel behind all those years ago, she'd left behind the childish idea that there was room for friendship in her life. Just like there hadn't been room for her family's worries. There was only room for one thing, and that was being a hero. So, she didn't need the weekend off. What if something happened while she was taking downtime? What if there was a major villain attack? Criminals didn't just keep to business hours, damn it.

"Let's go downtown to the open-air market," Dusk suggested, leaning over the back of the couch where Jericho was curled up, glaring at the dark TV screen. Why they'd needed a TV, she still didn't understand. She hadn't seen Dusk even turn it on since it had arrived.

"No."

"Why not?" Dusk grumbled, leaping over the back of the couch and very nearly landing in Jericho's lap in the process. "You can't just sit around here all weekend rereading your files from the office."

"Why not?" Jericho didn't turn to look at Dusk; she just kept staring straight ahead. Maybe if she didn't make eye contact, he would go away. That seemed to work with small animals. Squirrels. Birds. Yapping lap dogs.

"Well, for one, we need to go and pick up some supplies for dinner. We're completely out of protein after your full moon."

"We have eggs," Jericho said shortly.

Dusk huffed. "Eggs do not a dinner make. And besides, it would be good for you to get some fresh air."

Jericho finally turned to glare at Dusk. "And?"

"And . . . I want to pick up some books. Come on, Lettie, pleeeeaaaase?" Dusk dragged the last word out in a long, pitiful whine. "I'm bored. I can't just sit here all day staring at nothing. My mind needs stuff and things to think about."

"Stuff and things?" Jericho asked, doubtful. She gestured to the TV with her chin, one brow raised.

"Lettie," Dusk huffed. "I need intellectual stimulation! Stuff and things for my brain!" Dusk reached over, grabbing Jericho's shoulder to shake her roughly. "Come on!"

"If I take you, will you stop fucking shaking me?" She shrugged his hand off, ignoring how the familiarity threatened to settle into her skin. They weren't friends.

Dusk nodded eagerly.

"Fine." Jericho sighed heavily, standing from the couch to stretch. "Let me go change."

That was how Jericho found herself in a baggy band tee hanging loosely over a too-tight pair of ripped black jeans, which were tucked into a pair of heeled boots, walking through the open-air market, Dusk pressed close to her side.

"Ooooh, look at these, Lettie." He tugged Jericho unceremoniously over to a kiosk selling used clothes.

Jericho's eyes narrowed on the blush-colored blazer that Dusk had already begun holding up to himself. "You have clothes."

"No. I'm borrowing clothes. I'd like my own. Yours don't really fit my aesthetic. And since I'm not taking you back to my place to get mine . . . " Dusk shrugged, plucking a tweed mint-green vest from the rack. "Oh, this I need. Please, Lettie?"

"Where are you going to wear it?"

"To the station, of course." Dusk didn't even bother to sound defensive, just matter of fact.

Jericho raised a brow. "Really? You're gonna wear a mint-green vest to the station? Where you sit around in Ildri's lab most of the day while she tinkers with greasy machines? You wanna run that by me again?"

"It's not like I work there." Dusk glared. "I have few niceties in life right now. You could give me this one."

"You have few niceties in life because you were arrested. While trying to steal from a data bank. You're a criminal," Jericho pointed out, her tone bored.

Dusk huffed. His fingers tightened around the vest, clutching it to his chest.

"Fuck. Fine. Pick out a few things."

"Well, I'll need dress shirts, and ties, and slacks, and—"

"Fine! A few *outfits*," Jericho groaned, slouching into a chair in the corner of the stall to wait.

When all was said and done, there was a lightness in Dusk's step as he walked along beside her, his arm looped around hers. With a quick jerk, Dusk tugged Jericho into a fruit stand, eliciting a yelp.

"Look at these strawberries," Dusk breathed, eyes flicking excitedly over the red berries.

"We don't need strawberries." She tugged on the place where their arms were linked, trying to pull Dusk away and back onto the main path.

"We do," Dusk insisted, already beginning to examine the little cartons for the ripest of the lot.

A soft smile tugged at Jericho's lips as she watched the excitement flitter across Dusk's face. Jericho tried to shake off the feeling but she couldn't seem to. It was just *nice* seeing Dusk like this. So close to how they had been.

"We need your rent for the space," someone growled, dragging Jericho from her thoughts. Her eyes homed in on a gray-skinned gargoyle.

"I already paid for my space at the beginning of the month," the shop owner argued, his voice shaking a little.

"We don't have a receipt of that," the gargoyle's buddy—an elf of some sort—snorted. "Besides, the rent just went up."

The shop owner's eyes narrowed on them as if he were thinking for a long moment, then his mouth set in a hard line. "You don't work for Lord Feno."

"We do."

Jericho's hackles rose at the obvious confrontation about to happen. Her hands twitched for the weapons she'd left at home as she watched everything unfold. Not that she'd need them, but blades were so much cleaner than claws.

"No, you don't. I know all of Feno's boys. He doesn't have any gargoyles."

"Whatever. Just give us the fucking money." The elf reached forward to grab the shop owner over the counter. Her fingers twitched as magic sparked at their tips, and the smell of lightning filled the air, sharp and dangerous.

"All right, that's enough." Jericho stepped forward, reaching out to grip the elf's wrist hard enough to force her to release the man's shirt. "You guys come back with papers from the lord of this property and then we'll talk. 'Til then, scat. I don't want to see either of your ugly mugs around here again." Jericho bared her teeth, sharp incisors glittering in the late summer sun and green eyes flickering wolf-yellow in warning.

"And what're you gonna do about it?" the gargoyle asked, punching his stone-hardened fist into an open palm threateningly. "Wag your tail at us until we leave? Don't be stupid, Fido, this ain't your fight."

There was a moment, a brief one, where Jericho thought there would be a full-on fight in the middle of the little fruit stand, and she worried about the damage she'd do to the space. The shop owner hadn't asked for this, but he was going to—

Fear filled the gargoyle's eyes as he stared just past Jericho's shoulder, his hand turning back to a soft stone-gray—closer to human than statue. "We didn't—We weren't—" He aborted the words, shaking his head too quickly.

"Let's get out of here," the elf whispered, and the gargoyle nodded his quick agreement. They both turned, ducking hastily out of the stall to disappear into the crush of people beyond.

Jericho turned, blinking, to find Dusk scowling at the entrance. His hair was floating slightly, and his eyes had shifted from dark brown to a washed-out gray, as if he were just about to use his Voice. Shaking himself, Dusk took a breath before letting his hair settle and his eyes shift back.

"You should call the authorities, or they'll be back," Dusk said as an afterthought, then turned back to the fruit.

Jericho nodded, a little dumbfounded, and turned back to the stall owner, who was watching them both with a hint of fear. "He's right. The Alliance should double patrols for a bit to make sure it doesn't happen again. Those guys are probably shaking down everyone on the block."

The shop owner nodded weakly, his hands shaking as he pulled out his phone to make the call.

Dusk moved on from the strawberries to a big crate of apples. "Do you still like apple pie?"

"Yeah. I haven't had it in a while." Jericho sidled up to watch Dusk's long fingers pluck at the stack.

"Your mom used to make it every year for the fall equinox festival." Dusk smiled at the memory as he grabbed a tart apple from the pile, turning it over and over in his hands. "Hers was the best, with all the caramel she put in it."

"I think I have the recipe."

"When was the last time you went to an equinox festival?"

Jericho shrugged, looking away in embarrassment at the softness of the question. It hit a little too close to home. Especially when the answer was, "Not since your last festival." Jericho still remembered it vividly. Dusk's face had been painted red with the light of the lanterns around them, and Jericho had thought, maybe not for the first time, how beautiful he was. How much she liked him. How—

She was torn from those thoughts when two heroes entered the tent, both looking disgruntled at having been summoned. They took one look at Dusk, who was calmly adding apples to a little basket he'd hooked over his arm, and made their way to him.

"You're coming with us."

"Excuse you?" Dusk asked, looking up from the fruit he was carefully examining.

"We got a report of dangerous Unseelie activity in the area." The hero's words were gruff, and she wasted no time in grabbing Dusk's wrist to force it behind his back, making him drop the basket with a yelp.

"No, no, no. It wasn't the banshee!" the stall owner called from where he stood behind the counter.

"You're coming with us too." The other hero moved to grab the owner who, until that point, Jericho hadn't paid much attention to. *Hobgoblin.* "They said there were two of them, right?"

"Yeah. That's what the caller said."

Jericho blinked, looking between the two heroes for a moment, before she scowled deeply. "You two are fucking idiots."

"Excuse me, we didn't mean to intrude on your—"

"No. You two are literal fucking idiots. I want your badge numbers." It had all happened so fast, and it took Jericho a moment to process what the fuck she was actually seeing. But when she finally did, she was on the verge of snarling. Jericho dug out her phone, already pulling up her access to the Hero Alliance system. When they didn't answer, she looked up to narrow her eyes on them. "Badge numbers. Now. And I'd appreciate it if you'd stop trying to cuff my friend."

"We aren't obligated to—"

"Bullshit you aren't. That's procedure," Jericho hissed, reaching into her back pocket to pull out her wallet and show them her own badge. "As your superior, I want both your badge numbers so I can report that you both need sensitivity training."

The hero holding Dusk dropped his wrist, looking alarmed. "We're . . . We're really—"

"I don't give a fuck how sorry you are. You rushed in here, didn't ask any fucking questions, and tried to arrest the first two Unseelie you saw while the actual perpetrators are just escaping into the aether. You're being reported. Badge numbers."

They looked at each other, both shifting uncomfortably,

but obeyed. It only took a moment to report the two idiots to the higher-ups via her phone, and then she tucked it back into her pocket along with her wallet. "I want to see your sergeant when I get back into the office on Monday. We'll set up a new patrol schedule for Lord Feno's lands and have it cleared by him before next weekend's market."

"There already is a patrol." The hero's wings fluttered apprehensively. "We're it."

"Well, you two are clearly incompetent, so we'll see what your sergeant says when I have a chat with them, won't we?" Jericho's teeth ground hard enough to creak under the pressure, pointed incisors poking into her lower lip almost to the point of bleeding. The two heroes nodded, properly chastised, and skulked back out into the main thoroughfare to presumably do their jobs in the shittiest way possible.

"Great Merlin. Lettie, when did you get so cool?!" Dusk gushed, leaning in to grab at her forearm.

"Shut up." Jericho shook him off gently, ducking her head to hide the blush of embarrassment crawling across her nose. "Finish getting your shit so we can go home. I have a report to write up on this nonsense."

With a full basket of fruit, the pair made their way to the counter where the hobgoblin stood, still a little shaken. He looked over the produce and gave them a wobbly smile. "It's on the house."

"That's really not necessary," Jericho said, pulling out her wallet.

"It is," he insisted, holding up a hand. "I've been taken down to the hold for questioning more times than I can count. You just saved me a whole afternoon of hassle. That's the first time anyone has stopped it. I hope you enjoy your pie." He grinned broadly.

"Oh, I'm going to make her the best pie *ever*," Dusk assured him, a bright smile dimpling his cheeks. "Trust me."

"I'm Margog, and you two can come back whenever you like. I'll make sure to find you the best fruit every time." His smile crept a little too far up his face, almost touching his eyes where it pushed his cheeks up, giving his face a creepy quality that made Jericho's stomach turn. But she appreciated the sentiment, so she nodded.

"That's very sweet. Thank you." Dusk bowed his head politely. "Come on, Lettie, let's finish up our shopping and get home. I've got a pie to bake!"

"Right." Jericho nodded, running a hand through her blond hair. Then she let Dusk drag her back out into the throngs of people crowding the market's main alley, feeling a strangeness settle into her. How things seemed to have changed over the course of one afternoon.

CHAPTER TEN

Jericho had never striven to move into a position where he'd be in charge of other heroes for one simple reason: it seemed like a real pain in the ass. An opinion only proven fact by the tired, disheveled look of one Sergeant Loradove.

Greasy brown hair dangled around her ears, framing the broad features of a centaur and drawing attention to the dark bags under her eyes. She looked down at the badge numbers on the form Jericho had sent over and released a heavy sigh.

"What did these two dipshits do now?"

Jericho blinked. "Dipshits?"

"Yeah." Loradove scrubbed at her face for a moment before looking back down at the file. "They're from hero families, so we're pretty much stuck with them. But they've been nothing but trouble since they joined up."

Jericho's frown deepened, brows tugging together. "So why not just fire them?"

Loradove snorted, rolling her eyes. "Like I said, they come from hero families. You don't know how it is, you're not a legacy like some of these people. They have family high up in the Alliance, so it's tough to hold them accountable for anything."

"But they're idiots," Jericho argued. "They literally came in with a description of the suspects and then tried to arrest the first two Unseelie they saw. One of whom was the shop owner who called them."

"Right. I'll talk to them."

"Talk to them? They should have to go back through training. This isn't something that can be solved with a mere talking to." Jericho felt his fists tighten on the desk, but he forced his tone to remain level.

"Yeah. That's not going to happen. The best I can offer is to yell at them."

"Then I'll file the recommendation myself. Their families can't do anything to me, I'm not under their thumb." Jericho was loath to stick his nose further into this mess, but he didn't feel he had much choice. He couldn't let these two idiots continue to act as they had been. They were a threat to the established peace of Mythikos. And they made heroes look like morons.

"Whatever helps you sleep at night, but it's not going to help."

"And why wouldn't it? That's what that training is for." Jericho's jaw clenched. He couldn't fathom how someone could be so apathetic about their subordinates being positively useless. It was Loradove's job to keep them in line, and if she couldn't do it, it was her job to expel them from the Alliance—whether they had family in the organization or not.

Loradove sighed, her shoulders sagging. "Look kid, you seem like you have your heart in the right place, but you were never on a beat, were you? You didn't have to work your way up from the dregs. You came straight to this role out of an apprenticeship, right?"

"I . . . " Jericho frowned but nodded. "Yeah. My mentor got me this post." It seemed unfair when he said it that way, but this was different than Oakfur getting the job as captain because his father was on the council. Jericho *had* worked—he'd worked hard—it just hadn't been in basic training.

"Right. So you never had to work out on the streets, policing regular folks. You just hunt down the big bads. You don't protect the citizens on a daily basis." Jericho opened his mouth to argue, but Loradove stilled his words with a quick wave. "There's a lot of fear out there surrounding the Unseelie. It's not right. But many see it as justified, and that attitude isn't going to be changed through sensitivity training when these kids are taught from a young age that Unseelie tried to annihilate the human race and are thus evil. That idea isn't going anywhere. So just let it go."

"I'm writing the report," Jericho muttered through clenched teeth. "It's not much, but it's what I can do."

"Like I said, whatever helps you sleep at night." Loradove ran a hand through her lank hair and stood from the chair. "Just don't expect it to change anything."

●

"You know, if you want real change, maybe you should join my crew," Dusk offered once Jericho had finished explaining the details of his meeting with Loradove over dinner.

"Yeah, let me just join up with the villains," Jericho muttered sarcastically through a big bite of stir fry. "That's exactly what I want to do."

Dusk rolled his eyes, the couch cushions shifting under him as he leaned forward to force Jericho to meet his gaze. He set his bowl in his lap so he could sign along as they spoke. "Look, I get it. Is my method of enacting change right? Not really. But it's the way forward."

"*What* is the way forward?" Jericho stuffed a big piece of broccoli into his mouth to keep from snarling.

"We have to dismantle the council, break everything down to ground level. Start over." Dusk's movements were sharp, crisp, to the point. This was not a debate; it was abject fact as he saw it.

Jericho snorted, nearly choking on the vegetable, which quickly turned into a coughing fit. Dusk reached over to pat his back lightly, and Jericho shrugged him off. "And then what? Chaos? Anarchy?" he asked once he'd regained composure. "Let the Unseelie run amuck just like they did before? Do you remember how it was back then? Girls sleeping for hundreds of years, poison apples, curses, darkness."

"Well, first off, I'd like to abolish the distinction between Unseelie and Seelie. It's outdated. The war was centuries ago," Dusk offered with a shrug, as if it were the easiest thing in the world. Perhaps in his mind, it was.

"Yeah. Okay. And then what?"

"And then we start over. We build a system where Unseelie aren't considered to be evil by birth. But it has to start with the council."

"Right. That's bullshit, and you know it. It'll never happen, not in a million years." Jericho set aside his bowl, suddenly not very hungry at the idea of a world so full of gray. He liked how things were. He liked the black and white of it all. He liked knowing who was good and who was evil by the scent of their magic. He liked being able to say that if a redcap committed a crime, they were likely to commit another, and they should be taken off the streets.

"Oh, sweet, beautiful, naïve Lettie." Dusk tsked, shaking his head. His fingers began to move more languidly as the words left him in a purr. It was annoying. "The world is not as simple as we thought it was when we were children."

Jericho was quiet for a moment, desperately trying to

ignore the sentiment of that statement coming from a villain. "Are you ever going to tell me how you tricked your tracker?"

Dusk smirked, shaking his head again. "No. But I'll do you one better. I want you to meet someone."

"Someone who?" Jericho lifted his brows.

"You'll see." Dusk grabbed his bowl back up. "Finish your dinner. We'll go out after."

"I'm not hungry anymore."

"Then let me finish my dinner." Dusk laughed, taking another bite of his stir fry and releasing a soft, happy murmur.

"Right. Whatever."

•

AN HOUR LATER, Jericho was berating himself for the idiocy of letting a known villain lead him through the bad part of town in the pitch-black of night. But he had this nagging feeling that the person Dusk was about to introduce him to was important. Maybe they were a part of Dusk's "Team Eventide" as he'd called it. There was really only one way to find out.

What Jericho wasn't expecting was for them to wind up at the same building he'd followed Dusk to not a fortnight ago.

"We here to serve potatoes again?" Jericho asked, looking up at the darkened windows.

"Nah. The food pantry isn't open tonight. We're just here to meet with someone." Dusk headed for the door.

"It's not?" Jericho didn't try to hide the note of surprise—and concern—in his voice. "So, like, they just don't eat today?"

Dusk sighed, shoulders sagging. "We can't afford to run it every night. At least not yet."

"We?"

Dusk's eyes reflected the stuttering streetlight above them as he looked up to meet Jericho's gaze. "What? You think all I do is rob data banks to blackmail councilmen?"

"I mean, that seemed to be your shtick."

"You *would* think it was that simple." Dusk snorted. "Crime pays."

"Is that a confession?" Jericho couldn't help the little smirk tugging at his lips. They were getting closer to something he could use against Dusk. Something that would maybe lead him to Dusk's lab. Then he could have his apartment and his weekends back. And maybe he could convince Dusk to give this whole thing up. To go back to being a civilian. To go back to being just Soliel.

"That I help pay for the meals we serve here? Yes," Dusk said but would say nothing else. Instead, he unlocked the front door and headed inside, not waiting for Jericho to follow him. The lobby looked much the same as it had that night, but an eerie quiet clung to its walls without the soft chatter of people eating. Nervousness lifted the hairs on the back of Jericho's neck, wolf instincts on high alert.

"Dusk! I see you brought your friend again," the redcap's voice sounded from just to their right.

Not alert enough, Jericho thought bitterly. He hadn't even heard the redcap coming.

"I did." Dusk's tone was just as lighthearted as the redcap's. Like they were old friends. Maybe they were. Jericho hadn't been in Soliel's life for the better part of a decade now. Who knew who his friends were these days. But Jericho couldn't shake the feeling that there was another conversation going on beneath this seemingly normal, friendly exchange. "This is my old friend, Jericho. Jericho, this is Fizz. He holds down the fort here for us."

There was that word again, 'us.' There was more than just Dusk and Fizz in this whole thing. How large was Dusk's team? How big of a network had he woven across the city in the last eight years? And how long would it take Jericho to extract all of that information from him? Hopefully less time than it'd take for Oakfur to lose his patience.

"A pleasure," Fizz said with a smile, holding out his hand.

"Right," Jericho grunted, shaking and dropping it perhaps a little too quickly. "Is this who you wanted me to meet?" Jericho signed instead of saying the words out loud.

"To the point as always." Dusk's fingers formed the words with light and fluttering motions as he laughed fondly. "Yes. Fizz here comes from one of the oldest redcap families in Mythikos," he said aloud.

Jericho stiffened at the words, eyes narrowing on the man with the pointed, sharklike teeth split into a too-kind smile. "Oh yeah?"

Fizz held up his hands, chuckling softly. "Yes, but trust me, I was never interested in the family business. Murder and mayhem aren't really my thing."

"Your thing is running a soup kitchen for Unseelie?" Jericho asked, skeptical.

"My *thing* is helping people who need it," Fizz corrected, his tone a little harder than it had been before.

"All right. Down boys." Dusk stepped between the pair, one hand lifting to Jericho's shoulder as if to calm him down. "We aren't here for a brawl, and Jericho isn't here to arrest anyone. I just wanted you to show him your records."

Fizz's smile fell into a tight-lipped line. "Are you sure that's a good idea?"

"I trust him."

"Right. They're back in my office. Follow me." Fizz turned on his heel and headed back the way he'd come. The hallway was twisted and dark, and they made so many turns that Jericho wasn't sure he'd be able to find his way back out if he tried. He wondered if some kind of labyrinth spell had been placed on it to protect Fizz and his files.

"How'd you become friends with a *hero?*" Fizz said the word like it left a bad taste in his mouth.

"We grew up together," Dusk chirped. "We went to the same park when we were, like, three years old or something. And Lettie here bit a kid for picking on me."

"He was pulling your hair," Jericho muttered petulantly. "And he was three times your size."

"And at least twice yours," Dusk teased with a little grin.

Jericho shrugged.

"He's my knight in shining armor. Sometimes literally," Dusk bragged, his arm looping Jericho's neck to tug him down into a one-armed hug.

"Such a shame," Fizz mumbled, just loud enough for Jericho's delicate hearing to pick it up, shaking his head.

"Hmm?" Dusk asked.

"What is?" Jericho asked at the same time.

"Here we are," Fizz said without answering either of them. The office door swung open to reveal a cluttered space. A desk packed high with paperwork stood in front of a bookshelf loaded with overflowing binders and notebooks. "Should I just grab the book from this year?"

"Yeah. That's a good start." Dusk dropped his arm, moving to clear off the two chairs, then flopped himself into one before gesturing to the other. "You're going to want to get yourself comfortable. We'll be here a while."

"What? Why?"

Jericho didn't get an answer. What he got was a heavy binder dropped into his lap and a pointed look from Fizz. With a huff, Jericho opened the binder to the first page, which was a court file on the arrest of a young chimera who'd been picked up for shoplifting.

"His name is Shihiro. He's sixteen," Fizz supplied.

"It says he was found guilty of shoplifting."

"Read his testimony," Fizz urged, tapping a large paragraph farther down the page. Jericho did, frowning as he went. According to the young man, he'd been walking home and was in the area of the store where someone had shoplifted. The heroes found no merchandise on him but brought him in for questioning anyway. Despite a lack of evidence, the shop owner identified him, and the boy was given a year in prison.

"But the shop owner—" Jericho started.

"What's the first thing they taught you in your apprenticeship?" Dusk cut in. His posture was still carefully relaxed in the chair, but his hands, which were moving in time to the words, displayed something else. Irritation. "Eyewitness testimony is the least reliable. Especially with how many shapeshifters we have in the world. They had no other evidence. The Oracle cameras in the store didn't even catch the thief in the act. The case should have been dismissed." Dusk's tone turned short and clipped at the end, fingers moving angrily. Jericho hadn't ever heard him this way before. "Keep reading."

The next case was of an imp who had been given the maximum sentence of six months.

"Okay, but this one was guilty," Jericho argued.

"Yes, she was. They caught her in the act." Fizz nodded. "But if she'd been Seelie, she would have gotten community service."

"You have no proof of that."

"Actually, I do. Look at the back of the page, you'll see the statistics."

Jericho frowned, turning over the page to find a list of other Unseelie who had been imprisoned for similar offenses versus Seelie who had merely been given a slap on the wrist.

"Keep reading."

Jericho continued flipping through the binder to find case upon case of the same ilk. He wasn't sure how long they sat there as he read, but Dusk and Fizz stayed silent, only speaking to answer questions. When he shut the binder, Jericho sat back in the chair, closing his eyes for a moment to rub away the blurriness of too long reading under fluorescent lights.

"What does all this mean?" His throat had gone dry while they'd been sitting there, and he cleared it.

"It means exactly what I've been saying. Unseelie are not inherently evil, but they're treated like they are." Dusk didn't just say the words, he moved his fingers into them, and the effect of that made them heavier. Like each curve of a finger or twist of his wrist was another careful hole poked in everything Jericho had always thought to be true.

"And the solution is blackmailing councilmen?" Jericho asked, doubtful.

"That's not all we're doing." Dusk shrugged.

"What else are you doing?"

Dusk and Fizz met each other's eyes, holding a silent conversation that Jericho wasn't privy to. So much had changed. It used to be Jericho who could talk to Dusk with just his eyes and have a whole silent argument right in front of someone. But now, Jericho had no idea what the expressions flickering across Dusk's face could possibly mean.

"We should get back," Dusk said when he and Fizz were done arguing. "You have work in the morning." He stood, stretching his legs, then headed for the door without another word. The walk home was spent in silence, and once they were back at the apartment, Dusk ducked into his room without so much as a goodnight.

Jericho crumbled onto the couch, scrubbing at his face as he tried to process everything he'd learned in the span of a few hours. He'd seen similar cases at the station, had wondered about the difference in treatment, but there had been no hard evidence that Unseelie were treated differently. He hadn't had statistics to compare the two. Now . . . Now he'd seen the statistics himself, and he felt . . . He didn't know *how* he felt.

CHAPTER ELEVEN

"I want to help," Jericho said, and he was surprised to find he meant it. Although maybe not in the way Dusk wanted him to.

"What?" Dusk's hand stilled in its path to stuff an entire piece of bacon into his mouth.

"I want to do something to help your organization." Jericho sat up a little straighter on the couch, doing his best to look stalwart and resolute. Maybe this wasn't his best plan, but it was something. He needed information, and he'd already gotten Dusk to trust him a little. Helping to carry out an actual crime could push him over the edge.

Heroes undercover were allowed to take part in certain criminal activities to maintain their cover, and this would be no different, he was sure. And maybe if he learned more about what Dusk's actual end goal was, he could find a way to convince him to give up on the villainy. To be good again.

Dusk blinked at him for a long moment. "And how would you propose you do that?"

Jericho faltered. He wasn't really sure what Dusk and his organization did other than stealing incriminating photos of politicians. There had to be more to it than that, right? Dusk had said crime paid for the food pantry, so did they steal? Or was it more reappropriation of funds from people who had too much and would hardly notice? Was this a Robin Hood situation, or something more nefarious? Jericho wasn't sure, but he knew he had to do something to prove himself to Dusk.

"Whatever you need me to," he answered finally, thinking that was perhaps the safest answer.

"And if I needed you to assassinate a crooked judge?" There was a dark glint in Dusk's eyes that made the hair on Jericho's arms prick up and a shudder run down his spine. Surely Dusk wouldn't ask him to—

"Well . . . no," Jericho said lamely, pushing eggs across his plate with his fork.

"So not *whatever* I need then," Dusk said, finishing off his bacon.

"Do you need a crooked judge assassinated?" Jericho suddenly felt on edge. They had no record of Dusk ever committing murder, but Jericho was beginning to wonder if there were no bounds to what Dusk would do to usher in his vision of the new world, and that thought terrified him. What had happened to the sweet, soft-spoken boy who had cried when the other kids picked on him for his freckles? Who had defended Jericho when he'd started a fight and they'd both been suspended? Who had been trembling when he'd given Jericho his first kiss? Where had he gone?

Dusk didn't answer—which seemed to be becoming a habit, and was an answer in itself, Jericho supposed. Instead, he stared at Jericho for an uncomfortably long time, making Jericho squirm a little in his seat. Then he said, "Let me do some thinking. I'm sure I can come up with something for you."

Jericho wanted to push further, to ask more, but he knew

better. Dusk had closed himself off, and the only thing left to do was to wait. All Jericho could hope was that Dusk wouldn't have to think about it too long.

●

"Have you found anything?" Oakfur hissed, glaring at Dusk through the window in his office door before he turned that scathing look on Jericho.

"I'm getting close," Jericho said with a frown. "He's starting to trust me. But it's only been a little over a month. I need more time."

Oakfur's red brows narrowed in disbelief, a frown wrinkling his forehead into a ridiculously hideous bulldog expression.

He should really stop doing that with his face. It might stick that way, Jericho thought in mild hysteria.

Oakfur's patience with this idea was wearing thin already, and who knew what would happen to them if Jericho failed to placate the captain.

"This runs deeper than we thought. It's not just Dusk and his lab." Not a lie but a conveniently placed truth. A nugget of information to tide Oakfur over until Jericho could get him more. Maybe Dusk was rubbing off on him.

"He's got a whole crew of people working with him. I've started acquiring information on his network." Another nugget, and Jericho could see Oakfur's eyes gleaming a little at the idea that there would be more than one arrest. It would be a real feather in the captain's cap to bring down a whole group of villains. "We can either arrest one person or take down his entire organization." Jericho's voice remained calm, but he could feel the mania creeping in at the edges. He was desperate—to prove himself, to keep digging, to bring Dusk back to his side. Soliel could be good again, he *wanted* to be good. Jericho just needed more time to convince him!

"You're lucky this is up to the council, not me," was Oakfur's only response, then he dismissed Jericho with an irritated wave of his hand.

When Jericho returned to his desk, a smiling Dusk was waiting for him. "What's his problem?" Dusk signed, mouth twitching into a teasing tilt. "Did someone spit in his cornflakes?"

"Who the fuck knows," Jericho signed back, rolling his eyes.

"He looks like a socially repressed Shar-Pei."

"Bulldog."

"If he's not careful, it'll stick like that." Dusk's fingers danced over the words cheerfully.

"That's what I said!" Jericho exclaimed, unable to stop the words from leaving his lips.

"What's what you said?" Erling asked. His own face had scrunched up to look rather pug like.

"Oh shit, we're surrounded!" Dusk signed, biting his bottom lip hard to choke back his chortles.

"Nothing," Jericho said as he schooled his expression into a scowl to hide his own laughter. It was a struggle. *Such* a struggle.

Erling huffed.

Dusk shook his head. "Let's go out for lunch today."

"Where did you have in mind?" Jericho grabbed his jacket from the back of his chair and tugged it on.

"There's a cute little diner around the corner. I think we should try them out. I've heard they have really good milkshakes." Dusk hopped up from his chair and looped his arm through Jericho's on their way to the door.

"Yeah. Okay." Jericho let Dusk guide him out onto the street.

●

THE DINER that Dusk had described as cute was just that. With walls painted in pastels and shelves lining the ceiling laden with old teapots, Jericho would be hard pressed to find another word to describe the place. It was also extremely busy, and loud. Jericho's eyes swept the room, taking note of the tactical advantage a place like this could provide. It would be difficult for them to be overheard for the noise, and Jericho was sure none of the heroes from his division would be caught dead in a place that cutesy. It just wasn't their style.

Jericho shifted uncomfortably on his feet, afraid to touch anything for fear he'd dirty the dainty tablecloths or break one of the fine bone china teacups.

"Can I see you to a table, folks?" a waitress asked, offering a curtsy. Her deep blue dress featured ruffled white sleeves and a high white collar with a bow tied tight around the neck. She looked no older than eighteen, but her silver eyes glittered with an intelligence that set Jericho's teeth on edge. There was something condescending in their depths, like she was mocking the world.

"Yes. We'll take a table in the corner, if you can." Dusk smiled easily, dipping his head into a soft and respectful bow.

"Let me go see if we have anything available. I'll be back in a moment." She spun on one well-polished patent leather shoe, and that's when Jericho noticed the tails—all nine of them. Soft and fluffy, and although she'd shrunk them to be less obtrusive, they still stuck out of a hole in her dress clearly designed for that purpose.

"Kitsune," Jericho growled under his breath, eyes narrowing. Merlin, he hated foxes. They were all sneaky and manipulative, and you couldn't trust them as far as you could throw them.

"Hm?" Dusk asked, eyes flicking to the tails. Then he

shrugged. "I suppose she is. Please don't let that whole wolf-kitsune nonsense ruin our lunch."

"It's not nonsense."

"Lettie."

"Fine." Jericho sniffed.

The waitress returned a moment later and ushered them to a table in the back of the restaurant, tucked into a corner away from most of the other customers, right beside the door to the kitchen. "Here you are. The menus are on the table. I'll be back soon to take your order."

"Thank you." Dusk grinned brightly, eyes sparkling. She nodded, spinning on her heel again to tend to the other customers.

"Right. So, what's this really about?" Jericho flicked his eyes over the sandwich menu, not bothering to look at Dusk. *Does everything need to have honey on it? Fuck. And where are the milkshakes Dusk promised? Liar.*

"Try the quiche," Dusk advised, not answering the question as he peered over the tea menu.

"I thought you said they had milkshakes."

Dusk hummed, tapping his fingers on the sides of his menu without answering.

"You've been here before, haven't you? This isn't just lunch. This is a meet." Jericho lifted his gaze to narrow it on Dusk. He didn't get a response. A moment later, the waitress had joined them at their table, looking quite put out all of a sudden.

"I've got ten. What do you want?" Her once cheerful tone had dropped into something grumpy and irritated.

"Not happy to see me, Maz?" Dusk asked in return, setting down his menu so he could offer the girl another smile.

"What? She's the meet? She's, like, twelve!"

"Actually, I'm fifty-two." Maz turned to glare at him, one

white brow lifting high enough to disappear into her bangs. "Foxes don't age past a certain point. Unlike *wolves*," Max snarled, bearing sharp canines.

"Right." Jericho snorted, unimpressed by her little fangs.

"Let's not fight." Dusk held up his hands for peace. "Jericho, this is Maz. Maz, Jericho."

"A pleasure," Maz muttered sarcastically.

"Likewise." Jericho rolled his eyes.

"Jericho is going to be our lookout for the job on Friday," Dusk continued, as if his tablemates weren't both actively trying to intimidate one another by bearing their teeth and glaring.

"They're a hero." Maz leaned in, long white hair slipping from her braid to brush her chin as she inhaled deeply before wrinkling her dainty nose in disgust. "I can smell it on them. We can't trust them."

"Now, now, Maz. When have I ever steered you wrong?"

Maz's only response was an irritated grunt, but she was still looking suspiciously at Jericho.

"Jericho is an old friend. We can trust him."

"Fine. Here's the drop point." She slid a piece of paper over to Dusk, drawing no attention from the swarm of customers around them. "I'll see you two idiots there."

Dusk nodded, slipping the paper from the table and tucking it neatly into a pocket without a word.

"Now." Maz rose from her chair, a customer-service smile suddenly plastered onto her lips. Her posture shifted so one hip popped out to the side as she pulled a notepad from some hidden pocket along with a pen. "Can I take your order, gentlemen?"

"We'll have two slices of the vegetable quiche and a pot of raspberry tea, please." Dusk leaned back in his chair, returning her smile with one of his own. No hint that they knew one another remained, and Jericho frowned as Maz jotted everything down before leaving without giving him a second glance.

"I don't trust that fox."

"That's fair. In this game, we can't really trust anyone."

We. Were they a 'we' now? Jericho set that thought aside for later as their tea arrived, delivered by another waitress.

"What are we stealing?" Jericho poured himself a steaming cup and cringed when the sweet smell assaulted his nose.

"Probably better that you don't know that right away. Like I said, we can't trust anyone in this game." Dusk didn't meet his eyes, sipping from his own teacup carefully.

So. Not 'we' then.

"You don't trust me?"

"You haven't really given me a reason to." Dusk grabbed a sugar cube and popped it into his mouth with a soft hum, as if the words he'd just said weren't cruel in their way.

"I didn't think I had to, since we're friends." Jericho frowned, his fingers gripping the dainty teacup perhaps a little harder than need be.

Dusk reached over to pluck it from his fingers and set it gently onto the saucer once more. "As you keep reminding me, Jericho, we *were* friends. Now . . . Hmmm. Well, maybe we'll get back there one day."

Jericho winced, and oh, didn't that hurt? Having his words thrown back at him like that.

CHAPTER TWELVE

FRIDAY COULDN'T COME SOON ENOUGH. OVER THE NEXT three days, Jericho tried to drag answers from Dusk, but each time, he was met with a soft smile and a quick subject change. Whatever they were stealing was important but not exactly top secret, as they were entrusting Jericho with guarding them during the heist.

"He won't give you a location." Erling's tone was bland, his expression one of abject boredom. He was probably tired of talking about this. *Jericho* was tired of talking about this. But they needed the kinks worked out beforehand.

"No, he won't. But I need to make sure this thing goes well. Could you keep anyone from going out on calls tonight?" Jericho knew he was asking a lot. The captain had approved this, but that didn't mean someone who was as much a stickler for the rules as Erling was would be willing to bend them even just this once.

"No." Of course he wasn't fucking willing. Because why would anything in Jericho's life be easy? "I will not aid a criminal in getting away with a crime."

"Just . . . don't come out on any breaking and entering

calls. Or at least give us time to get away." Jericho rubbed at the bridge of his nose tiredly. "Actually, that would be better. If you don't come at all, it'll look suspicious. Just give us time to get away."

Erling's face hardened, eyes narrowing. Stubborn bastard. "I will not impede justice."

"Oh, for fuck's sake, Erling. At least give us a five-minute head start. I'll never be accepted into his organization if we don't do this. Which means we won't be able to get the rest of them or the lab." Jericho tugged at the end of his long braid in frustration.

Erling's wings rustled for a moment and then he sighed, one large hand rubbing down his face. "One-minute head start."

"Four."

"Three."

"Done!"

•

"You're wearing that?" Jericho asked, wrinkling her nose at the well-fitting slacks, tailored waistcoat, and overcoat with the sun and moon brooches on it.

"This is my villain costume." Dusk didn't bother to stop as he pulled on an expensive-looking pair of loafers.

"It's summer." Jericho shook her head.

"Point?"

"Won't you get hot?"

"Won't *you* get hot in that hoodie?"

"This is for stealth." Jericho pulled the hood up over her blond hair to hide it and her face from sight. "And those shoes . . . How the fuck did you run from me in those?"

"Stealth. Right." Dusk snorted, then smirked widely. "Wouldn't you like to know?"

"I would. That's why I asked."

Dusk tapped his nose conspiratorially. "The geniuses I work with don't just mess around with computers. They know other stuff too."

"Right. So how do I get myself a pair of expensive-ass loafers with tread that somehow magically keeps me from falling off rooftops?" Now that they were both dressed, Jericho tugged the door open, and they made their way down the hall toward the elevator.

"Stick around. They're standard issue." Dusk jabbed the button for the lobby.

•

THE LOAFERS WERE NOT REALLY standard issue—at least not in a loafer style. Maz was wearing a pair of shiny saddle shoes, a dress that was slightly less puffy than the one she'd been wearing at the diner, and tights in a deep brown. The tread on the bottom did look very similar, but Jericho was no shoe expert.

"Are we doing a mugging?" Maz asked, looking Jericho up and down.

"No." Dusk laughed, shaking his head. "She thinks she's being stealthy."

"Right." Maz snorted. "Stealthy. She's going to stick out like a sore thumb in the shopping district uptown."

"That's what I thought." Dusk shrugged. "At least it's not a ratty hoodie. Maybe no one will notice."

"Still standing right here, assholes," Jericho growled.

Maz didn't dignify that with an answer, nor did Dusk, and the trio hailed a cab to head uptown.

"What's in North Lilve that we need to steal?" Jericho asked as she squished between Dusk and the door in the back of the small cab now buzzing along the streets of Mythikos.

"Shut up, you idiot," Maz hissed. Her eyes narrowed on the lit-up console of the self-driving taxi.

"Why?"

Dusk leaned in close—too close—his lips brushing the shell of Jericho's ear as he whispered, "Our tech girl says these things are bugged to the nines."

"Paranoid much?" Jericho asked mockingly, but her voice was too high, and she couldn't ignore the way her ear tingled from the contact. Dusk could have signed the words—even in the dark, Jericho would have read them—but he'd chosen to invade Jericho's space . . .

Jericho shook it off and didn't push the subject any further until the car had pulled to a curb outside of a large department store. The people around them were carrying bags and going about their nightly shopping as if nothing was amiss. They didn't even take notice of the oddly dressed trio as they peered through windows at brightly colored displays of clothing and appliances. "This it?"

"Yeah. We're going shopping," Maz muttered.

"For a new toaster and some bath bombs." Dusk cackled, and Maz snickered right along with him, like an asshole.

"You know, you're both real shitheads," Jericho grumbled, following them down the street.

"No. We didn't know!" Maz gasped as if surprised. "Please, tell us more."

Dusk was still chortling softly, and Jericho fell silent, stuffing her hands into her pockets petulantly. They took a turn, and then another, and at some point, the crush of early evening shoppers gave way to quiet, more abandoned streets.

"What? We're stealing sales records?" Jericho asked.

"I told you. This is a need-to-know kind of thing, and you don't need to know." Dusk didn't even sound like he felt bad about it, which Jericho supposed was fair. They weren't friends.

Maz looked over at them, her lips lifting in twisted amusement.

"No one fucking asked you, fox," Jericho spat.

"Good thing I don't need your—"

"Both of you, shut up," Dusk ordered. He held up a hand to quiet them, then, grabbing their wrists, he tugged them into an alley off the main sidewalk. Just as they turned around to face the mouth of the alley, a figure swept past them.

"Do you think they were following us?" Maz's fingers clung onto the tails of Dusk's overcoat in an irritatingly familiar gesture. Everything, Jericho was realizing, was too familiar between them. And she didn't want to look too closely at the clenching feeling in her chest that might have been jealousy. It was not jealousy. She was *not* jealous.

"No. I think they were just walking the same way. But let's give it a minute to be sure. Jericho, what do you smell?" Dusk turned to Jericho, who wrinkled her nose a little.

"Am I your bloodhound now? Is that why you brought me?" Jericho huffed, crossing her arms over her chest.

Dusk shot her a pleading look, and Jericho sighed, her arms dropping as she lifted her nose to the air. Nothing. There was nothing but the subtle smell of grime from an alley that hadn't been cleaned in Merlin knew how long. Shutting her eyes, she focused more, digging deeper through the layers of scent. Underneath was the subtle, mild smell of human. No hint of the coppery metallic magic that clung to the Unseelie or the electric spring smell that came from the Seelie.

"Just a human."

"Probably on their way home from work." Dusk nodded. "This way." He turned on his heel, heading deeper into the darkness of the alley.

"That's a dead end," Jericho said, narrowing her eyes

through the darkness, but without the help of certain potions, her nighttime vision was only slightly better than a human's unless she forced a shift. Which she was not inclined to do, as that would be a real pain in the ass. So she couldn't see anything on the other end of the alley, just darkness.

"Is it?" Maz asked, and Jericho could make out the smug smile on her features clearly in the gloom. They walked deeper until they came out on the other side in a completely different part of the city. It had been the meatpacking district once, before the businesses in the shopping district had taken over, turning it into their headquarters for convenience's sake long ago.

"Don't be smug," Dusk chided softly. "We're a team. Remember?"

"Right. A team with a hero," Maz muttered under her breath, low enough that Dusk was apparently unable to hear her. Jericho scowled at Maz, green eyes narrowing, and she met Jericho's gaze with squinting silver irises. A challenge.

"This is it," Dusk announced. His hands were on his hips as he looked up to survey the towering building, a pleased tilt to his lips.

"What is it?" Jericho asked, breaking her silent staring contest with Maz to look up too.

"The offices of Bronzelhelm and Bristlehorn." Dusk's fingers twitched in his dark gloves.

"We're stealing from the miners? The dwarves? You mean, like, Snow's people?" Jericho felt her palms grow moist with sweat, and she rubbed them on her jeans to try to clear it away.

"Don't think of it as stealing, think of it as reappropriating. You know, like Snow's people did with the bluecap culture." Maz's face had twisted into a dark grin.

"The bluecaps are Seelie." Jericho blinked through the

darkness at the unlit sign that clearly declared the names of the miner partners.

"Yeah, and I'm sure they love being used by a corporation to inflate their profit margins." Maz rolled her eyes, pulling something from the satchel slung over her shoulder. It looked like an old calculator. "And don't get me started on what she did to rebrand the dwarves."

"What?"

"That is a discussion for another time," Dusk said, putting an end to the conversation. "Can you get us in, Maz?"

"If you would both shut up and let a girl work for about two seconds," Maz huffed, sidling closer to the building. Her gloved fingers moved quickly over her keypad for a moment, then she pressed a wire and a little sticker to the building and began to type again. "Keep an eye out, Jericho."

"I don't take orders from you." Jericho hissed but turned around to look up and down the street they were on. Not that she saw a reason to; no one would be bothering with office buildings this late in the evening. Only someone who was up to something would be on this street. Like them.

"And . . . we're in," Maz whispered, triumphant. She turned back to Dusk as the front door popped open a hair.

"Security system?" Dusk asked.

"Five minutes before it resets."

"Right. Before we get a move on then: Jericho, you stay here and keep an eye out. If anyone comes . . . " Dusk dug into his pocket and pulled out a tiny earbud. "This connects directly to my and Maz's headsets. Give us a howl."

"I'm not your fucking guard dog." Jericho scowled, but she took the small device and slid it into her ear before turning back to the street.

"Of course not. You're our lookout." Dusk pressed a hand to Jericho's shoulder for a moment, opening his mouth as if to say something else.

"We gotta go." Maz had moved to grab the door and start inside.

"Right." Dusk nodded and spun to follow her. The glass door shut behind them with the soft rush of central air, and Jericho moved to lean against the building. Crossing her arms over her chest again, she cast her eyes down toward her feet but perked her ears at the quiet street around her. Jericho wondered how long Erling would really give them. He'd said three minutes. But was that three minutes after the alarm was tripped, or three minutes after a call was made? Maz said they had five minutes, but Jericho wasn't sure what the alarm being reset really meant. She'd never needed to be particularly tech savvy in her position.

Either way, it took almost exactly five minutes for the pair to reappear.

"Do you think we tripped it?" Dusk's words were breathy and rushed, his eyes glittering in the darkness.

"Guess we'll see if it's in the news tomorrow." Maz shrugged.

"Did you get what you needed?" Jericho pushed off from the side of the building as she surveyed them both.

They didn't answer with words, but the conspiratorial smiles they offered Jericho were enough of a confirmation. Whatever they'd been after, they'd found it.

"Well, folks, I'm off. I'll see you when I see you." Maz saluted, slinging her bag over her shoulder again, and turned to head down the sidewalk.

"You don't want us to walk you back?" Dusk asked.

"Nah. You'll just slow me down." With that, the silver-haired kitsune melted into the shadows of the abandoned street.

"She's a fucking weirdo," Jericho grumbled.

"Yeah. She is. But she does good work." Dusk shook his head with a soft chuckle. "Come on, let's head home."

"Home," Jericho repeated. It wasn't the first time Dusk had referred to her apartment as such, but it still felt strange. She was about to say something to that effect when her nose caught an unusual scent—griffin. She grabbed Dusk's wrist and took off at a run. "Time to go."

Dusk whooped beside her, his shorter legs keeping pace as someone behind them yelled and gave chase. "Stop! You're under arrest!"

"You have to catch us first!" Dusk laughed breathlessly.

Jericho shook her head, but she couldn't keep the smile from her face. With a quick look around, she dragged Dusk into a dark alley, hoping it came out on the other side just like the one earlier had.

"Where are we going?" Dusk panted.

"I don't know." Jericho frowned. She listened for the tell-tale sounds of wings chasing them, eyes wild in the dark.

"You adorable moron," Dusk huffed, tapping a button the side of his headset. "Hey there, Pickle. We need an out. What have you got for me?"

"Pickle?"

"Shush." Dusk waved her off, nodding at whatever the person in his ear was saying. "That's perfect. You're a gem, Pickle. See you later." He tapped again on his ear, then tugged Jericho to a stop. "This way."

There was a faint click, and Dusk pulled open a door Jericho hadn't seen before yanking her inside. The door shut behind them with a soft thud. Jericho had to strain to hear the sounds outside over the soft huff of Dusk's harsh, panting breaths.

"Now we're trapped in here," Jericho grumbled.

"Oh ye of little faith." Dusk laughed, then took Jericho's hand, threading their fingers together. "Trust the Pickle."

"Who or what the fuck is Pickle, anyhow?"

"That's on a need-to-know—"

"And I don't need to know. Got it." Jericho rolled her eyes, ignoring the sting of that. "Where to now?"

"This way." Dusk tugged Jericho through a maze of densely packed cubicles, then up a set of stairs lit only by a glaring red exit sign.

"Up?" Jericho's boots trod softly on the cement steps.

"Up." Dusk nodded. They reached the fifth floor a few minutes later, and Dusk led them out to a wide-open floor with only a covered footbridge connecting it to another building and a handful of closed restaurants. "Food court."

"Are all of the buildings in this row connected?"

"No. But this one is connected to the one across the street. Then we can head down the alley into the block on the other side. It'll be more crowded."

Jericho pressed her mouth into a firm line, fighting the urge to argue, then followed behind Dusk without any further questions. Like Dusk had said, they headed through the building across the way. In no time, they were out on a crowded street, completely out of view of Erling, who had lost them in their trek through the buildings.

"That was . . . " Jericho's words drifted off in disbelief.

Dusk giggled, holding his free hand out to hail them a cab now that they were several blocks away from the Bronzel-helm and Bristlehorn offices. "Right? Thank Merlin for Pickle."

"How did you meet these people?" Jericho asked, flopping back into her seat and letting her tense muscles finally relax.

"Oh, I inherited Pickle from Mom." Dusk typed in the address for Jericho's apartment.

"Your mom?"

"Long story. One we really shouldn't talk about here. But once we're home, why don't we have a midnight snack and a chat?"

"Yeah. Okay."

They rode in silence the rest of the way.

When they finally reached Jericho's apartment—home—she was sure that Dusk would say he was too tired to talk about it. That seemed to be his go-to method to get out of tough conversations. But Dusk just rolled up the sleeves of his crisp white shirt and pulled a carton of ice cream from the freezer and two spoons from the drawer. He plopped the container onto the island and held a spoon out to Jericho.

"No bowls?" Jericho took the utensil, turning it over in her fingers.

"Just like old times." Dusk offered her a secretive smile, peeling the lid off the container and taking a big scoop.

"Auntie hated that."

"She said it was bad manners." Dusk chuckled fondly, but his eyes dimmed into melancholy. "But I caught her at it one night."

"Oh yeah?" Jericho smiled faintly. She remembered the scolding Dusk's mother had given them on multiple occasions for drinking from the milk bottle, eating from the ice cream carton, and stuffing their grubby hands into the cereal box instead of pouring a bowl.

"Yeah." Dusk's laugh had gone hollow. He shook his head. "Merlin, I miss her."

"What happened to her, anyway?"

Dusk took a moment, nibbling more ice cream from his spoon as he stared off into the space just over Jericho's shoulder. "Well, like I said, she pulled me out before I could—"

"Right. But then after that, Ildri said she just disappeared. She fell off the grid. It gave Ildri a real hard-on." Jericho scoffed, but there was no real heat behind it.

"Yeah, it would." Dusk muttered the words almost too softly to hear. Then he took a breath and straightened his shoulders a little. "Anyway, we went into hiding after that, and she taught me everything she knew. Pickle was someone she knew from her university days, and they helped us fall off the map, like Ildri said."

"So how did you get into doing . . . this?" Jericho gestured to the villain costume.

"Adelia Tsuki was always an activist. She just got more active when she gave birth to a banshee." Dusk shrugged. "When I couldn't be a hero, and I . . . Well, she'd had enough."

"She became a villain." Jericho frowned. Something about that didn't fit with the Adelia Tsuki she'd known.

"No. She became the hero *I* needed." Dusk looked away from the spot he'd been staring at to meet Jericho's eyes. Stone cold and serious. "She didn't start me off digging for information on council members. We started going to protests, and we still went to them even after we began digging around in the broken system. The fact is, the system *is* broken, and protesting wasn't enough."

Jericho shook her head, running the tip of her spoon through the steadily softening ice cream.

"I know what you're thinking. That isn't a good enough reason to do something illegal. I guess from where you sit, you'd be right. But from where I sit, from where Mama sat, it's a different story. She taught me everything she knew about technology, and keeping a low profile, and how to make the changes we wanted to see."

"If she taught you to keep a low profile, why did I catch you?"

Dusk smirked, dropping his half-melted spoonful of ice cream back into the tub so his fingers could work over the words, his voice low. "Because I decided it was time to put a face to the movement. We can dig up information all we want, but until we put it out there for the people to see, it's not going to do anything. The fact that we found the information, and the council knew we found it, was enough to scare them but not enough to make them change. No. If we're going to change anything, we have to expose them for what they really are."

"And you're going to do that by leaking dirt from dating sites?" Jericho snorted, rolling her eyes. "Seems a little petty, don't you think?"

"I guess it does. But that's not the only thing out there to find, it's just what I had on me that day."

"And what else is out there to find?"

Dusk shrugged, picking up his spoon again and cleaning it with his mouth before dropping it into the sink with a soft *tink* of metal on metal. "Guess you'll have to wait and see."

CHAPTER THIRTEEN

JERICHO DIDN'T HAVE TO WAIT LONG. IT HADN'T EVEN BEEN A full week when word that the Bronzelhelm and Bristlehorn mining company had been selling synthetic stones and passing them off as real came to light.

"That's what they're worried about?" Dusk scowled, glaring at the news anchor as he leaned forward, elbows pressed hard to his knees to keep him sitting on the couch.

"Bronzelhelm and Bristlehorn is also under investigation for unsafe work environments and unequal pay for their bluecap workers," the anchorperson continued.

"Investigation my left tit," Dusk muttered darkly. "I gave them all the proof they needed!"

"Well, you know what they say: innocent until—"

Dusk whipped his head around to glare hard at Jericho, who was in the kitchen cooking dinner, looking for all the world like a very pissed off owl. "No. Don't you throw that shit saying around at me."

Jericho lifted a brow, trying not to show the amusement on his face.

"I will scoop your vocal cords out with that ladle if you finish that sentence."

Jericho held his hands up in surrender, the ladle clattering against the pot. "Why do you care about the bluecaps, anyhow? I thought your whole shtick was justice for Unseelie. The bluecaps are Seelie."

Dusk's eyes narrowed, flicking over Jericho's face as if trying to make sense of something he was seeing. What that was, Jericho wasn't sure, but he remained quiet and waited.

"My whole *shtick*," he said slowly, using air-quotes around the word 'shtick' with no small amount of irritation, "is equality. The bluecaps are Seelie, but they're commonly mistreated and taken advantage of because of their redcap cousins. They're almost as badly discriminated against as Unseelie, and that's not equal." A hard edge lit Dusk's eyes, and he turned back to the television to scowl at the news anchor. "Merlin help me," he muttered under his breath. "I'm surrounded by idiots."

●

IT HAD BEEN two weeks since their little heist, and Jericho hadn't told anyone—or the Alliance was *pretending* like he hadn't told anyone. Two weeks of silence and boredom, complete with a boringly standard full moon, as Dusk glared at news anchors and the case against Bronzelhlem and Bristlehorn slowly progressed.

Two weeks, and then Dusk flopped down at his desk right before lunch. A wide grin stretched across his face, making his dark eyes crinkle to accommodate it. "It's time," he signed.

"Time? For what? You're going to have to be more specific," Jericho drawled, not bothering to look away from his computer.

"Time for coffee." Dusk's grin and squinting eyes couldn't hide the sly look that resided under the mask of playfulness. He was up to something.

"Coffee," Jericho repeated, his fingers only slowing slightly across the keys.

"Yeah, you look like you could use it." Dusk didn't bother with any other explanation, and Jericho didn't force the issue. He just rose from his chair, grabbed his jacket, and followed Dusk around the corner to a tiny hole-in-the-wall coffee place.

"This place has the shittiest coffee in the city," Jericho griped, loud enough to earn him a mildly annoyed look from the cashier as they walked up to the counter.

"I know." Dusk's tone was strangely gleeful given the context, but Jericho was learning to ignore the tone and focus on the sentiment. Dusk knew. Which meant . . . "That's why I picked it."

Jericho took a cursory glance around, noticing the lack of other patrons. *Ah, that's it.* No one would overhear them here because there was no one *to* overhear them.

"I'll just take a black coffee," Jericho told the girl, then headed to a table in the back. Jericho pressed his chair into the corner, his eyes flicking around to take in the barely awake barista filling his cup with what looked like lukewarm coffee.

Dusk hummed softly, his fingers drumming along to a disjointed tune before he made his way over to the table with their drinks.

"Your coffee, sir," he teased, sliding the thick looking sludge across the table before grabbing the sugar bowl to spoon a generous heap into his tea.

"So, it's time for what?" Jericho signed. He knew they wouldn't be overheard here, but he still wanted to be careful. He lifted the cup, its contents making a soft squelching sound as it moved, and then promptly replaced it on its saucer. Jericho was not drinking that. It'd probably kill him.

"For you to see my lab," Dusk signed, his lips twitching with a knowing smile. Then his long, thin fingers fell to spin his own drink around and around with a spoon, eyes fixated on the little whirlpool he was creating as he let the words sink in.

"Wait. Really?" Jericho asked out loud. He felt his heart pick up at the mention of the lab. He'd been waiting so long now, he'd almost thought that Dusk would never trust him enough to take him. "I'm going to get the location of the lab?"

Dusk nodded slowly. He lifted his cup to his lips, took a sip, and cringed. "Shit, that's bad." The cup settled back onto the saucer with a hollow *thunk* as he shook his head. "Anyway, yeah. I think you've earned it. You kept your mouth shut about our heist."

"You trust me now?" It seemed too simple. Way too simple.

Dusk snorted. "You're on your way."

He refused to answer any of Jericho's other questions, and soon they left their untouched drinks behind them to head back to the office.

"Sunday," Dusk promised before breaking off to head down to Ildri's workspace, a tiny K.N.I.G.H.T. unit buzzing along behind him.

Sunday.

Jericho had two days to set up the sting.

•

"THAT'S NOT enough time to set this up," Erling argued, his eyes narrowing on the projection set up in Oakfur's office. "For one thing, we don't know where we're going yet. For another, who's to say this isn't a trap?" Erling leaned back in his chair, his arms crossed over his chest as his wings rustled. He'd pressed his lips together hard. There was something he wasn't saying, and Jericho could only assume it was that Erling didn't trust *him*.

"I don't think we can take the chance that it's not." Jericho crossed his arms over his chest as well, settling in for a standoff.

"There isn't enough information to go off of," Erling spat, his eyes narrowing on Jericho next.

"And there will continue to not be enough information if I don't gain his trust." Jericho's lips peeled back off his teeth to snarl.

"Enough!" Oakfur shouted, his hands slamming on the desk. "Erling is right, this isn't enough information." Erling had the nerve to look smug. "Jericho is also right. Dusk has remained tight lipped the last month, and this seems to be our first in. We have to take it. Now, run the plan by me again."

Jericho nodded. "Ildri has outfitted my cell phone with a tracker app. All I have to do is hit the button once we reach the lab, and you'll have the location."

"And if he has jamming tech?" an elf, Gelwyn, asked. She'd raised her hand as if she had to be called upon to speak.

"Ildri has assured me that jammers can't stop this signal. All I have to do is push the button. I trust her."

"Where is Ildri in this? Why isn't she a part of this brief?" Erling's scowl was growing by the minute.

"She's keeping Dusk occupied," Jericho muttered, trying not to feel guilty about using Ildri as the babysitter for his criminal.

"And isn't that suspicious?" Erling asked. "He's taken quite a liking to her and that workshop, hasn't he?"

Jericho narrowed his eyes on Erling, his mouth opening to growl a response.

"I said enough, Erling. If you aren't going to be productive, you can go sit outside." Oakfur turned an annoyed look on him. Erling pressed his thin lips into an even thinner line to silence himself. "If there are no other questions . . ."

Gelwyn's hand shot up again.

"You don't have to raise your hand, Gelwyn." Jericho rolled his eyes.

"Uh . . . right. But . . . what will happen after we have the location of the lab? Will we be bringing the villain back in?" Gelwyn shrank in her seat, her shoulders hunching under the attention of the room.

"Jericho?" Oakfur asked, a smug tilt twitching at the corner of his lips. He knew the answer—of course he did—but he wanted Jericho to say it. He wanted Jericho to expose his bias to a room full of his peers. The rat bastard.

"Once the lab is located, I will send the location, but you are not to move in until Dusk and I have cleared the facility and are out of sight. We don't want him to know that we've infiltrated his lab, at least not yet." Jericho said the words more firmly than he felt them. The plan sounded so simple when he laid it all out that way, but he knew so much could go wrong so easily. All it would take was one overeager hero jumping the gun.

"Why?" Gelwyn pressed, her pale green eyes big and earnest. She was young. She'd likely just finished her apprenticeship, and now here she was, about to be a part of one of the biggest stings their unit had ever seen. Jericho almost felt bad for her. It was a lot of pressure for someone so new to all this.

"Because even if Dusk gives us the lab, he's still got a network of dangerous villains we need to apprehend, and he's only introduced me to a couple of them. If we show our hand too soon, he won't give me any more." Jericho let the words leave him in a calm, confident breath. He knew what he was doing. He was in charge of his own emotions. He was in charge of this situation. Whether Oakfur and Erling believed that or not didn't matter. He knew he was doing things the right way.

"That's logical." Gelwyn nodded.

And just like that, the other arguments died down. Jericho spent the rest of the meeting letting the unit know almost everything she knew of Dusk's network—from Maz to the mysterious Pickle. Although he left out Fizz and the food pantry. The redcap really wasn't doing anything wrong. He was just collecting information and helping those who needed it. He was harmless. A hero. At least from what Jericho had seen.

The meeting broke before lunch, and everyone had dispersed long before Dusk slunk out of the elevator toward Jericho's desk.

"Lunch?" Dusk chirped, eyes bright. "Ildri is coming with."

"Yeah, sure." Jericho nodded, grabbing his wallet and stuffing it into his back pocket. He pushed the briefing from his mind in favor of enjoying a meal with the only two people who he'd ever thought of as friends—even if one of them was a villain.

●

JERICHO STARTED FEELING twitchy on Saturday morning, and even the four-mile run she took couldn't settle her rattled nerves. What if Erling was right? What if it was a trap? Still, she pushed those things from her mind and focused instead on spending time with Dusk like it was the last time they'd have together, because it very well could be. Then, when the day finally came and the nerves were still very much prevalent, she put on what Ildri had taken to calling her 'war paint.'

Dusk took one look up and down, then smiled softly. "You know you have nothing to worry about, right?"

"I know that," Jericho huffed, adjusting the black skater dress self-consciously. "Do you think I don't know that?"

"Right, well, the lipstick is killer. Where'd you get it?" Dusk leaned in to get a better look at Jericho's heavily lined eyes and crimson painted lips, a knowing smirk stretching across his own face.

"Bite me," Jericho snarled, baring sharp incisors.

"Hmmm . . . Maybe later." Dusk laughed, shaking his head.

"What? No villain costume tonight?" Jericho tugged on the black hoodie she'd worn the night of their first heist. Stealth. It hung awkwardly over the skirt, but there was a certain amount of comfort in being able to pull a hood up over her telltale blond hair.

"We aren't doing anything villain-y tonight," Dusk said, sounding unbothered. "I'm just taking you to a building. Plus, the humidity index is super high tonight. I'd sweat through my shirt if I put on that overcoat." Even still, he'd pulled on the thin black gloves that accompanied his costume. They were in stark contrast to the brown skin and smattering of freckles along his forearms where he'd rolled up the sleeves of his dress shirt. "This is my casual look."

"That's supposed to be casual?" Jericho's eyes flicked over the trousers, pressed indigo dress shirt, and herringbone waistcoat before scoffing. "You're even wearing a fucking tie."

"But the sleeves are rolled up," Dusk signed, adjusting his hearing aids before slipping into his loafers as a final touch.

"Whatever. Let's just get this shit show on the road."

Dusk shook his head, reaching up to tug on the strings of Jericho's hoodie so the hood cinched around her face. "Cheer up, Lettie. After tonight, you'll be one of us," he muttered, much too close to Jericho's face, then pressed a quick kiss to her nose before spinning on his heel to head out the door. "Or you won't. Your choice."

Jericho stomped down on the feeling of unease that threatened to turn her stomach into a mess of butterflies and other unhappily fluttering insects. It was fine. This was fine. They had a plan in place. They could do this. *She* could do this.

"Are you at least going to tell me what part of the city we're heading to so I can tell the cab?" Jericho slammed the door behind her.

"Ilygroth." Dusk's lips spread into a knowing smirk, which did nothing to settle the fluttering in Jericho's stomach.

"Our old neighborhood?" Jericho frowned. It had been under her nose the whole time? Of course. Dusk *would* pick someplace sentimental. Soliel had always been a sap.

Dusk shrugged but said no more as Jericho typed in her old home address. It wasn't where they were going, but it would get them to Ilygroth and close enough to the lab.

●

THE TOWNHOUSE LOOMED over Jericho as she stood outside the white picket fence. It seemed smaller than it had the last time she'd visited, with its windows all dark and only a yellow streetlamp to cast light on the siding, which was much in need of a coat of paint.

"When did they move out?" Dusk asked from where he stood beside Jericho, his head tilted back to look up at the window of what had once been her room. Jericho remembered keenly all the times Sol had thrown pebbles up at that window to lure her out so they could run around the neighborhood like the hoodlums they were.

"Long time ago." Jericho jerked her head away to glare at the squeaking "for sale" sign on the front lawn. What she didn't say was that it hadn't been that long after Soliel had "died." What she didn't say was that it had been her own absence and anger that had ruined the home her parents had built for them.

"So, where's this place?" She fiddled with her phone, pretending to check the time as she sent a message to the app Ildri had set up to make sure Erling and the others would be in the area.

"Not far," Dusk answered vaguely. Then he turned and headed down the street. The neighborhood was quiet, eerily so, nothing like Jericho remembered it. "I think Mom said a lot of the neighbors stayed, so they're all older now."

"That makes sense." Jericho nodded. "It's still weird not seeing a bunch of rugrats running around after dark." Her eyes drifted over to the park across the street, swings empty and swaying in the light breeze. It felt like both forever ago and just yesterday that she and Soliel had challenged one another to jumping contests—leaping from the swings in reckless abandon that had led to a sprained wrist and a twisted ankle on two separate occasions. Or sat with their fingers intertwined as they watched the last of the summer's fireflies drift past.

"It was so simple then," Dusk whispered, following Jericho's gaze to the swings. "Before we knew the differences between us and what they would make us."

"Yeah, it was." Jericho stuffed her hands into the big pocket on the front of her hoodie, darting her gaze away from the playground. "C'mon. I don't have all fucking night."

Dusk nodded, and the ghost of an expression Jericho didn't recognize—something like loss, maybe—filtered over his face underneath one of the streetlamps. But by the time he reached the light of the next, it was gone. They walked past the park and the apartment buildings where Dusk had once lived. Past the empty storefront of what used to be their favorite tayaki shop, and the spray-painted wall of the grocers. So many things hadn't changed but were different at the same time. It left Jericho off balance, and a heavy feeling settled into her gut. When had all of this happened?

"Things went downhill a few years ago," Dusk answered the unasked question. "That's why we picked this place to move into. They needed someone to regulate it."

"Why?"

It was a vague question, but Dusk seemed to understand what Jericho was asking. "The Alliance doesn't care about these outlying neighborhoods unless one of their own lives here. But . . . " He gestured around, to the graffiti, and the streetlight that was flickering on and off, and the signpost from which someone had stolen the sign. "No one really important ever lived in Ilygroth."

There was a bitter note to his words that hadn't been there before, but Jericho decided not to push the conversation further. She wasn't there to delve into all the emotional bullshit from when they were kids, or the guilt that festered under her skin even now. She was there to find the lab and get the fuck out of Ilygroth.

They continued through the deserted storefronts until they reached a convenience store. Its bright windows lit the sidewalk outside, the only place within a three-block radius actually open, like a will-o-wisp calling to them in the night. Dusk stopped suddenly, just outside the square of light cast by the window, his hands on his hips as he lifted his chin.

"This is it," he declared almost proudly.

"This? Your lab is inside of a 24-7?" Jericho scoffed, tone incredulous.

"Round the back, actually." Dusk reached down to take

Jericho's hand, threading their fingers, then tugged her into the alley lined in metal trash cans and graffiti.

Nerves licked at Jericho's insides, making her palms damp and her muscles twitchy. Should she tell them now? Or was it too soon? She didn't want Dusk to know she'd given him up. But if she waited too long, she might give herself away calling them. And what if it was a trap? What if . . .

"Here we are." Dusk broke through Jericho's train of thought. He dropped her hand to reach for a keypad Jericho hadn't noticed and type in a quick series of numbers. A soft click, and the door sprung ajar. Dusk pressed the door open further. Without looking back to see if Jericho was following, he went inside.

Jericho took one quick glance around before heading in. Just inside, there was a narrow flight of stairs that led up to what seemed to be the third or perhaps fourth floor of the building. They creaked under Dusk's weight as he climbed them. At the top, there was another door. This one looked to be made of steel and was lined with intricate runes indicating heavy spellwork to accompany its matching keypad. Dusk's lean fingers typed in another passcode, too quick for Jericho to catch, and the door glowed faintly for a moment before the lock released and it opened inward.

When Dusk stepped inside, bright lights flickered to life, stinging Jericho's eyes for a long moment before she adjusted. Once she did, she got the full view of a wide-open room with several rows of work benches littered in items she didn't recognize, from the magical to the technological. The windows were boarded up, although that hadn't been obvious from the street, so there must have been some kind of spell in place to make them appear normal. And along the walls were several bookshelves stuffed too full with tomes in languages Jericho had thought long dead.

"Holy shit," Jericho breathed, her eyes widening.

"Welcome to Operation Ilygroth," Dusk chuckled, giving her a theatrical bow. He dropped into one of the wheeled chairs and pushed himself across the floor to an old computer. The soft clacking of the ancient keyboard filled the room as Jericho wandered, picking things up to examine them.

"So, what? This is where you guys make everything?"

Dusk nodded, only half listening to Jericho. He was muttering under his breath, things that sounded like calculations and instructions. Jericho could only just make some of them out. For all she knew, he could be hacking into the council building from here. She moved over to one of the bookshelves near the windows, grabbing a book that seemed to be in Spanish and flipping through its contents to look for pictures to make sense of the words. That's when her ears picked up the sound of someone stumbling into one of the garbage cans in the alley.

She was about to brush the sound off when she heard a soft, "Shit," in a voice that was all too familiar. Jericho turned her head to look at Dusk; she found him still ducked over the computer, focused solely on the screen before him. They were too early. Way too early. She needed to get Dusk—

The door flew open, and one by one, a group of heroes filed in, blocking the exit. Dusk's head jerked up, but he wasn't looking at the heroes, he was looking at Jericho. There was a moment, a split second, where he looked betrayed, and then a slow smirk split his features. *Cheeky little fucker. He knew all along.*

"No, don—" Jericho called out to stop him. But it was too late. Dusk pressed a button on the keyboard, and every screen in the room crackled with static before going entirely black. Another fizzling sound filled the room, and a charge went through the metal benches, this one tinted with magic, shocking one of the heroes who'd been touching it and frying every bit of electronic material sat on top of it.

"Good luck getting anything salvageable off them." Dusk leaned back in his chair, resting his hands behind his head, totally at ease.

"What did you do?!" Jericho roared, lunging to grab him by the lapels of his waistcoat and shaking him for all she was worth.

Dusk just stared back, a self-satisfied smirk on his lips, but the expression didn't quite reach his eyes. In those dark depths resided disappointment. Like he'd expected better of Jericho.

●

THEY DIDN'T SPEAK to each other the whole way back. Dusk picked at the cuffs on his wrists, fingers turning blue from how tight Erling had made them, while Jericho pretended not to notice, staring out the window at the blurring city lights.

"We didn't need an escort," Jericho grumbled softly as she shifted her hips in the back of the squad car, which was jammed full of herself, Dusk, an extra-large K.N.I.G.H.T. unit, and two other heroes.

"Sorry, J. Erling's orders," Keya—a dark haired mermaid—said with an apologetic smile.

"We'll be outside of your apartment building for the remainder of the evening," Imizael—a pixie—offered in a crisp, formal tone.

Jericho bit the tip of her tongue hard enough to draw blood. There was no point in arguing. Erling was being an ass, and there was nothing she could do about it. So, she stayed silent and led Dusk back up to the apartment, where she was finally allowed to uncuff him, although Imizael looked nervous at the very thought.

"He's not going to hurt anyone. And if he does, it'll be me first," Jericho said, unfazed.

"We should—" Imizael started, stepping toward the threshold.

"Oh no you fucking shouldn't." Jericho cut him off by slamming the door in his face before he could follow them inside. Then she rounded on Dusk. "You tricked me!"

"No. I trusted you." Dusk's face was a mask of impassivity. Jericho could only see the hurt in his eyes. "I trusted you to come to the lab and see what we were all about. And you betrayed me."

"Because we can't just—"

"Can't just what?" Dusk prompted, rage seeping into his features and casting his freckles in an angry red color. "Can't just *what, Jericho?*" He spat the name like it was a slur. "Change the world? Help people? Fight back?"

Jericho opened her mouth to answer, her fingernails digging harsh crescents into her palms. She was trying to hold back, trying to keep from completely flying off the handle at Dusk. Couldn't he see? Couldn't he understand that the way he was doing this wasn't right? That in order for this to work, for them to both come out of this unscathed, they had to do things the right way? The legal way? If they didn't, it went against everything Jericho thought they'd once believed in. And then . . . and then that would be the end. Soliel really would be dead.

"No." Dusk held up a hand to silence her. "*You*"—he pressed one boney finger to the center of Jericho's sternum, digging in hard enough that Jericho was sure it would bruise—"can't do what needs to be done. *You* can't help people. Because *you* can't get your head out of your ass long enough to realize that you've gotten complacent. Comfortable. The fact of the matter is, you don't want to upset the status quo because it might change your place in the world. You've become exactly the type of hero we said we'd never be. Too comfortable in the comforts of Mythikos, and out of touch with the world. *You* disgust me."

Then Dusk turned on his heel, stomped to his room, and slammed his door behind him. Jericho didn't need wolf hearing to hear the lock slam into place. Not that it would stop her from entering if she wanted to, but she wouldn't.

Dusk's words had left her cold.

Was he right? Had she gotten complacent? Was she the one who had grown lax on their moral code? No. *No*, that couldn't be right. It couldn't.

CHAPTER FOURTEEN

JERICHO DIDN'T BOTHER TO WAKE DUSK AND DRAG HIM TO THE station the following morning. With a K.N.I.G.H.T. unit in the hall, and two heroes posted in a car across the street, she was sure that Dusk wasn't going anywhere.

"You left him? Alone?" Erling asked, his eyes narrowing. "Have you lost your fucking mind?"

"You sent men to guard him. Are you telling me you don't trust your men?" Jericho countered. She wasn't particularly in the mood for whatever tirade Erling thought to go on. There were other things to worry about, like reading over the evidence list from the lab and seeing if anything had actually been salvaged. Although, Jericho knew there wouldn't be. If Dusk didn't want them to find anything, they wouldn't find anything.

"You should have brought him back in! He should be locked up in the hold right now for that little stunt he pulled last night!" Spittle flung from Erling's lips, his wings expanding behind him threateningly.

"And what good would that do? Huh?" Jericho crossed her arms over her chest, unperturbed. "He thinks he's got us all figured out now. He thinks he fooled us. What good would bringing him in do?"

"It would mean we wouldn't have to worry about him escaping from your custody." Erling stood taller—his height nearing two heads above Jericho—in an attempt to intimidate the werewolf. But Jericho had never been one to be bothered simply because she was smaller.

"Erling! Jericho!" Oakfur barked from his office door. "My office. Now." He turned without waiting for them to follow. "Sit," the captain ordered as they entered, pointing to the chairs across from his desk.

They dropped into the seats.

"Captain, I feel that Soliel Tsuki—villain name: Dusk—should be brought in and detained in the hold. It has been made clear that Jericho has lost control of the situation and is too close to all of this. Not to mention that all the information Jericho has gotten us through the investigation has—" Erling's words were cold, clipped, concise, but they were cut off by the captain's raised hand.

"Jericho?"

Jericho gritted her teeth, hands fisting in her lap. "The moment he's brought back into custody, he'll clam up. We won't get anything else out of him. I just—"

"Then he should be put into the custody of another hero. Someone who isn't so close." Erling wasn't looking at Jericho. He was focusing on pleading his case to the captain.

"Yes, and undo all of the work I've put into building a relationship with him." Jericho rolled her eyes.

"Which you just threw out the window by betraying him. Like he'd trust you now." Erling snorted.

"And whose fault was that?!" Jericho shouted. "You weren't supposed to—"

"Enough!" Oakfur slammed his hands on his desk,

scowling at the pair of them. "I had a meeting with the council this morning. This is an epic fuck-up, Jericho."

"Yes, sir." Jericho clenched her teeth to keep her tone respectful.

"But lucky for you, your exemplary record has spoken for itself," Oakfur continued as if Jericho hadn't spoken. "You have till this time next month to turn this around."

"Yes—"

"Let me finish," Oakfur cut her off. "If you cannot get us any viable information within that time, Soliel will be sent to the Isle, and you will be demoted and investigated for conspiracy."

Erling's expression turned smug as he leaned back further in his chair. "Sounds fair to me."

"It would," Jericho muttered, rolling her eyes again.

"What was that?" Oakfur asked.

"Nothing, sir. I'll have information for you as soon as possible." Jericho rose from her seat, bowing her head respectfully. "You can count on it."

"Yes, well, let's hope so." Oakfur nodded. "You're dismissed as well, Erling. Please do keep your bickering to a minimum from here on out."

"Yes, sir," Erling grumbled, rising from his chair. Then the duo was back out in the bullpen. "This isn't over," Elring growled under his breath, sitting down stiffly.

"No, it's not," Jericho agreed, her hands clutching the arms of her chair so hard her knuckles turned white.

●

THEY WORKED in silence for the remainder of the morning until Jericho decided to take her lunch down to Ildri's workshop.

"Now is not a good time," Ildri called through the door when she knocked.

When Jericho opened it, she was rubbing a bit of grease from her nose, smearing it in a way that only seemed to make matters worse.

"We're in quite a bind, J. A bind indeed!" A near hysterical laugh left Ildri at the words, and she shook her two-toned head, wisps of blue and pink hair falling into her face.

Jericho dropped onto one of the stools and prodded at her mushy bowl of ramen with a fork. "What's it this time?"

"It's all fried! Everything! The blast he sent through the tables destroyed every bit of information we may have gotten from what was there." There was a contradiction in Ildri's tone—it *should* be bad that they could get nothing from the lab equipment, but she looked almost thrilled by it. "Impressive, very impressive."

"So, we've got nothing." Jericho sighed, her stomach rolling as she set down her bowl. Nothing. They'd gotten *nothing*. Fuck. How was she going to turn this around in a month? Cold sweat crawled down her spine. What if she couldn't?

"Don't put that there," Ildri said sharply, her eyes narrowing on the bowl of broth. "In fact, get that out of my lab. Now."

"You let Dusk eat in here all the time."

"Dusk understands how fragile this equipment is."

"Fine. I'll hold it," Jericho snapped, her hands wrapping tightly around the bowl and setting it in her lap. "Better?"

Ildri didn't answer, she just turned back to whatever she was tinkering with. It was something from Dusk's lab, though Jericho wasn't sure what it was for, and it had a distinct burn mark on the outer shell. "I don't know where your boy learned all this."

"He's not *my* anything," Jericho hissed, but it sounded

weak even to her own ears. Dusk was her . . . something. Just . . . she didn't know what.

Ildri made a noise in the back of her throat like she didn't agree, but she didn't say anything to contradict Jericho.

"He said his mom taught him." Jericho scooted closer to get a better look at the device Ildri was working on. It looked to be some kind of recorder, like one might use for surveilling an office. "What's this?"

"A bug," Ildri said, confirming her suspicions. "Long-range would be my guess, much better than anything we use here. Basically, he can stick it on a person or in a room and listen from anywhere in the city."

"How?" Jericho blinked down at it. It didn't look like much. Just one little hole to indicate the microphone.

"It runs off the wireless network in Mythikos. Which is extraordinary." She unscrewed the shell, setting it aside and poking at the innards with a pair of needle-nose tweezers. "But that's not the best part."

"What's the best part?"

"The battery," Ildri whispered as if she'd come across something miraculous.

"The battery," Jericho repeated blandly. "What about it?"

"There isn't one!" she blurted, throwing her hands up in excitement and nearly knocking Jericho's bowl of ramen out of her lap in the process. A wild look gleamed in Ildri's eyes.

"I'm sorry?"

"It runs entirely off the latent magical energy in the air." Ildri's bright eyes had gone wide as saucers.

"Can that be done?" Jericho moved closer, squinting down at the little device. With the shell removed, it was even less impressive, just a tiny bed of circuits and wiring. Jericho couldn't see what was so special about it, but the air buzzed with Ildri's excitement.

"Clearly! I mean, every fae excretes a certain amount of

latent magic—that's how we've managed to cut back our energy consumption for things like cars and cell phones. But I've never seen anything that runs exclusively off of it. It must be incredibly efficient. If we could harness this kind of technology, we could get rid of our dependency on the solar fields almost entirely."

"Right." Jericho's brows knit together. How much of a genius *was* Dusk? Or had this been another of Adelia's gifts? "So, I have an evil genius living in my apartment?"

"I mean . . . yeah. If you're looking at him through the lens of the council." Ildri ducked over the device again, eagerly prodding the wires.

"And if I'm not?"

Ildri looked up, blinking behind safety goggles that magnified her eyes by about a hundred. "If you're not . . . " She bit the inside of her cheek for a moment. "If you're not, then I guess you have to decide what Dusk is, don't you?"

"And what are my options?" Jericho asked, more to herself than to Ildri. It was a question she'd struggled with since the moment she'd brought Dusk to the hold. What *was* Dusk? His methods were skewed, yes. But his ideals . . . They were something Jericho felt she could get behind. Was Dusk the hero of the people, or the villain of the council? At this point, was there a difference? Jericho didn't hear Ildri's reply as she left the workshop and headed back to her desk.

She had some thinking to do.

•

BY THE TIME Jericho left for the evening, she still hadn't decided what Dusk was. She *had* decided that Soliel would never have grown into a villain. So, she supposed that was something. But if he wasn't a villain, and he wasn't a hero, what was he? Maybe he didn't have to be one or the other.

Maybe he was just a good person doing bad things for the right reasons . . .

Jericho shook herself. She'd deal with that later.

Two heroes were still parked in front of her apartment building when she arrived, and she went over to knock on the roof of their cruiser.

"You two can take off for the night. I got this."

The younger of the two frowned. "But Erling said that—"

"I don't give a fuck what Erling said," Jericho interrupted. "The captain said this is still my case, so get gone."

The girl's face scrunched up as if she were deciding who she was more afraid of pissing off. After a moment, she seemed to decide it was Jericho. "Do you still want the K.N.I.G.H.T.?"

"No. I'll send it down when I get up there, and then you lot can fuck off somewhere."

"Yes, sir." She nodded and rolled up the window before her partner could argue with the decision she'd just made for the both of them. Jericho didn't wait for her partner to get up the balls to say anything either; she just turned and headed into her building.

The elevator ride went much too quickly as she breathed the recycled air, trying to calm her nerves. Dusk had been pissed. What if he still was? What if they couldn't have a civilized conversation? What if Jericho couldn't get Dusk to trust her again? That would be the end of everything, wouldn't it?

A soft hiss told her that the doors had opened, and she shook her head to clear her thoughts before heading down the hall to her apartment. A large robot waited outside, its head turning and luminescent eyes giving an unneeded blink as it tracked her approach.

"Jericho," it said in its dry, stilted fashion.

"You're relieved. The heroes are waiting downstairs to take you back to the hold."

With a soft whirr, the K.N.I.G.H.T. headed toward the elevator. That was the good thing about robots: they didn't argue about orders, they just followed them. Jericho pressed her palm to the pad by the door, and it opened with a soft click.

"Dusk. I brought home pizza. It's pineapple and ham, your favorite." A peace offering that she could only hope he'd accept. Jericho dropped the cardboard box onto the island with a soft thump.

Lights flickered on as Jericho walked deeper into the apartment. Not a single sound greeted her, and everything was as she remembered it from when she'd left that morning.

"Dusk?" Jericho poked her head down the hall as the hallway lights lit at her approach. She frowned, pacing to Dusk's door and taking hold of the handle. Surprise drew her brows together when it turned without resistance. "Sol?" Jericho pressed the door open, and her stomach dropped. Fuck. The room was empty. "That little fucker. How did he get past the robot?"

It took only a handful of minutes to search the rest of the apartment and find no sign of the villain. Dusk hadn't packed a bag; he'd just slipped on his fancy shoes and left. He hadn't even worn his overcoat. In fact, judging by the lack of empty hangers in his closet, Dusk hadn't worn any of his new clothes.

Jericho pulled out her phone and dialed Ildri as she slipped into her own shoes and back out into the hall.

"Talk to me," the voice of Ildri greeted through the tinny speaker.

"I need the GPS on Dusk's tracker pinged." Jericho jabbed the button for the elevator a couple of times, willing it to move more quickly.

"Is he missing?" Ildri asked, and Jericho could hear the click-clacking of keys in the background.

"Is he miss—Of course he's fucking missing!" Jericho hissed, pinching the bridge of her nose where a headache was starting. "Tell me where the little fuckwit is."

All sounds of clicking stopped for a moment, and Ildri let out a long, slow breath. "Are you sure that's a good idea, J?"

"Why wouldn't it be?" Jericho felt her hands grip the phone dangerously hard, glass and metal cutting into her palm hard enough to leave a sharp red indent. This is exactly what Erling had been talking about. Exactly what would prove that fucking birdbrain right. And what if something happened to Dusk? What if someone else found him first? There would be no way for Jericho to protect him then.

"Because," Ildri said slowly, her voice like someone speaking to a wounded animal, "if I track him for you using that, I have to report it. That means Oakfur will know that he got out. You know what he'll do if he finds out."

Teeth ground together painfully. Jericho squeezed her eyes shut. *Fuck.* "Cancel that then. I'll find the little fucker on my own."

"Probably for the best. You have any idea where he might be?"

"Not really, but—" She stopped, a thought striking her. "No. I know exactly where he is. Thanks, Ildri. I'll talk to you later."

"Right. Just . . . let me know once you've found him and he's safe, yeah?"

"Yeah."

•

IT TOOK over an hour to hail a cab and make it to Ilygroth. By the time Jericho reached the old playground, the clouds had opened up. Late summer rain pinged softly against the metal of the crooked slide, and the ground squelched beneath Jericho's boots.

"You're not even wearing a fucking coat." Jericho glared at the darkly clad figure hunched on a swing.

"I've got a hood." Dusk tugged at the strings of the black hoodie he'd clearly pulled out of Jericho's collection.

"How long have you been sitting out here?" Jericho moved to sit in the swing beside Dusk, ignoring the water seeping through her jeans.

Dusk tilted his head to the side as if to consider the question and then said, "Little while."

"Are you ready to come home?"

A heavy sigh, the oversized hoodie shifting with the movement of his narrow chest. "I have something for you."

"You can give to me at ho—"

"No." Dusk rooted around in the big pocket at the front of the hoodie for whatever it was.

"No?"

"No. Because if this doesn't work, then I'm not going back with you."

"If what doesn't work?"

Dusk didn't answer. He just pulled out a small handheld screen, not much bigger than the cellphone Jericho had tucked into her pocket. A video began playing, the sound barely audible above the rain.

"Is that Councilman Pendragon?" His face was out of focus, and the sound quality wasn't great, but Jericho would recognize that man anywhere. He was the head of the Council of Elders in Mythikos. He'd been in office for longer than Jericho had been alive. "Or did you hire some fucking shifter—"

"You know shifts don't show up on Oracle cameras," Dusk muttered, sounding tired. "Just watch."

Jericho grunted, skeptical.

"No," Pendragon's voice cut through the gentle patter of the rain. "I don't care what you have to do. I want that property."

"It isn't a high crime neighborhood," another voice responded, one Jericho didn't recognize. "We can't just make it look like crime spiked out of—"

"What's its Unseelie population?" There was a rustling of papers as the other person slid them across to Pendragon. He adjusted his glasses on his nose, looking over the numbers. "Higher than average."

"Well, it is a lower income—"

"It's perfect," Pendragon cut in, a smug smile tinging his voice.

"What do you plan to do with the property?"

"Does it matter?" Pendragon asked, an edge to the question.

"No. I suppose not. How soon do you need it cleared out?"

Pendragon tapped a finger on his chin, muttering to himself for a moment before deciding on, "Five years."

"Sir, that's—"

"That's what I want."

"We'll have to get the heroes involved."

"Whatever it takes. I want Ilygroth cleared out in five years. That's where I'm building my new estate. Maybe if we stage a murd—" Pendragon drawled, but the video cut out before he could finish.

Jericho stared at the dark screen as water splattered it. "So that was . . . " She let the words drift off, scrubbing at her damp face.

"A plot to blame the Unseelie for increased crime in our neighborhood so a member of the ruling political class could purchase the land cheaply and build himself yet another fucking mansion?" Dusk asked, tone bitter. "Yes, it was."

"That could have been a shapeshifter."

"It's an Oracle camera. I can show you the base file when we get back. It'll have all the spell markings to prove it's shifter-proof."

"Fine. But there's not enough there to be conclusive—"

"No, there is no concrete proof," Dusk agreed. "But it's a start. And imagine what the public would do with this—"

"We can't show anyone this. Not yet. Not until we have concrete evidence. Not until we know everyone who's involved." Jericho frowned, her mind already working on what they'd need for this to not blow up in their faces or be brushed off as a hoax. "Otherwise, people will just think it's a stunt."

Dusk nodded in understanding. "You'll help?"

"For Ilygroth," Jericho said.

Dusk chuckled, shaking his head. "No, for Mythikos. Pendragon isn't the only one twisting the facts here. You saw Fizz's records. So, are you in?"

Jericho bit her lip, thinking. Then she nodded. "Yeah, Sol, I'm in."

"Then let's go home."

CHAPTER FIFTEEN

"WHERE DO WE GO LOOKING FOR MORE PROOF?" JERICHO asked, cereal crunching between her teeth loudly. She hated eating dry cereal, but she needed something to settle her stomach after the shocking news Dusk had given her. Pendragon had always seemed to be a pillar of the community, someone who wanted to help the disadvantaged. Now, seeing him in this new light, Jericho felt strangely off balance and wrong-footed. Still, she couldn't deny the proof of what she'd seen.

Dusk tugged his feet onto the couch, curling his arms around his knees as if to make himself smaller and smaller. "We're going to have to find some documents in his files. Definitely more video." His words were soft and thoughtful, fingers signing along to them more and more slowly as his mind turned inward. "Oh, and maybe Pickle can get a look at any recent transfers. He has to be paying someone off."

"Right." Jericho nodded. She swallowed the dry cereal, letting it scratch all the way down, and chewed on her lip when there was nothing left. Their time was short, and there was so much to do. "We've got a month."

Dark hair fell across Dusk's eyes as he jerked his head up to look at Jericho. "What?"

"Oakfur says the council is giving me a month to get my head out of my ass and prove to them I'm capable. Maybe a little less. If I can't do it in a month, you're off to the Isle, and I'll be investigated as an accomplice." The words tasted like lead on her tongue—heavy, metallic, poisonous—and despite her best efforts, they trembled from her like a death knell.

"That's it then," Dusk said with an air of finality, his hands moving without any of their usual flourish. As if Jericho had made her choice, and there was nothing Dusk could do about it. "You're just going to help me do this, bring down a prominent family, and then you're going to . . . What? Go back to your life like nothing happened?"

Jericho shrugged. It had felt stupid even before Dusk said the words. She knew there was really no going back to how things had been. She *saw* it now, the corruption that had been spreading through Mythikos like a cancer since . . . How long? Before she'd been born? Since the war itself that decided on Unseelie and Seelie? "It is what it is. I'm not like you. I'm not a rebel."

That's not what she meant to say. She meant to say she wasn't brave. She meant to say she was too scared. *Rebel.* It tasted like chalk on her tongue. *More like hero.*

"Right." Dusk's jaw clenched tight, the tensed muscle near his ear a harsh contrast to the rest of his soft, freckled face. He'd heard the words Jericho hadn't said. He always did. "Well, I guess we better get to work then, huh? I'll set us up a meet with Maz and Fizz."

"What about the rest of your crew?"

Dusk snorted. "Like I'd trust their identities to you. It's bad enough I've given you Maz and Fizz. No, we do this my way or not at all. You want to help, don't you?"

"Yeah."

Dusk nodded. "I'm going to get some sleep. I've got a lot of shit to plan tomorrow. You should sleep too; you've got work in the morning." He rose from the couch, tugging the sleeves of Jericho's hoodie down over his hands like mittens. It was still soaking wet, but he'd refused to strip it off when Jericho had changed into a set of dry clothes.

"Good night," Jericho muttered, the words barely above a whisper, but she knew Dusk would hear them.

"Things were different once, you know," Dusk said as if it were an afterthought. "There was a time when you were going to . . . When we were . . . When I . . . " He shook his head. "Sweet dreams."

Jericho frowned after him, scrubbing at her eyes. Dusk didn't have to say it; she knew. She knew what Dusk was thinking. They'd been seventeen, just old enough to make stupid promises that neither would ever keep, and high off their certainty of success in the hero exam. And love. Or at least they'd thought that's what it was. But who was to say now if it'd been love or hormones?

"It won't hurt, will it?" Soliel shifted where he sat on the floor of his room, his knees curled up to his chest.

"Fuck. I don't know. Probably." Jericho rolled her eyes, but her fingers twitched nervously. "But you're going to be a hero. What's a little bite compared to the injuries we'll probably deal with?"

"That's true." Soliel nodded, his hair flopping into his eyes. He peered up at Jericho through the dark strands, a little smile twitching at his lips. "You know it means forever, right?"

"I fucking know! I'm not stupid, Sol! I know what a fucking mating bite does!" Heat crawled up Jericho's neck and across her cheeks. Why was she so embarrassed? She'd never been embarrassed with Sol before. He was her best friend. Her partner. Her

everything. The bite would just seal the deal. "But we're . . . We're a
. . ."

"We're a team," Soliel finished with a gentle hum. "And this
way, we always will be."

"Right."

"After graduation."

Jericho just nodded.

IT HAD BEEN STUPID. Jericho hadn't known it at the time, but
she did now. And it would have hurt like shit. She'd gone on
to learn later how badly werewolf saliva could hurt another
person. But in those days, everything had been swallowed up
by Soliel. When Jericho had looked into the future, all she
could see was that bright smile and those bright eyes. She
couldn't have imagined a day, much less a life, where they
were on opposing sides. Where Soliel would become Dusk, a
villain. She'd been such a child. Immature and foolish.

Jericho shook herself, rising to throw away the rest of the
forgotten cereal and head to bed. She didn't know how long
she'd been sitting there. Long enough for the phone in her
pocket to be nearly dead. Glancing at it, she noticed the
missed calls from Ildri. Shit. Would she even still be up?
Jericho sighed and dialed anyway. If all else failed, she could
leave a voicemail.

"J, tell me you found him," Ildri ordered in a voice tinged
with worry and too much caffeine. Jericho wondered if she
was still sitting up in her workshop at . . . whatever fucking
time it was.

"Yeah, sorry. I meant to call earlier, but we had a lot of
shit to talk about."

A relieved breath left Ildri. "Good. I'm glad it was you
who found him and not someone else."

"Me too." Jericho tried not to think about what would

have become of Dusk had Erling found him as silence settled between them. He would have been . . . Erling would have . . . No. Her grip tightened on the device in her hands. No, she'd let Dusk go before that happened. She'd take whatever heat came her way for it, and she'd let Dusk go. Because she couldn't bear to see him end up on the Isle, or worse. He was too fucking *good* for that.

"J, it's late. You need to get to sleep," Ildri whispered, finally breaking the silence.

"Yeah. Good night, Ildri. I'll see you tomorrow." She hung up, then went to pour herself into bed where she tossed and turned the remainder of the night. The voice of Pendragon played through her mind over and over again.

•

BREAKFAST the next morning was a hazy, silent affair. Dusk made eggs with cheese—just the way Jericho liked them—but Jericho was hardly awake enough to enjoy it until he was on his second cup of coffee. They were on their way out when Dusk turned to Jericho, stopping him in the middle of reaching for the door.

"You're going to have to give them something," Dusk insisted softly, his hands gripping Jericho's wrist tightly.

"We'll cross that bridge when we come to it," Jericho said, putting an end to the conversation. He didn't need to think about what he'd give the Alliance and the council when the month was through. He already knew. He may not have the courage to leave the comfort of his life behind, but he could give Dusk this. He could tell the Alliance that he hadn't found anything. He could let Dusk and his little group of bandits escape into the night to continue wreaking havoc. He'd take whatever punishment came out of it. His career would take a hit, but maybe one day he'd work himself back up to his current position, or maybe he'd just retire and take on an apprentice. That's what washed-up heroes did.

The ride to the hold took forever as the quiet stretched between them. Dusk was mumbling under his breath, fingers working furiously in signs too fast for Jericho to catch as he sorted something out in his head. And Jericho stared forward as if he didn't notice, because it was easier than thinking about the warmth pressed into his side.

They parted ways at the threshold of the bullpen, Dusk muttering something about going to see Ildri and meeting Jericho for lunch. A small K.N.I.G.H.T. trailed behind Dusk to keep him out of trouble, and Jericho turned to head to his desk, where Erling was waiting. The broad-shouldered griffin was leaning against it, his thick arms crossed over his chest.

"You called off my patrol," he accused without preamble.

"And would you look at that? He didn't escape," Jericho retorted, pushing past Erling and jamming his shoulder into the other man's with a soft grunt. "It's almost like I have the situation under control."

"You better watch yourself, Jericho. The clout from your master will only carry you so far." Erling straightened, back stiff.

"Thanks for the warning, I'll make a note." Jericho dropped into his chair and set to work. There was a case file from a breaking and entering last week in Ilygroth to handle, and some other petty crimes near there. Knowing what he knew now cast them all in a different light, and Jericho wondered how many of them were staged and how many were actual crimes. One way or the other, an Unseelie had been arrested for each and would spend time in prison as a consequence.

Jericho pulled his phone from his pocket and typed their names into it so he could do more research on his own time.

Maybe Fizz would have some answers on what had really happened.

●

IT WAS ALMOST noon two days later when the call came in. Jericho and Erling were the only two heroes still hanging around the bullpen, as the rest had drifted off for an early lunch, likely to escape the tension between them. There had been a bank robbery reported in the area of Manluna.

"Damn it. And I was just about to head out for lunch too," Erling griped, but neither he nor Jericho hesitated to head down to the locker room and suit up.

"What are the civilian numbers?" Jericho asked the K.N.I.G.H.T. hovering over them as she pulled her armor over her head, ready to go to battle. With two katana strapped to her back, Jericho lifted her chin, her hands steady.

"It appears the bank was mostly empty," the robot replied, tinny voice just barely audible over the buzz of its wings. "They close for lunch hours."

"Perfect, no hostages." Erling's smirk turned sharp as he tugged on his boots.

"Two hostages," the robot corrected.

"Send the full workup to my phone," Jericho ordered. "We'll review it in the car." They loaded into the vehicle, and Jericho let her eyes fly over the information they had so far, her lip between her teeth. "It looks like they've been holed up inside for ten minutes."

"Fuck. What took them so long to send it our way?" The self-driving car swerved too fast down a side street, making Jericho and Erling both lean with the movement.

"It looks like the alarm wasn't automatically triggered for some reason. They had to push the panic button under the counter." Jericho scrubbed at her face. The car pulled up to a curb, stopping abruptly, the doors swinging open.

"What's our play?" Erling adjusted the broadsword on his hip.

"We go in, try to take them down, get the people out. I'm not looking to draw any more attention to this than I've gotta."

"How are we getting in?" Erling eyed the doors, which remained shut despite the fact that there was nothing and no one blocking them.

"It looks like they've hacked into the main system and activated the nighttime locks. But Ildri sent over the schematics for the building. We can go in through a back door down the alley. It'll bring us in through the employee entrance of the neighboring café. There's a connecting door that was sealed off on a separate electrical system when the bank moved in."

"Has she gotten it open?"

Jericho rolled her eyes. "It's Ildri. Of course she's fucking gotten it open. What do you take her for? A fucking amateur?"

"Great Merlin, chill out! I was just asking."

Jericho didn't respond. Instead, she led the way around the corner and down the alley. It was out of view of the front door, and she could only hope the thief hadn't taken it into their head to look outside and notice the hovering car parked on the curb. If they were lucky, very lucky, the robber would be distracted. Their report had nothing on if they were armed, and Jericho prayed they did not have a gun. Fuck. She hated guns. They were loud, messy, and made it too easy to cause an accident where innocent bystanders could get hurt.

The café next door was empty when they entered, having been evacuated by a quick notice from Ildri, and the door into the bank was sitting unlocked before them. Erling went first, opening the door a crack to peek into the break room of the bank before he nodded. He and Jericho crept inside. Their soft boots made no sound on the way across the tile floor. Then they were there, looking into the wide-open lobby of the bank.

Jericho's eyes caught sight of the fluffy white tails poking out of the robber's dark getup, and the girl turned to flash a knowing grin at Jericho.

"So that's the way out," the girl whispered, hardly loud enough for even Jericho's sensitive ears to hear. Her face was a blur, and looking at it made Jericho's head throb. She couldn't make out any of the features. A cloaking spell of some kind. That would make things difficult. Especially if the robbers had turned off the Oracle cameras in the bank.

"Get the hostages out," Jericho ordered, pulling one of the long thin blades from her back. "I'll round up the suspect."

Erling didn't waste a moment. He nodded and headed for the people huddled behind an upturned table. Jericho heard him mutter a quick, "Ildri, I need an out," into his earpiece.

Then she turned to the kitsune, planting her feet and cocking her head. "Why don't you make this easy for me and come in quietly?"

The kitsune tapped her jaw as Jericho had seen Dusk do that night on the rooftops that felt like it had been so long ago. "Pickle," she said in an annoyingly familiar voice. And just like that, the veil dropped from between them, and Jericho watched as the girl's face came into sharp focus. *Maz.*

"Wh—" Jericho started to ask, her brain trying to piece together why Maz would be robbing a bank. The kitsune didn't need money. Right? But all thoughts were stopped when the sound of a gunshot echoed off the marble walls and counters. Jericho only had a second to register the sound before searing pain lit up her right leg. "You little bitch!"

Maz smirked, slamming her shoulder into Jericho's,

sending her staggering onto her injured leg. It caved under her weight, pain lancing up her hip and making her eyes blur. Gritting her teeth, Jericho forced herself upright. But Maz was already brushing past her toward the open door.

"See ya later, puppy." Maz saluted, then she jetted through the break room behind Jericho. Jericho moved to follow, ignoring the dizzying effect of the pain to run after Maz. She knew it was futile. Pickle would find Maz an out much quicker than Ildri had found them an in.

The street outside the café was empty by the time Jericho limped out onto it. Not a soul lined the sidewalks, and she snarled at having lost even the fox's scent.

"Fucking fox," she hissed.

Erling joined her a moment later. "Come on, we've got to get you back to the hold to see the medic. The K.N.I.G.H.T.s can handle the clean-up."

Jericho didn't fight him as Erling helped her into the car. A medic was waiting for them with a wheelchair when they got to the hold. Jericho didn't fight them either. She was too busy seething internally about her lack of insight into this part of Dusk's plan.

Dusk rushed down to the medic, his eyes wild with worry and glittering wetly as they flicked over the blood seeping into Jericho's pant leg.

"You were shot," Dusk signed with a frown as he sat beside the exam table. His hands were shaking so much, Jericho could hardly understand the words. "Maybe we should push off the meet for next week."

"No," Jericho signed back, motions sharp and decisive. "I have a few words for Maz." That was the end of that.

•

THE MEETING WAS SET for late that evening, and all Jericho could do in the meantime, according to the medic and an annoyingly worried Dusk, was fill out his report and wait.

So wait he did.

After dinner of a half-frozen lasagna that sat heavily in his stomach, he and Dusk grabbed a cab to Oralthyr—a small borough at the heart of Mythikos' business district. America-town was what the locals called it, and it was lined in old-style diners, general stores, and small dinner theatres that showed westerns every other night. One such dinner theatre was closed for the evening—or at least that's what the sign said, but it looked like it'd been closed for much longer. Long enough for dust to collect on the windows.

"This another lab?" Jericho asked with a frown.

"You thought I had just one?" Dusk's lips twitched as he cocked his head. "Try not to destroy this one, yeah?"

"*Someone* thought you had just one."

"The shit the council knows couldn't fill a thimble," a voice said from the darkness of the alley to their right. Fizz poked his head around the corner with that sharp-toothed smile of his. "You two idiots just gonna stand there, or are you coming in?"

"We're coming." Dusk followed Fizz into the darkness, leaving Jericho behind.

A moment later, Jericho shook himself and followed as well. The door swung shut behind them, and although the outside of the building looked like an old-timey saloon, the inside was an open warehouse full of tables, much like the lab over the 24/7 in Ilygroth.

Maz was waiting for them, a smug smile on her lips as her fingers drummed on one of the cold metal tables. "Good to see you up and about, puppy."

"You fucking shot me!" Jericho growled, hobbling toward her in fury. No one stopped him as he grabbed the front of

Maz's ridiculously puffy dress and gave her a good hard shake. "Why the fuck did you shoot me?!"

"Oh, darling, you're as bad as a dog with a bone." She shook her head, clicking her tongue, condescension lining her features. "I had to make it look good."

"Look good? Look good! I'm on desk duty for the next week because of you!"

"That seems an overreaction. I only grazed you." Maz's silver eyes filled with faux innocence, widening and shifting into something large and almost doll like.

"How do we know we can trust her?" Jericho spat, dropping his hold on her dress.

Maz scoffed, pressing the wrinkles out with her thin fingers. "Me? How do we know we can trust *you*? You're a hero. You led them right to our operation in Ilygroth!"

"And you shot me!"

"You know, you keep bringing that up like I actually *care*."

"You—"

"Look. You're both pretty. This doesn't need to turn into a pissing competition," Fizz said reasonably. He stepped between them to try to stop any further fighting. Jericho's eyes flicked over to Dusk, who was watching them with an expression of mild amusement.

"Tch." Jericho stepped back with a little wobble. "What'd we get from that little stunt anyway? The incident report said nothing was stolen."

"Nothing that would be on an incident report." Maz rolled her eyes.

Jericho huffed.

Dusk turned to grab a tablet from the metal bench. With quick motions, he typed something in and then held it out for Jericho to inspect. "Account records."

"So that was Pendragon's bank?" Jericho's eyes flicked over the list of transactions thoughtfully. There was no definitive proof there, not yet, but once it had been cross checked with other accounts, they could easily find the bribes. The question would then be *how* to cross check them.

"Well . . . no." Dusk shifted his weight on his feet.

"Then how did you get these?" Jericho asked, holding up the tablet.

"All the banks in Mythikos are connected by a single network so that transfers can be instantaneous. Pickle just needed an access point."

"I think that could have been achieved without taking hostages." Jericho rubbed at his eyes tiredly, dropping the tablet back to the table.

"Where's the fun in that?" Maz smirked. Jericho turned to scowl at her, eyes narrowing, and she stuck her tongue out in retaliation. "And what have you got for us? I mean, you're in the office. Surely you've got—"

"A list of names," Jericho said, pulling his phone from his pocket. "Look into these. I think these are the latest crimes Pendragon is using to lower Ilygroth's property values. I can get more, I have access to all the previous files, I just need to have a moment when someone isn't *shooting* at me to research them. We should be able to cross reference these with any suspected bribe transfers."

Maz mouthed 'when someone isn't shooting at me' mockingly.

Fizz took the phone, looking over the names with a little grin. "This is really helpful," he said, not looking up from the names as he typed them into his own phone. "Good work, Jericho."

"Hey! Where's *my* pat on the back?" Maz huffed, sulking.

"You shot one of our own," Dusk said, tone cold, one brow raised as if begging her to challenge him. "You don't *get* a pat on the back."

"I'll get more names for you," Jericho said, taking back his phone when Fizz was done with it.

"You can't send them through this device." Fizz frowned a little. "Does he have access to the closed network?"

"I'll have Pickle set him up on it." Dusk nodded. "Now, if that's all?" He looked around, waiting for someone to add something else, but no one did. "Right then, meeting adjourned. I've got to go home and take care of my friend because *someone* shot him."

Max shrugged, not looking even a little contrite.

Jericho frowned. "What about the bug on Pendragon? We need more footage."

"I'm still putting together a plan for that. I'll have something for you all soon. Till then, let's get out of here." Dusk didn't wait for the others to respond. He took Jericho's arm and helped him hobble toward the door.

•

WHEN JERICHO WOKE up the next morning, Dusk was gone again. He hobbled into the kitchen to find a quickly scrawled note on the counter.

"When the fuck did he decide it was a good idea to start coming and going as he pleased?" Jericho scowled, snatching up the note.

> *Running errands. Be back before work.*
> *Love,*
> *Sol*

Jericho smoothed the crinkled paper with his fingers, tracing the curling letters of Sol's name slowly. It'd been so long since he'd seen Dusk sign his name, or even call himself by it. It was like when Soliel had started this whole thing, he'd signed off as Sol and never looked back. Like Sol had really died in the river all those years ago. An image of the dark-haired boy floating facedown flashed through Jericho's mind, and he quickly shook it away. No. Sol was still around. Sol was safe.

Jericho dragged himself to the shower, taking care not to get his bandages too wet. When he hobbled out with a towel wrapped around his waist, Dusk had returned. Soft jazz music filled the kitchen, and Dusk was swaying to it as he flipped a pancake.

"Morning, sunshine," Dusk chirped.

"You're awfully chipper this morning." Jericho moved to lean heavily against the counter beside Dusk, letting the hard edge take some of the weight off his injured leg.

"It was a productive morning." A pancake flopped loudly onto the plate, joining the slowly growing stack. "Cinnamon sugar, your favorite."

"Productive how?" Jericho swallowed around the sensation of his mouth watering. When was the last time he'd had pancakes? Especially Tsuki cinnamon sugar pancakes.

"How many do you want?"

"Too much sugar for breakfast is bad for you." Jericho shrugged, moving to grab a coffee cup to fill it from the pot. He grabbed the creamer from the fridge, threw in an ungodly amount of sugar, and headed for his bedroom with the mug still in his hands. "I'll just have coffee."

"I'll make up your normal three then," Dusk called after him.

Dusk kept good to his word. There was a plate of three fluffy pancakes waiting for Jericho upon his return. Alongside the plate sat an older looking cellphone.

"What's this?" Jericho asked.

"I told you, I had a productive morning. That's your new phone, provided to you by the genius of Pickle. It's untraceable by the Alliance and already has Fizz's number in it." Dusk cut into his pancakes and stuffed a tall bite into his mouth.

"What about Pickle's number?" With quick thumbs, Jericho opened the phone to look through it. It was minimal: two numbers labeled Fizz and Dusk, and no apps to speak of.

"Don't download anything on that. And no pictures either. If you do, Pickle will just delete them. It's for communication only."

"Your techie has full access to this device?" Jericho didn't know how he felt about that. No, wait, he did know how he felt about that. He felt . . . unsettled. "Meaning they could be tracking me at all times. Or listening. Or doing some other crazy shit when I'm not looking, like downloading information from the Alliance servers." Jericho's knuckles turned white as he gripped the device harder.

"Yeah, Pickle could do all of those things," Dusk said, unbothered. "If you don't trust it, leave it here. Only use it when you've got names for Fizz. It's no skin off our nose. Just don't use your personal device to contact Fizz, that's the only rule."

"When do I get to meet the rest of your crew?"

Dusk was already halfway through his stack of pancakes, syrup smeared across the plate. He shrugged.

"Hungry?" Jericho sipped his now-cold coffee, trying not to grimace.

"It was a long night." Dusk's knife scraped against ceramic. Now that Jericho was really looking at him, he could see the dark circles lining the banshee's eyes. "Evil never sleeps, you know." Dusk winked.

"Right. You're about as evil as a fucking bunny rabbit." Jericho swallowed a chuckle, finally deigning to cut off a small piece of his pancakes and take a bite. They weren't quite the same as he remembered them, but they were good.

And they brought back all manner of memories from his childhood that Jericho wasn't sure he was ready to face quite yet.

"Hey. Bunnicula." Dusk pointed his sticky fork at Jericho.

"Bunnicula? That's what you're going with? He wasn't even properly evil." Jericho chortled.

Dusk hummed noncommittally around another big bite of pancake, and then they were both laughing. Deep belly laughs that made Jericho's sides ache.

"How're the pancakes?" Dusk asked when they'd calmed down.

"Auntie made them better."

"Yeah, Mama made everything better." A look of longing crossed Dusk's features. He shook himself after a moment, stuffing the last bite of pancake—arguably a quarter of the whole stack—into his mouth, making his cheeks puff out.

"To your other question," Dusk said through a full mouth. It was kind of cute—gross, but cute. "You get to meet the rest of the crew when we're sure we can trust you. Or right before we need you for a mission. Whichever comes first."

CHAPTER SIXTEEN

NECESSITY, BEING THE MOTHER OF ALL INVENTION, CAME first.

They were most of the way through the following week, and Jericho was getting antsy. Dusk had been busy the last couple days, off in his own head half the time. So much so that he'd taken to leaving his hearing aids out so Jericho's constant rambling about account numbers, case files, and what it all meant couldn't distract him from his thoughts.

A pile of files had taken up residence next to their couch, stacked so high it could be used as a side table, and Jericho was rifling through the pages of another case Fizz had wanted him to look into. He'd been cross checking them with the bank transactions Pickle had sent over for what felt like months but in reality hadn't been more than a few hours. Still, it all lined up. The evidence was there. Money was changing hands, and Unseelie were being arrested for crimes that there was little evidence they'd committed. It was hard to deny the truth when it was right in front of Jericho's eyes.

"There is no other way," Dusk muttered, barely audible,

dragging Jericho's attention away from the paper in front of him.

"What?" Jericho looked up from the file, settling it in his lap.

"There just isn't any other way," Dusk repeated, adjusting his hearing aid carefully. "We're going to need to include you."

"Oh? So, I've proven myself now, have I?" Jericho smirked a little. Progress at last! Something warm bloomed in Jericho's chest at the thought that maybe, just maybe, Dusk trusted him again. Like a balloon full of hot air.

"No," Dusk said flatly. The balloon burst. "You're just the only person I can see being able to get close enough to Pendragon to plant the bug. So I'll set up a meet with Pickle."

Jericho perked back up at this, brows lifting. "Yeah? When?"

Dusk looked down at the clock on his phone, sighing. "An hour. We should go now if we're going to catch her before she heads home."

"Heads home?" Jericho frowned.

"Yeah. Once she leaves work, we won't be able to find her. Pickle goes off grid." Dusk stood from the couch to stretch his joints till they popped lightly. "Come on, then. No need to make yourself presentable. She won't care."

They were down in a cab not five minutes later, giving Jericho no time to argue or growl about Dusk insulting his clothes. Not that he would have even if there'd been time; he was too nervous at the thought of meeting the infamous Pickle. The person behind the curtain who seemed to be Dusk's most trusted and well-guarded secret. Maybe even Dusk's closest friend.

"What are we going to do with all this proof once we have it?" Jericho asked, aiming to fend off the nervousness in the air. "I mean, clearly we'll need a judge who we can—"

"We're not giving this over to a judge," Dusk said plainly.

"What?" Jericho balked, and Dusk jerked his head to blink at Jericho as if he'd suddenly sprouted another head.

"We can't trust them with this."

"But if we—"

"Lettie, no. The only ones we can trust with this information are the people. They need to see, and know, and vote accordingly. We can't just—" Dusk stopped himself, frustration suddenly thinning his lips. His fingers started moving instead, probably for the best since the cab could be listening. He signed the words so quickly and sharply, Jericho almost missed them. "We can't just expect this to go away because we prosecute. Pendragon can just pay the judge off. Or have us scooped up as villains and sent off to rot somewhere before our message ever gets out. No. We have to expose him for what he is."

"Sol." Jericho said the name softly, fear lacing his tone as he met Dusk's eyes. Dusk looked . . . He looked . . . Jericho had never seen him this fanatical. Yes, Dusk had talked a big game this whole time, but he'd never seemed so totally unhinged before, eyes wild and teeth bared. "We have to do this the right way, or they'll just cover it up. They'll cast it aside as conspiracy."

Dusk's gaze narrowed on Jericho, lips pressed in a hard, thin line.

"Please," Jericho pressed. "Sol, please." Without giving any thought to the urge, Jericho reached over to take Dusk's hands in his own, squeezing the brown, freckled skin lightly. "Please, I can't bear to see you locked up again. I can't sit and watch you fucking fade away like that. I lost—" His throat tightened, and he swallowed around the feeling, forcing down a lump.

"Fine." Dusk sighed heavily, pulling one of his hands from Jericho's to run through his hair. "Fine. We'll try to come up with a more legal way of getting the information out."

Jericho nodded, breathing in through his nose and out through his lips to calm his nerves. "Th—"

"We're here." The car had stopped. Dusk pulled away entirely to open the door and get out. "Time to go."

Jericho looked up at the building they'd stopped in front of and frowned. "This is across from the hold."

"Yes, you're very observant."

"Cheeky little shit," Jericho grumbled, climbing out behind Dusk. The car buzzed off after the door shut, and Jericho crossed his arms over his chest to keep from fidgeting. "Now what?"

"Now, we wait." Dusk looked down at his watch. "Pickle should be out any minute."

"Pickle works at the hold?"

"Clearly."

Dusk moved to lean against the office building, his eyes fixed on the massive structure across the street. Jericho leaned beside him, ignoring the trickle of people making their way to and from wherever people went at this time of night.

"She works late," Dusk said without prompting.

Minutes ticked by, and gradually, the foot traffic on the sidewalk died away until only one or two people were passing them every few minutes. Jericho yawned into his hand and rubbed at his eyes. "I should have brought my files."

"That wouldn't have looked suspicious," Dusk said sarcastically.

"And us just standing here doesn't?"

"You'd draw far more attention to yourself standing there holding a manilla folder than us just standing here chatting." Dusk rolled his eyes and pulled his phone out to check the time again. "Come on, Pickle." Jericho looked over to watch

Dusk wear on his lip, and then a wide smile lit his face. "Ah. There she is."

Jericho's gaze jerked over to see the bright blue-and-pink head of Ildri exiting the hold. Her eyes flicked over to them, and she smirked. Jericho saw her tilt her head to the side, and then she turned to walk down the sidewalk. He blinked, confusion making his heart race. "Ildri?"

"Let's go." Dusk pushed off from the wall. He led Jericho down the sidewalk, following Ildri from across the street. They walked for a while before Ildri ducked into the shitty little coffee shop Dusk had taken Jericho to. The pair crossed the street and followed her inside. "You want—?" Dusk offered, pointing to the chalkboard menu above the register.

"Fuck no. It's awful." Jericho looked over to the table in the back corner where Ildri was waiting, her hands folded neatly around a chipped mug. His heart was still pounding loudly in his ears, palms sweating enough to make his jeans damp where he'd tucked them into his pockets. Ildri. It was Ildri. Ildri was Pickle.

Dusk shrugged, going to the counter to order himself a cup of tea while Jericho waited beside him. "You could go."

"No. I'll wait for you." Jericho shifted his weight nervously on his heels.

"Okay." Dusk glanced over at Ildri, smirking a little, then tapped on the counter in a lazy rhythm. "Nervous?"

"No."

Dusk chuckled, grabbed his tea, and they headed over to the little table. "Pickle." He offered her a genuine smile, his cheeks dimpling.

"Dusk." Ildri nodded. "What can I do for you boys?"

"Wait. So, this whole—" Jericho tried to get the words past the rapid confusion tearing at his insides. He needed confirmation—now.

"Clearly. This whole time." Ildri was laughing at him,

even if she wasn't making any sound. Her eyes danced with amusement. "Now, can we get a move on? I want to go home and have a proper cup of tea." She spun her mug round and round on the saucer, watching its contents spiral.

"Lettie is going to be our bug setter," Dusk said. "He needs the bug, and we need information for him to bring to Pendragon's attention that will get him a meet."

"Anything else you'd like from me, Dusk? How about I pull a rabbit out of my ass while we're at it?" Ildri asked, tone bland.

"You won't do it." Jericho frowned, his hands clenching in his lap.

"Never said that." Ildri tilted her head to one side as if she were inspecting Jericho. He'd never seen her look so . . . calculating before. How long had she been hiding this persona under the friendly, bubbly veneer he'd always known? How long had she been working with—Oh. Dusk had inherited Pickle from Adelia. Ildri and Adelia had—*Oh.*

"Just wanted to make clear the relative difficultly of what you're asking of me. The bug will be the easy part." She turned to dig around in the messenger bag she'd slung over the back of her chair. From it she produced a small black device, holding it between her index finger and thumb as it glinted in the light. "Just stick this to the underside of his desk, and we're good to go."

"That looks like—"

"Who do you think made it, Lettie?" Dusk asked, a little grin on his lips. "I'm pretty good, but Pickle here has been at it much longer than I have. She's definitely got a leg up on me."

"Right. And how will I get a meeting with him?"

"That . . . will take a little more doing." Ildri wrinkled her nose in thought. "I know they've been looking at you to try to bring you into the fold, but lately, because of your history with Dusk . . . they don't actually trust you."

"Why don't you just tell him you have some information on me that you'll only tell the council?" Dusk offered, and Jericho felt his stomach sink at the mere suggestion. "Say you're going to expose one of my assets."

"And then what? Give them Fizz on a fucking silver platter?" It made Jericho sick to even think about it, and he wondered when the thought of turning Dusk and his people in had started turning his stomach.

"No. We have contingency plans for this sort of thing. We've got someone else inside who we can expose."

"And risk their job?" Jericho's head jerked to look at Dusk, horror and ice replacing the rolling feeling in his gut.

"No, idiot." Ildri sighed, rubbing at the bridge of her nose. "They won't get in any trouble. There isn't any proof that they've done anything at all. Believe me, I've checked their records. And we think exposing them will only make Pendragon want to bring them into his little organization. You've just got to spin it the right way. It'll be easy."

"Easy," Jericho repeated, though he didn't feel it was true.

Dusk reached out to take one of Jericho's hands from his lap and give it a firm squeeze. "Look, I'll give you an ear bud, one they won't see. Then I'll be right there with you the whole time. Trust us, we've got this."

"And you trust me with this?" Jericho asked, ignoring how his hands had begun to sweat more and more, sliding against Dusk's dry palm.

"Not like we have a whole lot of other options," Dusk said, but he gave Jericho's hand another reassuring squeeze.

"Your other guy, he could do it. Or Ildri."

"No." Ildri shook her head. "It's got to be you. Since you're the one who's been with Dusk this whole time, you're the one who'd know." She pulled a tablet from her bag, tapping on it too quickly for Jericho's eyes to follow. "All right, file sent."

The phone Dusk had given Jericho pinged, and he pulled it out to look at the information. At the top of the file was a picture of golden eyes set into a too-young face. "Imizael?" he asked, frowning. "But he just started. He's a rookie."

"We know that." Ildri didn't sound like she cared. She probably didn't.

"This could ruin his career."

"Trust me," Dusk said, his voice bitter. "This is going to *make* his career. Plus, this is what he signed on for. He might be a kid, but he's a kid who Pickle has been training from the get-go. He became a hero for this exact purpose." Dusk brushed his thumb along Jericho's knuckles as if trying to comfort him. It didn't really help. "He knows it's coming, he just doesn't know when, so he'll know how to respond when it does. He's not going to panic on us."

"You've been training him?"

Ildri put her tablet away again, her fingers returning to drum on the teacup. "No one at the hold knows, but he's my cousin. So yeah, when he found out we needed someone in this role, he was eager to join up. We can trust him."

Jericho nodded, closing out the file and tucking his phone away again.

"The question remains though . . . " Ildri leaned forward. Her eyes were wide, manic, that fanatical expression Jericho had seen on Dusk's face in the car lighting up her features now. "Can we trust *you*?"

"Yeah," Jericho whispered. He cleared his throat. "I'll get us what we need." He forced his voice to be strong in a way he didn't quite feel. Resolute. Determined. Even as his insides writhed with panic. "Then we find a judge to give it to?"

Ildri and Dusk shared a look, and Dusk threaded his

fingers with Jericho's as if to ground them both. "Then we find a judge," he agreed.

Jericho nodded again, taking the bug from Ildri's fingers and setting it in the palm of his hand. "Tomorrow?"

Ildri shook her head. "Monday after next. Your full moon is coming up, we can't take that chance. And we need time to bait the hook." The manic glint had faded, and she looked at him a little more closely, assessing. "Will you be all right, J?"

"I'll be fine. I've got this." Jericho swallowed, his hand closing around the bug. "You got a case for this thing, so I don't lose it?"

"Don't lose the bug," Ildri deadpanned, a threat in her eyes.

"Right. Careful with the tech. Got it."

"All right boys, good luck! I'll see you when I see you." Ildri leaned in to brush a soft kiss to Dusk's cheek, warm and familiar. "Your mother would be so proud," she whispered to him, and Jericho looked away, sure he wasn't supposed to hear the soft sadness in Ildri's voice.

They waited until she'd gone, sitting in silence together. When enough time had passed, Dusk turned to Jericho with a wide smile. "Pizza for dinner?"

Jericho let out a breath and nodded, then laughed. "Yeah, let's get it on the way home. But no fucking pineapple this time."

"Awww, you're no fun!" Dusk pouted. He rose from his seat and offered his hand to Jericho again. Jericho took it, and out they went.

●

THE NEXT WEEK was spent baiting the hook, as Ildri had said, and getting ready for the full moon. Which felt . . . weird this time. The last two full moons, although Dusk had been in

Jericho's home, Dusk had left him alone in his preparations. This month, something had changed.

"You know, I think if I'm there, you really won't need the patches," Dusk said as he packed another steak into the fridge. "We're already giving you more space than you had these last two times. And the wolf hasn't gotten territorial with me yet."

"I'd rather not take the chance." Jericho shrugged, moving the extra pillows off the couch to stuff into the TV cabinet. Dusk had picked out the pillows himself, and he was sure the wolf would love nothing more than to rip them open and tear every bit of fluff out of them. "Plus, they take the edge off of the initial change."

"We need you at your best on Monday."

"I'll have the weekend to recover."

"Lettie."

"Sol."

Dusk huffed, slamming the refrigerator door shut. "You're as stubborn as ever."

"So are you."

"Cut back then. Just use one." Dusk crossed his arms over his chest, planting his feet in a show of resistance.

"One doesn't really work anymore. Not now that I've been using them so long," Jericho said absently as he turned in a circle to make sure he'd hidden away everything the wolf might want to destroy. Well, except the couch and the armchair. But there wasn't much he could do about those. "I still don't like the idea of you being so easily accessible. Why can't I just lock myself in my room again?"

"Because you're going to make the poor thing fucking feral if you keep locking it up in a two-by-two cell every full moon." Dusk huffed, blowing at his bangs. "It doesn't deserve that just because you're scared."

"I'm not scared!"

Dusk leveled him with a look of disbelief. "I'll be locked in my room. It won't get at me if that's what you're worried about."

"That's not what I'm worried about."

"All right. Well. You're all set. So, I'm just going to go to my room and do some reading. Please don't fuck up the couch." Dusk moved to press his shoulder into Jericho's companionably. "Have fun."

"Fuck off." But there was no real bite to it, and Jericho had to tamp down on a weird feeling of loneliness when Dusk shut and locked his door behind him.

●

THE PATCHES DID HELP. They took the edge off the change, kept Jericho mostly coherent in the end. At least coherent enough not to run out into the street and start stalking the nearest fluffy bunny. What they didn't do was dull the wolf's senses.

So when the storm rolled in, the wolf felt the shift in the air. Electricity, sharp and metallic, rolling through the apartment.

The first crack of thunder shook its den, making Jericho jolt and cower. A soft whimper left him as the noise hurt his ears. He'd never liked thunderstorms. The change in pressure and the thunder gave him headaches, but it was worse in wolf form because his senses were heightened, and his instincts took over. Another crack, another whine.

A few minutes later, Dusk emerged from his room to find the hulking blond wolf tucked into the corner between the TV stand and the wall. Dusk took one look at him and frowned. Jericho let out another whimper, tucking his paws over his ears. Footsteps alerted him to Dusk's approach, and he shied away from the man's seeking fingers.

"It's all right, Lettie. I'm here," Dusk whispered soothingly. Then he dropped to his knees in front of Jericho, an arm's length between them. He sat back on his heels and waited. Not meeting Jericho's eyes but not lowering his chin either. "I'm not going anywhere."

Jericho lost himself then to the wolf. To the instinct, and the low hum of the full moon.

When he came to the next morning, his head was pillowed on Dusk's thigh, and Dusk's fingers were buried in his long blond hair. Dusk's back was leaned against the wall, his head tilted back, mouth open, and he was snoring lightly. Taking a deep breath, Jericho went to extricate himself from the all too familiar position, but when he pulled his hair away, Dusk mumbled awake.

Dusk made a low, tired, questioning sound in the back of his throat.

"Thanks," Jericho said softly.

Dusk just nodded and offered him a little smile. And that was that.

CHAPTER SEVENTEEN

"YOU'LL BE AMAZING," DUSK WHISPERED, TAKING JERICHO'S shaking hands into his own. It was Monday, the bait was set, and Pendragon had set up a meeting with Jericho. "I have complete faith in you."

"I'm glad one of us does." Jericho let out a breath that shook on the exhale. "What if he suspects?"

"He has no reason to," Dusk said, moving to stand behind Jericho as she inspected herself in the mirror.

"I look like a fucking narc." Jericho smoothed her hands down the charcoal pencil skirt she'd pulled from the back of a drawer to try to look more presentable. She did another careful turn in the mirror. The bandage from her gunshot wound had been removed days ago, the werewolf venom running through her veins working to heal her quickly. At least now she wouldn't have to try to pull off leggings with the skirt.

"You look no different than you normally do." Dusk chuckled, fingers brushing over Jericho's shoulders in a soothing motion that flattened the wrinkles in her band tee.

"I always look like a fucking narc?"

"Pretty much." Dusk smirked, pulling Jericho's long blond braid over her shoulder to give it a soft tug. "Come on, or we'll be late. You'd hate to look apprehensive about what you're doing."

"Tch. I definitely should look apprehensive. I'm about to possibly ruin a young man's future." Jericho turned from the mirror, grabbed her wallet, and headed for the front door. At this point, she was just delaying the inevitable. It wouldn't do any of them any good to try to put this off. They didn't have much longer to finish this. If it wasn't done soon, Jericho would lose her only chance to really help Sol, and that just wasn't an option.

The soft hum of the cab was loud in Jericho's ears as she picked at her cuticles until they were red and sore. Dusk sat beside her, his own hands folded neatly in his lap as he looked out the window. There was a comfort in his presence now, but Jericho would never admit to that. Dusk was steady, calming, quiet. Like he had no doubts about what they were about to do. And Jericho supposed he didn't. It felt like everything that had happened up to this point had just been another step in Dusk's grand plan. Jericho was just a cog in the great machine engineered and run by the man sitting calmly beside her.

"Oh, but Lettie, I'm right where I want to be. It's just that, as always, you're missing the bigger picture."

Dusk had said those words so, so long ago. It felt like it'd been decades since Jericho had brought in her old friend and faced him across the interrogation table. But really, it hadn't been more than a couple of months, had it? Yet here they were, set to topple a councilman, something Jericho had never thought she'd even consider, much less attempt.

It wasn't the danger of the thing that was making Jericho nervous. Or the consequences of what would happen to her if this all went to shit. It was what would happen to Pickle, to

Fizz, to Dusk if she wasn't good enough. It was having to lie when she'd never been particularly adept at lying. That was what turned her stomach.

Jericho hissed, looking down at her hands to see a short, bloody stripe where her nervous picking had pulled her cuticle too deeply. "Shit."

She went to wipe it on her skirt, but a hand stopped her. Dusk's freckled fingers held a clean white handkerchief to the injury, sopping up the blood and applying pressure to stop any further bleeding.

"Calm down. You're making me nervous," Dusk chided softly.

"Calm down. Yeah. I'll just do that," she mumbled, licking dry lips as she took over holding the handkerchief to the wound. It had a little pale blue moonflower embroidered into the corner with the initials S.D.T. in the same color stitching just above it. Jericho recognized Adelia Tsuki's neat lettering, and her fingers brushed idly over the design.

"You're going to do splendidly." Dusk leaned in to brush a kiss to Jericho's cheek just before the car stuttered to a stop outside of the hold.

"You going to hang out with Ildri?" Jericho asked, pulling the hanky away to see if the bleeding had stopped. It had. She held it back out to Dusk, but he'd already moved to climb out of the car, so she tucked it into the pocket of her jacket instead.

"Yeah. She's having a grand ol' time trying to reconstruct some of the stuff from my lab. I figured I'd see how she was doing." Dusk smirked knowingly at Jericho as he held out a hand to help her out of the car.

"I can get out of a car on my own." Jericho huffed, climbing out and stuffing her hands into her pockets.

"I know." Dusk shrugged, shutting the door behind her. They walked into the hold side by side, and then Dusk stopped next to the K.N.I.G.H.T. unit waiting for him. "I'll see you for lunch."

Jericho didn't bother to answer, and Dusk didn't push it before he turned to head in the direction of Ildri's lab. Jericho watched him walk away for a moment, feeling a strange sense of contentment wash over her. She'd see Dusk for lunch.

"What're you smiling about?" Erling asked, half growling as he slammed his shoulder into Jericho's, making her stumble.

"Nothing." Jericho shook herself and followed Erling to the elevator. A ping drew her attention just as the doors slid shut. With some fiddling, she stuffed the handkerchief further into her pocket, then pulled out her phone to look at the notification.

"Why've you got a meeting with Pendragon?" Erling peeked over her shoulder to read the text quickly. "Are you about to be discharged?"

"Or I'm about to be promoted."

"Tch." Erling's face turned a violent shade of red, but he turned his head to focus on the elevator doors and studiously ignored Jericho as she reviewed the meeting information.

The meeting was in thirty minutes, leaving her little time to dwell on all the things that could go wrong. A nervous smile tugged at the corners of her lips. It was happening. She could do this. *Just breathe.* Locking her phone, she tucked it back into her pocket and willed herself to be calm. What was the worst that could happen?

●

THE WORST THAT could happen was that she'd fumble as she sat down in the chair opposite Pendragon, her knee banging the desk painfully and knocking over his full cup of coffee.

"Shit! I'm so sorry, sir!" Jericho yelped, standing again to try to wrangle the coffee into submission with no way to clean it up. She grabbed up papers and electronics to try to salvage them.

Pendragon laughed softly, grabbing some napkins from a drawer on the other side of his desk. "Don't worry about it, happens all the time." His gray eyes twinkled with mirth as he sopped up the mess.

"All the time?" she squeaked.

Pendragon shrugged, barely even creasing the well-tailored, expensive looking suit that clung to his form. His face was lined with age, but Jericho knew well enough that with fae, there was no true way to tell someone's age.

"I make people nervous. Please, sit." He gestured to the chair again.

This was it. This was her chance. "No, let me at least . . . " She let the words drift off, one hand grabbing some of the napkins to help clean up, the other pulling the tiny bug from her pocket to press it onto the briefcase beside the desk as she bent over the mess. She heard a soft beep echo in the earpiece as it activated. "There, that's better." She forced a nervous smile once most of the now-cold liquid was cleared away. "Can I get you—?"

"No need." Pendragon waved her off. "Let's try this again."

She nodded, sitting on the edge of her chair, her knee bouncing. "I really am sorry," she muttered.

"It's quite all right." Pendragon pushed the rest of the mess into a waste bin, and everything returned to normal on his desk with a few quick motions. "Now, what is it you wanted to meet with me about, Jericho?"

Jericho twisted her fingers in her lap, taking a deep breath to silence the nervous energy jittering through her muscles.

"Relax, Lettie. You've got this," Dusk whispered in her ear.

Jericho wasn't sure how he knew that she was fidgeting. Maybe he could hear it. "You've already set the bug. Now it's just a matter of telling the lie."

Jericho wanted to tell Dusk to shut the fuck up. That she knew all of that. But instead, she offered Pendragon another tight smile. "As you know, sir, I've been tasked with extracting information from the villain known as Dusk these last few weeks."

"I do." Pendragon nodded. "From what I understand, we have been able to find at least one of his lab facilities, and your captain says you have a short list of some of his known associates. Although it's my understanding that you've been playing them close to the vest."

"I have been, sir." Jericho ducked her head to look at her hands in her lap, pressing her thumb into the red skin where she'd ripped the cuticle. It stung, but it helped to ground her.

Dusk snorted, and Jericho wanted nothing more than to rip the tiny ear bud out so she didn't have to hear his snarky retorts anymore. But that would look suspicious. She pulled her braid over her shoulder, covering her ear with it as she fiddled nervously with the ends of her hair.

"May I ask why?"

"I, uh—" Jericho broke off, swallowing roughly.

"Just like we practiced, Lettie," Dusk murmured encouragingly into her ear. "Just breathe."

"It's all right, my dear." Pendragon smiled sharply. Like this, she could see his elven lineage even more clearly. "Whatever it is, you can tell me."

Jericho nodded to herself, taking a deep breath and then releasing it in a shaky exhale. "I have only shared this with our tech, so that I could get his file. You understand."

"I understand." Pendragon's tone was calm, sympathetic. "Please, this is a safe space. You can speak freely here."

Jericho looked up to meet Pendragon's eyes and nodded.

If this old geezer was going to simper, smile, and lie to her face, then she could do the same. *For Ilygroth*, she reminded herself. "I have reason to believe Dusk may have an inside man amongst us. His name is Imizael Lachlan. He's a rookie who just joined the Alliance about eight months ago. I had Ildri send over his file."

Pendragon turned to his computer, tapping away on the keyboard for a moment before he nodded. "I see. And why do you suspect him?"

Jericho gulped.

"This is the easy part, Lettie," Dusk whispered soothingly. "You just tell him that we've—"

"Dusk has been introducing me to his inner circle," Jericho lied, silencing Dusk before he could finish. "We met with Imizael a couple of weeks ago."

"And you waited till now to bring this to me?"

"I knew if I told you right away, it would blow my cover with Dusk. It needs to look like you found this information on your own. I've almost gained his trust enough to give me the rest of the—"

"You have till next week," Pendragon cut her off, not looking up from the file on his computer. He had fixated on the words, the picture of Imizael reflecting in his glassy eyes. A soft smirk lifted the corner of his mouth, like he'd struck gold.

"I know that's what Oakfur said, but I thou—"

"You have until next week," Pendragon said sharply, looking from his computer screen finally to fix Jericho with a disinterested glare. "That is all you have. I would suggest you stop dillydallying and take your villain on some trust building exercises. I'll schedule you off the rest of the week. Maybe go for a hike now that you're healed. Or show a little leg. I'm sure Dusk wouldn't mind. Use what few charms you have," Pendragon suggested with a meaningful look. "You know. Bonding."

"Yes, sir." Jericho swallowed, praying Dusk hadn't been listening just then, but the soft hiss in her ear told her he had. Dusk must have pulled the mic away from his mouth, but Jericho could hear him muttering angry swear words in the distance.

"You're dismissed." Pendragon turned back to the computer without another word, his eyes roving over the file.

"Yes, sir." Jericho rose from her chair, brushing her fingers down her skirt to straighten it. "If you need anything else—"

"I know where to find you."

Jericho nodded. She tried to ignore how her hands shook when she reached for the elevator controls but didn't quite manage.

"It's over now," Dusk whispered, back in her ear. He seemed to have calmed his anger, if just for the moment. "You did so well."

"Yeah. It's over now."

"I'll meet you at your desk. You want coffee?"

Jericho shook her head, then realized Dusk couldn't see her. "No. I'm jittery enough."

The elevator moved at a snail's pace back to the bullpen. She'd gotten away with it. She'd set the bug, and she'd gotten away with it. Now, all that was left was to listen in as Pendragon met with whoever he was meeting with, and find the information they needed. Jericho wondered if they'd have to do that manually, or if Ildri would have some kind of program to weed out only the important things. Not that it mattered; she didn't think she could do anything else this weekend. There would be no resting, no relaxing, no *bonding* as Pendragon had so politely put it.

Dusk was waiting for her with a mug of something steaming on her desk. "Tea." He held the mug out with a soft smile.

"Thanks." Jericho took it, letting the heat warm her clammy hands and settle her back into this time, this place. Her skin was starting to feel too tight for her body. If she stayed in the bullpen any longer, she felt she very well might fly apart. "So. You wanna get out of here?"

"What? Don't you have to work?" Dusk frowned, tilting his head.

Jericho shook her head. "I've been given leave the rest of the week by Pendragon. No sense sitting around here when we could be out enjoying the fresh air. Maybe go for a hike?" Jericho asked, taking a careful sip of the still steaming tea.

"Yeah. A hike sounds good." Dusk laughed, a soft, secret sound.

CHAPTER EIGHTEEN

AND THAT WAS HOW JERICHO FOUND HIMSELF CURLED UP ON his couch, his shoulder pressed to Dusk's as they shared one set of headphones to listen to everything that had happened after he'd left Pendragon's office.

"Maybe we should actually go for a hike," Dusk suggested, and Jericho couldn't tell if he was kidding or not.

"And miss all the riveting typing noises?" Jericho asked, his eyes closing as he leaned his head against Dusk's.

"Pickle could listen to this bit. She's good at multitasking."

Jericho sighed, burying his face in Dusk's hair for a moment.

"Or I could sit and listen, and you could go for a hike." Dusk's fingers were typing away at something on his tablet, but Jericho studiously avoided the dim light of the screen, not wanting to be nosey.

"Like hell I'm leaving you here by yourself. What if he says something important?"

Dusk huffed, rolling his eyes. "You still don't trust me."

"You don't trust me either, so I guess we're square."

"Suit yourself." Dusk shrugged, the motion jostling Jericho's comfortable position and making him grumble softly. "Can we order ramen?"

"Not dinner time yet."

"Later then."

"Sure. Later." Jericho sighed, rubbing at his temples. Who knew typing could be so fucking annoying? "Merlin, is he going to do anything fucking interesting today?"

"Maybe not. But we've got all week."

"I should go to the grocery store and get some shit to make food since we won't be going out."

"What time is it?" Dusk asked, pulling out his phone to answer his own question. "Three. Why don't we go out for a couple of hours and head to the store? He's probably not going to do any shady shit until dinner."

"You think?" Jericho pulled away, blinking.

"I mean, isn't that how this stuff works? People do bad things in the dark?"

"Is that when you committed all of your crimes?" Jericho smirked.

"Well, it's not *not* when I committed most of my crimes." Dusk huffed. "But that's different."

"How?"

"Just get up and let's go to the damn store to get shit for dinner." Dusk scowled, shutting down his tablet and standing up to stretch. He dug through a satchel set in front of the couch and pulled out a set of wireless headphones, setting them up quickly with his phone. "We can keep listening."

"Why weren't we using those all along?" Jericho eyed the earbud with suspicion.

"Didn't want to wear down the battery."

"What if something interesting happens while we're out?" Jericho took one of the little earbuds and slid it into his ear to replace the headphone.

"We're recording everything," Dusk said, sounding offended. "What do you think I am? An amateur?"

"Then how the fuck are we supposed to know where the good shit is?" Jericho frowned, rooting himself to the spot on the couch.

"I just told you, I'm no amateur. I can mark it with my phone. Now, come on. I changed my mind. I want home-made ramen for dinner." Dusk reached down to grab Jericho's wrists and yanked him to his feet. "Pleeeeeassse."

"Tch. Fine." Jericho rolled his eyes.

●

JERICHO DEDICATED his focus to two things while they were in the store: getting everything on his mental shopping list and listening to Pendragon slurp down his fifth cup of coffee. Honestly, the man could be dying of an ulcer with how much coffee he drank. Maybe he was. Maybe he'd die before they could even prosecute him. The thought made Jericho's ears ring, drawing the color from his face. He clenched his fingers around the cart's handle hard enough to make the metal creak softly.

"Are you all right, young man?" an older woman asked, pushing her cart up against theirs as she sidled in closer. "Is it because you're fighting with your boyfriend?"

"My *boyfriend*?" Jericho croaked, brows knitting to try to understand her meaning. Her brown eyes flicked meaning-fully to where Dusk was sorting through the broccoli, his mouth twisted in concentration as he tried to find the best bits. "Oh, he's not—" Jericho stumbled, shaking his head. "We're not—"

"We're not fighting." Dusk came over, setting a bag of green vegetables into the cart before looping his arm around Jericho's waist and kissing his cheek. Jericho felt heat crawl up the back of his neck and settle into the tips of his ears, but he ignored it. "He's just on a work call," Dusk lied, gesturing to the earbud in Jericho's ear. "Very important meeting, you know?"

"Oh. Of course." She nodded, a little smile on her lips. "I'm so sorry for intruding," she whispered, patting Jericho's hand where it was still gripping the cart perhaps a little too hard.

"No problem. Just . . . Excuse me," Jericho muttered, putting some distance between them as he tried to focus on the sound of Pendragon's voice. When had he started—? Oh, he was singing along to some stupid pop song. What a fucking letdown.

"I just wanted to check on you both," the woman said to Dusk, keeping her voice down so as not to disturb Jericho's "work call." "I see you two in here all the time, and you're just so cute together."

"Why thank you!" Dusk laughed softly, turning a knowing grin to Jericho, who just stared irritably back. Fan-fucking-tastic. Now he had crazy old cat ladies in their neighborhood *shipping* them. He'd have to pick another grocery store after all of this was over, or face explaining how he and Dusk had "broken up." What a fucking nuisance. And it wasn't even like . . . They weren't even . . . Well, they weren't *together*, that was for damn sure. But did he want that? Did Jericho want them to be together again? Like they'd been before? He didn't think Dusk would want that. No. There was too much else going on. Too much else to worry about to get tangled up in what might have been or might be again.

"Sir, you wanted me to set up a meeting with Captain Oakfur and Captain Bryndis?" The familiar voice of Pendragon's secretary filtered in through Jericho's earpiece, making the rest of the world fade into a blur around him.

"Ah, Soroya," Pendragon's delighted voice followed, and Jericho looked up to see if Dusk was paying attention. His freckled fingers had pulled his phone from his pocket, thumb pressing against something Jericho couldn't see on the screen as he continued to chat away with the old lady—her name, Jericho overheard while his focus was on Dusk, was Mrs. Bonifacy, and she thought they were absolutely the cutest thing she'd ever seen.

"Yes, a dinner meeting," Pendragon continued, cutting through Jericho's thoughts again.

"It looks like they will be free tomorrow evening, if that is to your liking." Soroya's voice was quiet, and Jericho couldn't tell if it was because they were standing too far from the listening device or if it was just in their nature to be soft-spoken.

"Yes, that will do nicely. Tell them to meet me at my usual table at Gideon's."

"Yes, sir." Soroya's words were followed by the soft sound of a door closing. Pendragon let out a loud breath, and Jericho heard his chair creak under his weight as he leaned back, but otherwise, there was silence.

Jericho looked up at Dusk, eyes wide. Dusk nodded. "You're very sweet, Mrs. Bonifacy, but I'm afraid Lettie and I have to go. He's making me ramen tonight, and I'm quite eager to get home."

"Oh, of course." Mrs. Bonifacy giggled. "You boys have fun."

"But not too much fun, right?" Dusk teased, and she blushed. With a shake of her gray head, she turned her cart away from theirs and made her way to the deli at the back of the store.

"Okay. How the fuck do you do that?" Jericho groused, grabbing a bundle of bok choy and stuffing it into the cart.

"Do what?" Dusk looked up, eyes wide and innocent.

"Make friends wherever we fucking go. It's like your superpower." He turned to inspect a selection of carrots critically. "Do you still not eat carrots?"

"Not cooked carrots." Dusk swatted Jericho's hand away from the vegetable he had referred to as "heinous" for much of his youth. "And I'm just nice to people. Honestly, if you didn't have the personality of a constipated goldfish, maybe you'd be able to charm the pants off anyone around you too."

Jericho snorted, and before he could stop it, he was all-out laughing as he watched Dusk slowly cock his head in confusion. "What kind of"—he wheezed, hands still clutching the cart—"personality does a constipated goldfish have?"

"Yours. Obviously." Dusk's lips twitched in amusement.

"Asshole," Jericho muttered fondly, bumping Dusk's hip with the cart, causing him to stumble a little. But he'd given up by then and was laughing along with Jericho. "No carrots then," Jericho said once he'd caught his breath.

"No carrots."

Dusk had gone quiet when they left the vegetables, his fingers working in furious signs as he thought to himself. It wasn't until they reached the checkout and Jericho was scanning their purchases that he finally spoke up, his fingers moving in front of them so only Jericho could see the movements. "What did you put the bug on?"

"His briefcase. I thought he'd probably have it with him most of the time." Jericho shrugged. The machine beeped at him as it weighed their bok choy, and then he moved on to the next item. A frown marred the freckled face beside him, and Jericho caught the movement out of the corner of his eyes. "Did I pick the wrong thing?"

"No," Dusk signed, his shoulders sagging a little. "I mean, there is no guarantee that he'll have anything on him at all times, and we don't want the bug to go through the wash. It's water-resistant, not waterproof."

"So?" Jericho asked, scanning a container of broth. Someone behind them in line coughed to try to hurry the pair, and the glare Jericho shot them made the whole line take a cautious step back. "What do we do if he doesn't have it with him?"

"We're going to have to get someone into the restaurant," Dusk signed, already pulling his phone from his pocket to make the arrangements.

Jericho hefted their bags up into his arms and led Dusk back out onto the sidewalk, careful to keep him from bumping into anyone in his distraction. Instead of calling for a cab, Jericho's free hand reached down to take Dusk's and pull him down the sidewalk. "How can we be sure they'll be seated near him?"

"Gideon's keeps everything on their internal network, from seating charts to schedules to employee files. Ideally, I would get someone at a table and a member of the wait staff in there." Dusk was muttering to himself as he typed away at his phone. Jericho glanced down to see that he was texting two numbers Jericho didn't recognize. "How do you feel about having some friends over for an early dinner?"

Jericho's nose scrunched in distaste. "I don't have friends."

"No. Of course not." Dusk laughed, shaking his head.

"I don't think we have enough ingredients to make dinner for more than just us," Jericho said, swallowing down the reminder and the guilt. He didn't have friends. He didn't need friends. What good were friends when they couldn't keep their promises? Just as he hadn't kept his to Dusk. He decided it was best not to argue about having people over. It was clearly more than just dinner with friends. It was a meet. At his home.

"We'll order takeout."

"Who all is coming?"

Dusk shrugged, continuing to type on his phone.

●

"DUSK!" Jericho shouted from the front door, where he was holding it from being pushed open the rest of the way.

"Yeah?" Dusk asked from the kitchen.

"You invited this bitch to our *house?*" Jericho scowled down at Maz, who was rocking on her heels with a large duffle looped over her shoulder.

Dusk shoved Jericho aside to peek around the door, then smiled wide. "Hi, Maz. Come on in!"

"Come in?!" Jericho shouted, his hands fisting at his sides. "This is my house. I don't want a fox in my house!"

"Maz is our only shifter. We need her." Reasonable, that's what that was. It was also annoying as fuck. "Let her in."

Jericho huffed, stepping away from the door and heading into the kitchen. "I'm not feeding her."

"Don't worry, I already ate." Maz kicked her shoes off at the door and padded past Dusk.

"Wait for me!" Fizz called, rushing down the hall toward them.

"Is that it?" Jericho asked from the kitchen, grabbing a stack of plates from the cabinet. "Or are we squeezing anyone else into this clown car?"

"We're waiting on one more." Dusk shut the door behind Fizz.

"My date," Fizz chirped with a flash of sharp teeth.

"You have a girlfriend now?" Maz asked, her lips curling up in disgust. "Who would date you?"

Fizz just laughed, then grabbed a plate from the stack and loaded it with pizza. "So, what's the plan, boss?" he asked, voicing the question that had been running through

Jericho's mind for the last hour as Dusk put everything together.

Dusk set his tablet on the counter between them, opening up the couple of screenshots he'd taken from the restaurant's intranet. "This is where Pendragon will be sitting." He tapped a rounded booth along the wall on the seating chart. "He reserves this table every weekday evening for 'important' business meetings."

"Every evening?" Maz asked, her nose now curling in disgust. Dusk nodded, and Maz scowled more. "What a jackass."

"Right?! You know he told Lettie to—"

"So where are we putting Fizz and his girlfriend?" Jericho asked, shooting Dusk a meaningful look. He wasn't sure why, but the idea of sharing what Pendragon had said to him made him feel gross, like it was somehow his fault. Dusk reached over to take his hand, giving it a firm squeeze before nodding.

"We're going to put them here." Dusk tapped one of the booths behind Pendragon's. "There will be lots of interference, but I think Pickle should be able to adjust the bug settings so we can hear Pendragon and his guests above it. Maz will be their server. A girl named Olivia usually takes that section, and I've already had Pickle call her to tell her not to come in." He pulled up a picture of a young ginger woman named Olivia Caoimhe. "All you have to do is show up in your uniform and pretend you lost your name tag."

"Won't she get suspicious when she gets paid for those hours?" Fizz piped up.

"If you got paid for hours you didn't work, would you be suspicious?" Maz deadpanned, quirking a silver brow.

Fizz laughed. "I guess not." There was a knock, and he straightened. "I'll get it!" When he returned, it was with a green-haired young woman with scales clinging to her cheekbones and pupils narrowed into slits. "Astra, this is Jericho."

"Hi." Astra gave an awkward little wave, leaning more heavily into Fizz's side as if trying to hide behind him.

"She's shy," Fizz supplied. "All right, show me the rest of it."

Dusk nodded, pulling a few devices from his pocket. "These won't be as clear as the bug Lettie stuck on Pendragon, but they're longer range, so they should pick up whatever is going on in the next booth over. You've just got to get in close enough."

"Put it on your coat and hang it on the coat rack between the booths." Maz flicked through the pictures of the restaurant on the tablet to show them what she meant. "That ought to be close enough."

"Good thinking." Dusk nodded. "Lettie and I will be here, listening and marking anything important."

"You aren't going with us?" Astra asked, her voice soft as she picked at the crust of a slice of pizza.

"He'd recognize us right off." Jericho shook his head. "We can't take that risk."

"I mean, you could go in and pretend you're on a date. Aren't you two like . . . supposed to be playing each other?" Maz mumbled around a mouth full of cheese she'd peeled off her own pizza.

Jericho's jaw clenched, eyes narrowing. He'd said he wasn't going to be feeding her. Yet there she was, ruining a perfectly good piece of pizza. Just as he inhaled to shout at her, Dusk cut him off. "We can't take the chance that us being there will influence what they talk about. Drop it."

Maz huffed like a scolded child. "Fine. I was just asking," she muttered, shoving her plate away.

"Where are the clothes?" Dusk gave Jericho's hand another knowing squeeze before he dropped the hold.

Maz rolled her eyes and scooped up the large duffle again. The pizza was pushed to the side as she began to unload dress clothes for Astra and Fizz, and a uniform perfectly matching those that Gideon's waitstaff wore for herself.

"Do I even want to know where those came from?" Jericho rubbed the bridge of his nose before stuffing his hands into the pockets of his sweatpants.

"Probably not." Maz offered him a sharp smile.

●

THE NEXT EVENING, they all met at Jericho's again to get the three made up for the mission. It was easy enough for Maz to shift her appearance to that of Olivia's. The hard part was finding clothes that Fizz could fit his long legs into and getting Astra into the slinky purple dress. Jericho was just finishing up the intricate braid she'd chosen to weave into Astra's green hair when the alarm went off.

"That's time, folks." Dusk tapped his phone to quiet the noise. "Maz, you need to get to the restaurant to help open. Astra and Fizz, reservations are in an hour. You should probably get there before him and get settled in with drinks. Pickle has already set up some funds for you, so be sure to order the most expensive thing on the menu." He winked at them.

Astra giggled.

Jericho ushered them out the door, her shoulders sagging as she leaned heavily against the wall beside it. "Do you think it'll work?"

"We don't have much choice. Come on, let's get comfortable. It's going to be a long night of listening." Dusk took Jericho's hands and tugged her over to the couch. Jericho didn't fight him. She simply collapsed onto the sofa, her head tilting back against the overstuffed cushions.

"We better get something good from this mess."

"Famous last words," Dusk laughed tiredly, pulling up the program on his tablet to monitor the different bug streams and set markers on the parts that were important. Then he held an ear bud out to Jericho.

•

IT WAS A LONG NIGHT. Pendragon sat for an hour by himself, hassling Maz—which was arguably hilarious, as Jericho listened to her try not to snap at him—and nursing a glass of whiskey.

"Ah! Bryndis! Nice of you to join me," Pendragon called at last. The leather of the booth shifted beneath him as he presumably stood to shake hands with the other person.

"Can we get video?" Jericho asked.

"Hmm . . . If I can tap into the restaurant security maybe. Hang on." Dusk's tongue poked out of the side of his lips as he typed away at his screen for a moment. "Haha! There it is. Now we just need popcorn."

"I got it." Jericho rose, heading back to the kitchen.

"Who is Bryndis?" Dusk called over the soft pop of kernels in the microwave.

"She's in charge of the Ilygroth Hero Division."

"That makes sense." Dusk nodded, his fingers drumming on the edge of the tablet as he watched.

"Oakfur is late," Pendragon complained. "But let's get you a drink."

"No, thank you." Bryndis waved off the offer. "Water is fine."

"Nonsense. The lady will have a glass of your house red," Pendragon insisted.

"Oakfur is always fucking late," Jericho muttered irritably under her breath.

"Don't forget the popcorn bowl. I hate eating it out of the bag. It gets my hand all greasy," Dusk called toward the kitchen.

Jericho grunted, grabbing the bowl from the cabinet and pouring in the popcorn.

"I bet she doesn't even like red wine," Dusk grumbled darkly.

"Probably not."

"Oh. Oakfur is here." Dusk sat up straighter. "Hurry up, things are about to get interesting." Jericho rolled her eyes and dropped down onto the couch with the popcorn in her lap. They fell silent, munching on their snack as Dusk switched the cameras to follow the leprechaun across the restaurant.

"Oakfur." Pendragon stood, sounding more jovial than he had when the other captain arrived. "You'll have a whiskey with me, surely."

Jericho focused on the soft crunch of popcorn in her ears as she did her very best to tune out the inane bullshit that was Pendragon's little circle jerk. It wasn't useful, and she didn't have the patience for it. What felt like hours ticked by as they shot the shit, but only half the bowl of popcorn was gone before Bryndis got tired of glaring at her untouched glass of wine. "All right, Pendragon, what did you call us down here for?"

Pendragon chuckled, pulling a tablet from the briefcase sitting beside him in the booth. He fiddled with it for a moment before turning it over for the two captains to see what was on the screen.

"Any way we can get a look at that?" Jericho asked, squinting at their screen.

"Astra? Fizz?" Dusk tapped on his jaw, and static rippled over the earbud in Jericho's ear as it connected to Fizz.

"No luck. The booths are too high," Fizz answered. "Maz?"

"Yeah, sure. Let me just go over there and peer over his shoulder. That's not going to draw attention. And for your information, this place is packed tonight. I've got six tables, and one of them has *ten* people." Maz's voice was rushed and annoyed.

"Everyone, quiet. Maybe he'll say what it is," Jericho ordered.

"You're the one who suggested it." Maz grunted. "Hey! Watch—"

Dusk tapped again, and the connection to Fizz and Maz cut out, focusing once more solely on the conversation at the booth.

"I want this hero transferred to Bryndis' jurisdiction." Pendragon tapped on the screen. "His name is Lachlan. A reliable source tells me that he's in league with a villain."

"And you want him brought onto my beat . . . why?" Bryndis frowned, picking up her glass and taking a sip. The video was too grainy to see her expression, but she coughed softly, clearly not enjoying it.

"He's a bad hero anyway, right?" Pendragon's voice had gone soft, leading.

"Presumably. We'd have to do an investigation," Oakfur said. For the first time in their limited acquaintance, Jericho could say that Oakfur sounded reasonable. It was not a word she usually associated with him. "Who's your source?"

"Not important." Pendragon brushed it aside. "Either way, he's very likely on the wrong side of things, so he'll need to go. Why not do it in such a way as to be profitable?"

"Your hold on Ilygroth is already fairly strong, sir," Bryndis argued.

"I want to move faster." Pendragon suddenly sounded petulant and childish. Like a little boy who wasn't getting his way.

"Sir, we're moving as fa—"

"Not fast enough!" Pendragon growled. He slammed the tablet onto the table, rattling their glasses.

"Yes, sir," Bryndis said tightly. "What's the plan?"

Pendragon sat back in his chair, his arms crossing over his chest. His posture had turned smug suddenly. The man-baby had won. "There is a business owner holding out on me. Next week, there will be a robbery that will result in the death of the owner and an officer who happens to be on the scene. It'll be a tragedy." Jericho's stomach dropped. Dusk was holding a bit of popcorn halfway up to his mouth, but his hand had started to tremble. "The neighborhood will mourn, and an Unseelie will be suspected. Ultimately, we'll never find the person who did it."

"Property values will tank," Oakfur added.

"There will be a panic." Bryndis sighed. She sounded more tired than anything else. "I'll need more men to deal with it."

"Oakfur will supply you with support." Pendragon sipped from his glass, relaxed.

"Yes, sir." Oakfur nodded.

"And you both will be generously compensated by my people, of course. The transfers will be in your accounts before the end of the week. I trust you can work out getting Lachlan transferred on your own?"

"Yes, sir," Oakfur and Bryndis answered in unison.

"That's it. That's all we need," Dusk said, his words soft. He lifted his face from the screen of the tablet to look at Jericho, that fanatical smile painted on his face again. "This is all we need to bring Pendragon down and cast shade on all the other council members."

Jericho nodded, swallowing roughly. "We just have to find a judge to give it to."

Dusk tapped on the screen in silence, that smile still splitting his lips.

"Right? A judge?" Jericho pressed.

"Right. A judge."

CHAPTER NINETEEN

DUSK TUCKED HIMSELF INTO BED EARLY THAT EVENING.

"I have a lot to think about," he said by way of explanation before he shut his bedroom door with a little wave and a soft click. He'd left the tablet sitting on the couch for Jericho to review the footage if she so chose, and Jericho did choose.

She quickly lost track of how many times she rewound and replayed the video, listening to Pendragon casually plan the death of a boy not much more than eighteen. As if he were talking about the weather or what he planned to make for dinner the following day. It made Jericho nauseous, but she couldn't seem to stop watching. How was it so easy? How had they fallen so far? The Pendragons had been a noble lineage, dating all the way back to Arthur—the king who abdicated his throne to make way for the new world order after the war. They were good people, or they had been anyway. And now, there sat Councilman Pendragon, washing all that honor down the drain.

At some point, Jericho's hands had started to shake so badly that she had to sit the tablet down on her lap to keep from dropping it. She sighed, running her hands roughly down her face, dragging the soft skin of her cheeks and eyes down with her fingers. When faced with information like this, it was easy to see how Dusk was right. How they should just demolish the system and start fresh. But there were rules in place for a reason, and that reason was to protect the general populace. Jericho still believed in the system; it was flawed but not broken. So, before she could let her heart sink any further, she grabbed her own tablet and got to work.

By the time Dusk hobbled, half asleep, out of his room, Jericho had consumed three cups of coffee, made French toast, and had a plan in place. She ignored the tremor running through her arm as she poured a mug for Dusk, sliding it across to the sleep-rumpled banshee.

"Morning," Jericho said with a pasted-on smile that was too bright, too happy, and very fake.

"Mhm," Dusk hummed. His freckled fingers grasped the mug, holding it closer to himself as he tried to get his bearings. "You're up early."

"Didn't sleep. How many pieces do you want?"

"Just two—Wait. Did you say you didn't sleep?" Dusk's eyes widened, then he looked over Jericho more closely. Jericho could feel him taking her in, from the bags under her eyes to her jittering hands as she flipped a piece of bread on the griddle. "Are you okay?"

"I'm fine. Just couldn't sleep." Jericho shrugged, sliding a plate over to Dusk. "Eat. It always sucks after it's gone cold."

Dusk eyed the plate critically for a moment before turning his gaze to Jericho again. "It didn't rattle you that much, did it?"

"No," Jericho grunted, starting a couple of pieces for herself. "I just had a lot to think about."

"Yeah. Me too. That's why I went to sleep." Dusk narrowed his eyes on Jericho critically. *Great. Here comes the lecture.* "So I could spend today looking at it with fresh eyes. I know it's tempting to set your sights on something and not let up until it's finished, but we can't be like that, Lettie. We're playing the long game here, and if we tire ourselves out, we won't get anywhere."

"We literally have less than a week to figure this shit out before they take you away from me again," Jericho hissed, not turning from the stove. Her shoulders hunched, fingers clenching the spatula hard enough that the cheap plastic bent in her grasp. She hadn't heard Dusk move, but suddenly there was a hand on her shoulder, brushing down her back as if to soothe her. It helped a little. Jericho found herself standing up straighter again, nodding to herself.

"We're going to think of something. It'll all work out in the end," Dusk insisted, his hand resting on the small of Jericho's back as he leaned his weight into her side.

"Go eat your breakfast before it gets cold," Jericho ordered again. She squeezed her eyes shut, trying to will away the strange coldness left behind when Dusk removed himself and headed back to the island. Once she had a plate for herself, she moved to stand across the counter from Dusk and grabbed her tablet from where she'd discarded it earlier.

"What's this?" Dusk asked through a mouthful of breakfast.

Jericho tapped for a few moments, not answering. Then she pulled up the list she'd worked on for hours. The list that had kept her up all through the night as she gulped down coffee and tried to keep herself focused. The list that would be Dusk's savior—or at least she thought so. "These are all the officials in Mythikos who I think could be of some help to us. These are the people I think have high enough moral standards not to be bought off by Pendragon. They should be safe."

Dusk's fingers skimmed the cool surface of the tablet, eyes flicking over the list of names. "Can I edit this?"

"Yeah, sure." Jericho shrugged, going back to her breakfast.

Dusk fell silent. His fingers flew over the screen, and his breakfast sat beside the device, forgotten. After several minutes, he pulled his fingers away and scooted the tablet over to show Jericho his work. "There. These are the ones I don't have information on so far."

"Three?" Jericho asked with a frown. "I give you a list of fifty-some names, and you leave me with three options?"

With a shrug of his narrow shoulders, Dusk ducked his head back to his plate. He grimaced a little at the bite of now-cold syrup but kept eating anyway.

"What about all the others?" Jericho growled through her teeth, her fist tightening on the countertop. "What happened to them?"

Dusk sighed, his shoulders sagging. "They're not as good as you think they are. Mom was at this a long while before I even came into it, and she had information on a lot of people in power. I've gathered some of my own." He reached over to take Jericho's hand, gently prying her fingers apart and relaxing her fist. "These are the three people I don't have intel on so far. But we'll get information on them—Pickle will get us some—and then we can pick someone."

"We need it now," Jericho insisted, though it came out as a croak.

"I know." Dusk hummed softly. "She'll be quick, I promise." He moved to wrap one arm around Jericho, pulling her into a tight half-hug. Jericho leaned into the comfort it provided, closing her eyes and doing her best to forget what it meant. She tried to tamp down the feeling that this was a goodbye. That this was the end. *No.* It wasn't. It couldn't be. "How about we just spend the day watching old cartoons and binging junk food?"

"I don't have any junk food."

"Then we'll go buy some!" Dusk laughed, pushing away his half-finished breakfast. "Let me just go get dressed, yeah?"

"Yeah . . . Okay," Jericho agreed, probably too easily

"Great." Dusk smiled brightly. He brushed a strand of blond hair back from Jericho's face and leaned in to brush a kiss over her cheek. "See you in a second."

Jericho nodded. With Dusk tucked into his room to change, Jericho made herself busy cleaning up and changing into a fresh set of joggers and a hoodie.

"All set?" Jericho asked when he heard Dusk join him.

"Yup!"

Jericho turned to eye the smaller man, now drowning in a hoodie that was obviously Jericho's, with the sleeves pulled down over his hands like paws.

"Did I say you could borrow my stuff?"

"Did I ask?"

"Cheeky little shit," Jericho grumbled. "C'mon, we don't have all day."

"Actually, we do."

Jericho huffed a laugh, reaching over to ruffle Dusk's hair, giving his head a hearty shove when he was done. "Stop being an ass."

"Never."

⬤

THE GROCERY STORE was too crowded, they decided with a quick glance through the sliding glass doors. Instead, they made their way to a convenience store on the corner to buy all of their favorites. Dusk's arms were piled high with bags of chips and candies, and his smile was bigger than Jericho had seen it since they were children.

"Is that it?" Jericho asked sarcastically, pulling his wallet from his pocket after setting a bag of chocolates onto the counter.

Dusk nodded, scooting closer so he could dump everything in front of the cashier. "Oh. Wait. One more thing." He pulled a package of sour straws out of his pocket and added them to the stack. "That's it." He grinned proudly at his haul.

"Right." Jericho bit the inside of his cheek to keep from being snarky. It would be so easy, but seeing Dusk this happy —he couldn't bear to ruin it. He paid for their purchases, took the cloth sack, and soon enough, they were back on their way to his apartment.

"We're going to have to watch it from the beginning," Dusk muttered, bouncing along beside him.

"What?"

"*The Shadow* animated series." Dusk looked up at Jericho, his eyes wide. And for the first time since all of this had started, Jericho could see his friend there in those eyes. Not just the face of the boy he'd known but the real person. Sol. "Are you telling me you forgot about *The Shadow*? It was like our favorite—"

"Of course I didn't forget about *The Shadow*," Jericho grumbled, cutting him off. "I remember very vividly how obsessed you were with them."

"*I* was obsessed?" Sol laughed, throwing his head back in glee. "You had the whole getup right down to the utility belt!"

"Shut up." Jericho cleared his throat around a chuckle, shoving Sol hard enough that he stumbled toward the buildings beside them.

"Oh no. You, sir, are never going to live that shit down. I still have pictures!" Freckled fingers pulled Sol's phone from his pocket, and he began to flip through images. "I have the proof right here! You wanna see?"

"Hey! Give me that!" Jericho reached for the device, intent

on deleting any incriminating images before Sol could share them with anyone.

"Noooooo. You were so precious!" Sol chortled, holding up the phone so Jericho could see a picture of himself on the screen. He was four, maybe five, and he had a long purple cape tied around his neck, his hands braced on his hips in the classic hero stance as the deep plum fabric blew out behind him. "You made me hold the fan."

"Shut up," Jericho grunted, finally giving up his attempts at stealing the device.

"Oh, how he blushes." Sol tucked his phone away, a smile still stitched into the corners of his lips. "You were a cute kid."

"Tch. Whatever." Jericho shook his head, refusing to meet Sol's eyes as they made their way up to the apartment.

Once there, Sol piled their load of snacks onto the coffee table, flopped down on the couch, and turned on the TV, already searching for the first season of *The Shadow*.

"I hope it holds up. I haven't been able to watch it in a few years," Sol muttered thoughtfully, already chewing on the end of a sour straw.

"It probably won't." Jericho propped his feet up on the table as he got comfortable.

"No. Maybe not. But a guy can hope." Sol turned to give him a wide grin, then hit play on the first episode of the first season of the first show that had made them both want to be heroes.

It didn't hold up.

The fight scenes were comical at best. The dialogue felt like it had been written by a teenager who didn't quite understand how adults spoke. And some of the villain costumes . . . Well, Jericho decided Sol's getup was far superior.

At some point, well past lunchtime, Jericho had leaned

heavily into Sol, his lids drooping as the sugar high finally wore off. He didn't even remember dozing, but suddenly he was being awoken by soft voices from the door.

"I know what I'm doing, Pickle," Sol whispered sharply.

The person in the hall was muffled, but Jericho could make out the worried warble of Ildri's voice.

Sol let out a loud sigh, deflating, and Jericho heard him shift against the door frame. "I don't have any other choice. This is what has to be done."

More softly spoken words.

"I know. I love you too, Pickle." Sol sounded tired, so tired. When had he gotten so tired? There was some more rustling of fabric and then the door shut softly. Jericho waited, his eyes closed as he listened to Sol shuffle back toward the living room. He lowered himself back to the couch slowly, probably being careful not to wake Jericho, but it was much too late for that.

"Time's it?" Jericho asked, scrubbing at his eyes as if he'd just woken up.

"Getting close to dinner time." Sol was fiddling with something in his hands. Jericho had to sit up to get a better look at it. It was a folder. Gray in color, and thin enough that there couldn't be more than a couple of sheets inside.

"What's that?" Jericho sat up straighter, his stomach clenching as he watched Sol tighten his hold on the folder enough to bend it.

"Nothing. Just information Ildri got us on those three people you picked out." Sol set the folder off to his other side, onto their stack of files, keeping his body between it and Jericho. "Will you make me ramen for dinner? You promised."

Jericho's eyes remained fixed on the folder for a long moment before he nodded. "Yeah, I will. You want it with the egg in it?"

Sol nodded quickly, a slow smile spreading across his lips. It didn't reach his eyes, and something about that unsettled Jericho impossibly more than the weight of that folder ever could.

"Afterward, we can dig out what's left of the ice cream and watch *The Shadow: The Animated Feature*," Sol said in an exaggerated voice, his eyes shining.

"That sounds like fun." Jericho forced a laugh, then pulled himself from the couch.

●

THAT NIGHT, after dinner was eaten, as an empty tub of cookie dough ice cream sat on the coffee table inevitably leaving a ring, Jericho and Sol curled up together on the couch. Sol leaned more and more heavily into Jericho's side, his arms wrapped around Jericho's waist, head on his shoulder. His bright eyes were blinking blearily, lids growing heavier. If they didn't get to bed soon, Sol would fall asleep on top of Jericho's already tingling arm.

"We should go to bed," Jericho suggested.

"One more," Sol pleaded.

"In the morning." Sol looked up at him with wide eyes, and Jericho relented. "One more."

Sol was asleep by the time the final credits rolled, and Jericho had to shake him awake. "Mmmm up. Mm up," Sol mumbled, still half asleep.

"Go to bed, Sol."

Sol huffed but rose from his seat. He wobbled on his feet, like his legs had fallen asleep, and Jericho stood to steady him before he could fall.

"Thanks for this, Lettie. It was a lot of fun." Sol rubbed a hand over his eyes, offering Jericho a tired smile.

Jericho nodded, helping Sol hobble toward his room, arm

firmly around the small man's waist. "Don't forget to take out your hearing aids."

"Right." One freckled hand reached for the knob to his door, and then Sol stopped. He whirled around, flinging himself more firmly into Jericho's arms. Jericho only just caught him as Sol hugged him tightly, pressing his face into Jericho's shoulder and inhaling deeply for a moment. "Good night," he mumbled into the fabric.

Jericho rolled his eyes, hugging Sol tighter, then pulling him back by the hood of his sweatshirt to untangle them. "Good night."

Sol nodded, but he wouldn't meet Jericho's eyes. There was something in the gesture, something like a goodbye. It made Jericho's gut twist violently. Was this it? Was this the end? No. They'd get everything sorted tomorrow. It would all work out just fine. Sol had said as much, hadn't he?

"See you in the morning," Jericho said.

"Yeah. See you." Sol turned, shutting the door behind him with a soft thump.

Jericho turned and made his way back into the living room to clean up the mess they'd left behind. Amongst the crinkled chip bags and powdered sugar left behind by sour sweets sat the gray folder. It had crumbs on it, and the condensation from the ice cream tub was creeping dangerously close.

"Tch." Jericho shook his head. Sol would show him when he was ready. This was their plan, after all. It wouldn't do either of them any good to have secrets now. Still, it haunted him.

With shaking fingers, he rescued the folder from the little puddle gravitating toward it. And then once he had it in his hands . . . Well, he may as well take a look, right? Casually flipping it open, he peered inside at four sheets of paper. The first three were printed records of the people Jericho had chosen, thinking they could trust them. At the top of each page was bold lettering that read NOT SUITABLE, and below, Ildri had proceeded to show their financial records, prior dealings with Pendragon, and holdings they had in companies relating to his. Evidence to prove they couldn't be trusted with the information Sol and Jericho had on Pendragon.

That on its own sent Jericho's heart into his throat, but the fourth page had him swallowing back bile. It was printed front and back with a detailed markup of the back doors into Mythikos' mainframe, and how to release the information directly to the public on every tablet, cell phone, television, and any other screen available within the city limits. There was even a script. Ildri was . . . she was suggesting . . . *No!*

Jericho tore off to Sol's room, knocking hard against the door. When Sol didn't answer, he forced it open.

"Lettie?" Sol asked, sitting up, face set into a bewildered scowl. He grabbed one of his hearing aids, putting it in his ear quickly to prepare for the shouting match that was likely on the way. "What th—" he started, and then his eyes fell on the file folder clutched in Jericho's shaking hands.

"'What the fuck' is exactly what I'm thinking!" Jericho nearly screamed. Sol winced, hand lifting to cover his ear. "What is this shit?! Ildri wants you to do a video? Like some kind of . . . some kind of . . . " He couldn't even get the word past his teeth.

"Terrorist?" Sol supplied unhelpfully.

"They'll arrest you on the spot!" Panic had gripped Jericho's insides like ice. *Terrorist.* That's exactly what they'd see Sol as. He wouldn't just be a villain. He'd be evil in the eyes of everyone who mattered. Everyone who could exercise power over him.

Sol shrugged. "They're going to take me back there anyway. Why not take someone down with me?"

"You can't!" Jericho's voice broke, but his fury hadn't abated. He couldn't lose Sol, not like *this*, not *now*. They'd finally just gotten close to what they'd been. Jericho had friends again. He had people in his life again. He had *Sol* in his life again. If Sol did this, that'd be gone. All of it. There would be no saving Sol. Not from this. There was no coming back from being labelled a terrorist. "There has to be another way. A *legal* way. A way that keeps you off the Isle."

Jericho wasn't sure when, but his gaze had flicked down to the trembling folder in his hands. His eyes were blurry and itchy with tears. He heard Sol open a drawer and then shuffle closer. "Look. It's sweet that you care, but—"

"I don't *just* care!" Jericho shouted, finally letting the useless folder and papers drop to the floor with a soft swish, only half noticing when he stepped on them in his rush to scoop Sol up into his arms again. Just as they'd been not ten minutes ago. Or had it been longer? How long had Jericho sat there reading that damnable file? It didn't matter, none of it fucking mattered! Sol couldn't do this. He couldn't leave. Not now! Not when Jericho had just gotten him back.

"This is the only w—"

"Don't go," Jericho cut him off, hands moving to clutch at Sol's jaw instead of his waist. Fingers still trembling as he ran a thumb over a darkly freckled cheek. "Stay with me. Let's do this together," he breathed. "We're a team."

A broken, tired sigh left Sol, his eyes growing sad as his own fingers lifted to brush across Jericho's jaw, then down the column of his throat, brushing blond hair away from the skin to keep the path of his fingers unhindered.

"I've waited years to hear you say that. But now is not the time for us to get sentimental." Sol inhaled deeply, swallowing roughly around some emotion, then nodded to himself. He'd made up his mind. Whatever he was going to do, he'd made up his mind. "Where I'm going, you can't follow."

"Wha—"

Sol cut off the words with a soft, lingering kiss to Jericho's lips. Chaste as it was, the tingle reached all the way down to his toes, turning every organ in his body into a puddle of goo as he eagerly returned it. They stayed that way for a long moment—lips pressed together, Jericho holding Sol tightly like he'd disappear if Jericho didn't hold on—before Sol finally pulled back.

He pressed his forehead to Jericho's, inhaling again. "No buts. You see it now. You see the wrong in the world and how we can make it better. We need people like you in the Alliance. We need—no, *I* need to know you're free. *Safe.*" The words were soft but firm, not a hint of emotion choking them. Sol had decided this long ago it seemed. Possibly before Jericho had even brought him home for the rehab program.

"So, you're going to take this wolfsbane," he whispered, pressing the tip of a needle into Jericho's neck close enough to Jericho's ear that he could hear the soft whoosh of the plunger as the drug was forced into his system. He didn't struggle. Merlin, why didn't he *struggle*? It was like all the fight had left him.

"And you're going to go to sleep for a little while. I'm going to go and make that video. When you wake up, I won't be here. I'll have escaped into the night. And then everything will be back to normal for you. Maybe we'll see each other in a decade or so . . . " Sol's words were growing softer, but Jericho couldn't tell if it was because he was upset or if it was the damn drug racing through his veins, dragging him down into sleep as his vision turned black around the edges. He stumbled. Sol caught him, keeping him upright. "When the dust settles, maybe we can try this again," Sol was saying as he forced Jericho toward the bed.

Jericho felt his body fall onto the covers, hard.

"Sol," he rasped, or maybe it didn't even get past the thickness of his tongue, he wasn't sure.

"Shhh. I know," Sol whispered, pulling the covers up to Jericho's chin before pressing a soft kiss to his lips. "Thank you for today, Lettie. It's all I've ever wanted."

"Sssss . . . " Jericho definitely couldn't get the name past his lips now. His tongue was much too heavy, and every time his lids slid shut, it was a struggle to tug them upward again. But Sol was still there. Looking at him. He had to try.

"I know, Lettie. Me too." Sol sighed into another lingering kiss against Jericho's lips. And then that was it. The darkness took everything with it, even Sol's dark eyes.

CHAPTER TWENTY

WHEN JERICHO WOKE UP, SOL'S MESSAGE WAS PLAYING ON loop over every screen in Mythikos.

"The world changes now, or else," Sol said before the video of Pendragon played, showing everyone who the councilman was and just what he was willing to do to get his way. Then it flashed to pictures of the councilman's bank records and news headlines that corresponded with his shady dealings. "This is who we've elected to represent us. This is who rules us. Those in power have become corrupt and complacent. The only option left for us is—"

"—a complete restructuring of our society. As people, magical and nonmagical alike," Jericho said along with Sol. He'd seen the video so many times now that he could recite the script in his sleep if he wanted to. He did not want to. He was sure Sol's face would be burned into the backs of his eyelids when he went to bed that evening.

"We must set aside the differences between Seelie and Unseelie—human and fae—and strive to do better. If you are one of these corrupt officials, I want you to know the sun is setting on your rule. Eventide is—"

Jericho muted the TV, unable to listen to Sol's diatribe any further. He was sure he ought to feel something about this. Pride, or anger, or betrayal. But all he was left with was a hollow feeling. Sol had left him behind, just as Jericho had done to him so many years ago. The villain was still clothed in that damnable hoodie—Jericho's hoodie—but he didn't look the same as Jericho remembered him in those final moments. There was a hard, determined set to his eyes, and his mouth moved in a twisted, confident smirk as he spoke, doing his best to instill fear. Gone was the soft young man who had curled up beside Jericho on the couch as they gorged on snack foods till they were sick, and in his place was this . . . this . . . Jericho shook himself, unable to finish the thought.

When the silence got the better of him, Jericho turned the sound back on, hoping to fill the void Sol had left behind. It did nothing for the hollow feeling, but at least it made his apartment feel less quiet. He wasn't sure how long he sat there, just listening to Sol repeat the same speech over and over and over, watching and re-watching the footage of Pendragon making a deal that would end a young man's life. By the time the networks somehow got Sol's message off TV, Jericho felt his stomach churning with hunger. A glance at his phone told him it was dinner time.

Jericho rose mechanically and went to dig two-day-old cold pizza from the fridge. He didn't even bother heating it before taking a bite of the rubbery cheese and chewy crust. He hardly noticed the taste. It was easy to ignore one's own senses when there was a part of oneself missing, Jericho found.

"This just in: The villain Dusk has been captured," the news anchor said, ripping Jericho from his emptiness and into a world of ache. The rest of the anchor's words were lost to the ringing in Jericho's ears as he watched the footage of

Sol being apprehended. He went down without much of a fight, and to the camera hovering in a drone above the scene, it looked as if one of the heroes detaining him did nothing more than shoot him with a tranquilizer and cart off his limp body. "Dusk has been brought in alive for further questioning on the Pendragon scandal."

"Off," Jericho ordered the television, unable to continue watching the scene they were playing on repeat now. Sol fell limply to the ground, over and over. Jericho's hands twitched to do something, anything. To go after his friend and bring him back. But that would only make matters worse. Instead, not wanting to worry about the computer mishearing him, he grabbed the remote and queued up another episode of *The Shadow*, letting the cheesy one-liners and ridiculous sound effects fill the space Sol had left. He threw away the now-slightly-warmer pizza and dragged himself down the hall toward the bedrooms. With one glance at his own closed door, he ducked into the room Sol had been using for the last couple of months. The bed was still unmade from when Jericho had woken from his drugged slumber, and he curled up on the fitted sheet, not bothering to drag the covers over himself. With a soft rumble, his wolf urged Jericho to press his nose closer to the pillow, and he inhaled what was left of Sol's scent greedily.

He began to doze, surrounded by the lingering smell of Sol and the ebbing darkness of the room. At some point, the sound of knocking dragged him from his half-asleep state.

"Coming," Jericho muttered, feet scuffing against the hardwood floor as he made his way to the door. When he opened it, he came face to face with two extra-large K.N.I.G.H.T. units. "What do you want?"

"Colette Jericho, we are under orders to bring you down to the hold for a statement on the villain known as Dusk. We request that you come quietly," one of them said in that stilted, stiff way that all robots spoke.

"Can I put on real pants first?"

The android looked him up and down for a moment before repeating, "We request that you come quietly."

Jericho huffed. "Fine." He stuffed his feet into the shoes sitting by the door and tightened the string on his joggers to keep them from slipping down off his hips. "Lead the fucking way."

It nodded curtly and turned to guide them back to the elevator. The second robot brought up the rear. They rode in silence to the hold, Jericho watching the lights of Mythikos flash by him in a rush. When they reached the large fortress of a building, the two androids stuck close to his side.

"I can get there on my fucking own," he complained, but they refused to answer, and the trio climbed into the elevator, shoulder to shoulder.

He resisted the urge to roll his eyes as he was led to an interrogation room. "An officer will be with you shortly."

"Right. Can I get some water?" All the answer he got was the door shutting in his face with a soft whoosh of air. "Thanks for nothing, asshole." He flopped down into the chair facing the wall of glass and waited.

It didn't take long at all for Oakfur and Erling to join him.

"Jericho," Oakfur said with a curt nod as he sat across from the hero. Erling didn't say anything; he just stood behind the captain with his arms crossed, doing his best impression of a bouncer at a club who'd seen one too many drunk girls.

"Oakfur." Jericho lifted a brow. "Erling."

Erling sneered, refusing to speak.

"So, boys." Jericho smirked, leaning back in his seat, completely at ease. If he was going down for what Sol had done, so be it. But he wasn't going to look panicked when it happened. "What's this about?"

"Oh, I think you know what this is about," Erling spat, slamming his hands on the acrylic table hard enough to shake it. *Ah, so it's good hero, bad hero,* Jericho thought.

Jericho tilted his head, the smirk still comfortably on his face. "Down boy," he cooed playfully.

"That's enough, Erling." Oakfur sighed heavily, shaking his head. He was definitely the good hero in this.

"Sir?"

"I said, enough." Oakfur's words were firm, and Erling stood back up, his arms crossing over his chest again as his face twisted into an expression that was equal parts stricken and chastised. "Now, Jericho," Oakfur continued, tapping on the tablet in front of him. "Dusk gave us a statement earlier this evening. He says that you had no knowledge of his activities. We're just not sure how that's possible."

Jericho swallowed, his hands clenching in his lap where he hoped the others wouldn't notice. "I must have been drugged."

"And you didn't notice? I find that doubtful," Erling scoffed.

Jericho shrugged. "I noticed I was sleeping better, but I didn't think much of it. I just thought it was because I wasn't drinking as much coffee."

"Right." Erling's wings rustled behind him. "But you suspected he'd try to drug you in the beginning."

"Yes, and then I didn't get sick. Honestly, I felt fine. I was just sleeping better." Jericho let his eyes flick up first to meet Erling's, then down to Oakfur. Innocent. He was innocent.

"That would certainly explain things." Oakfur nodded, typing away at the tablet. With his eyes downcast, Jericho couldn't tell if he believed the lie or not, but he supposed so long as Oakfur wasn't calling him on it, it wouldn't matter. "How long has this been going on?"

"A few weeks, I guess. I had switched to tea in the evenings shortly after you asked me to start working with Dusk. My doctor said I should cut back on the caffeine at my last physical." It wasn't a lie; his doctor had said that. It was just that Jericho had laughed in his face when he did.

"I see," Oakfur said, followed by more typing. "So, you had no knowledge of this scandal involving Pendragon?"

"No, sir."

"And you have no information on who was a part of this mission to slander the councilman?"

"Is it really slander if it's true?" Jericho asked, fighting the urge to sneer.

"Answer the question."

"No, sir. I have no information on which of Dusk's people were involved," Jericho muttered through gritted teeth. His hands clenched harder beneath the table.

"Do you have anything you can provide us in regard to this event?"

"No, sir."

Oakfur hummed softly, his fingers flying across the screen, then after a moment, he nodded. "Very well then, you are free to go."

"Yes, you are free—Wait. He's free to go?!" Erling shouted.

"Yes, he's free to go," Oakfur repeated.

Jericho stood from his chair, refusing to let the relief show on his face.

"Thank you, sir."

"But," Oakfur said, stopping Jericho as he reached for the door, "you will be under formal investigation, and until this is sorted out, you're on desk duty."

Jericho felt his shoulders tense, but he took a deep breath and refused to cave under the weight of that accusation.

They didn't have proof he'd been involved but they thought he had been anyway. Now, every moment of his life would be scrutinized until they could prove he'd helped Sol. And they *would* prove it. As far as they were concerned, it was just a matter of time. Fuck. "Yes, sir. I understand. Where should I report in the morning?"

"You'll still be at your desk in the bullpen, you just won't be allowed out on calls until we can prove that you didn't help the villain."

Jericho nodded. "Good night, sir."

"Good night."

The ride back to his apartment went by in another blur. Sol's voice filtered down the hall as Jericho opened the door. Jericho's heart beat wildly in his chest, crashing against his rib cage. "Sol—" he started, rushing toward the voice, but then his eyes fell on the television. There was Sol's face, the words of his diatribe playing again on the news.

"This video was aired early this morning," the anchorperson said, their voice talking over Sol's as they lowered the volume on his video. "Sources say Dusk and his people were also behind the recent data leak of Bronzelhlem and Bristlehorn, and a number of other leaks. Although we do not have information yet on why he is—"

"Off!" Jericho growled, and the apartment was bathed in silence. He dragged himself down the dark hall to Dusk's room and curled up on the bed.

●

LIGHT FILTERED in through the windows, burning the thin skin of Jericho's eyelids.

"Fuck," he grunted, rolling over and kicking at the blankets to try to get them up over his head. When that didn't work, his eyes flew open, and he sat up to reach for the blan-

kets. What greeted him was the emptiness of Sol's room. Jericho's eyes flicked from the scattered papers left behind on
the floor to the empty closet, then to the clutter of Alliance-
issue electronics on the nightstand. Sol had left nothing of
his own behind except the hole where he used to be, and the
phone and hearing aids the Alliance had given him.

Jericho frowned, rolling over to hide away from the truth
of what was in front of him. Sol was gone—again. Except this
time, there was no faking it. There would be no miraculous,
phoenix-like rebirth. There would just be emptiness. "What
fucking time is it?"

"The time is seven thirty-two," the computer set into the
wall said, her voice robotic.

"Fucking hell." Grinding the heels of his hands into his
eyes, Jericho pulled himself from the bed, ignoring the
wolfish instinct to bury his nose in the pillows again. He
dragged himself down the hall and rushed through a freezing
shower. Then, a breakfast of Sol's favorite sugary-as-shit
cereal was the least Jericho could do to feed his body. He
crunched loudly, looking around at the dirty apartment with
their trash still littering the coffee table.

"I need to clean up," he muttered but couldn't will himself
to bother.

The television's light glinted off something on the table,
and Jericho moved to investigate further. What he found was
the cell phone Sol had given him. Somehow, when Sol had
cleared all his stuff out, he'd missed this. His fingers twitched
to reach for it, but he stuffed them in his pockets. Why had
Sol left that behind? It was evidence. A reminder of what
they'd done.

Or perhaps it was a way to contact them. That thought
had Jericho's hand shooting out and snatching up the device,
scattering what was left of the hard-candy-shelled chocolates
onto the floor in a rush.

With a few taps, a glaring light filled his eyes from the screen. A red symbol in the upper corner showed that the battery was nearly dead, and Jericho tripped over the coffee table in his haste to get to the counter and drop it onto the charging pad. Then his fingers skimmed the screen to open the contacts. None had been added. The only numbers in there were still Fizz and Dusk's. But Sol was in the hold.

Jericho's fingers were moving before he could process the thought, typing out a message to the redcap that he hoped would get a reply. Although he wasn't sure what he expected of Fizz. Sol, their leader, had been captured, and it wasn't as if he'd be getting out any time soon. The little team he'd gathered wouldn't still be running without him. Even if they were, Jericho wasn't exactly keen on leaving his world behind in favor of them. Was he?

J 7:46AM: What next?

HE DIDN'T EXACTLY EXPECT a reply right away, but still he stood watching the screen for several minutes with bated breath. When no reply came, and the clock finally read eight o'clock, it was time to head to work.

Jericho wasn't sure what he'd been anticipating when he got to the hold. Perhaps he'd thought that everything would go back to normal, but what he found was the opposite. Erling looked up from his paperwork as Jericho moved to hang his jacket on the back of his chair. A sneer lined the griffin's face, and then he promptly looked away. That trend carried on. Every hero in the bullpen would meet his eyes for a moment, sneer, and then promptly go back to ignoring him as if he didn't exist. There was no proof at all that he'd helped

Sol but it didn't seem that there needed to be. He'd already been tried by the court of his peers and found guilty. He would now be treated as such, whether or not the investigation came back proving his innocence.

What felt like a century later, lunch rolled around. Jericho went to the vending machine to purchase something but found the damn thing out of order, and instead of facing a cafeteria full of people who would continue to ignore him, he headed for Ildri's workshop. She always had extra food, and surely she'd be more welcoming.

Nerves fluttered through him as he raised his hand to knock on the door. He took a moment to breathe. It wouldn't do anyone any good if he continued to avoid this situation. Whether Ildri was pissed or not for what had happened, they still had to work together, and Jericho wasn't about to lose the only person he had in the hold who he truly respected. He knocked softly.

"Enter at your own risk," Ildri called from inside, her voice a little duller than normal.

"Why? Is something going to explo—" Jericho started with a hollow chuckle, but the sight of the pixie stilled his tongue. Ildri's arguably ridiculous wardrobe of overalls and goggles had been replaced with a pair of sweatpants and a T-shirt that draped off her shoulders, making her look small. So small. Dark circles smudged the skin beneath her eyes, and there was an unhealthy pallor to her already pale face that made his gut twist. "Ildri?"

"Oh. It's you." Her wings bristled behind her, hands clenching harder around a pair of needle-nose pliers.

"What happened?"

"I think you know what happened." Ildri's tone was cold, detached, hard. Unlike he'd ever heard it before. She was furious with him. But it wasn't just that. Sadness seemed to make her sag.

"I didn't—It wasn't my choice," he whispered, shutting the door behind him, lest someone overhear them.

Ildri laughed, but the sound wasn't whimsical or light; it sounded half-choked, as if she were forcing it from her throat. "Oh no. I know it wasn't." She finally turned around fully, letting him see the red-rimmed puffiness of her eyes and how her hands trembled around the pliers. "And maybe it was my words and my tech that got him there. But he did this for *you*. If *you* hadn't stormed back into his life like a fucking hurricane, he wouldn't have been caught in the first place. He wouldn't have been so worried about how all of this would affect you and your precious career. But no . . . you just had to get involved. Didn't you?"

"I didn't ask him to." Anger and guilt welled up inside of him, and Jericho stuffed his hands in his pockets to keep her from seeing how they shook. He wasn't sure who he was most angry with: himself, Ildri, or Sol. "I would never have asked him to."

"No. I don't suppose you did. But pray tell, what did you think was going to happen when all of this was over?"

The chill of her words swept up Jericho's spine, making him shudder. "I don't know," he answered, tone soft. He didn't know. He hadn't really thought about where this whole thing was heading. But he supposed it was true that this was going to be the outcome from the beginning. One way or another, Sol was always going to wind up back behind bars.

"I thought I was saving him." Jericho hunched his shoulders, making himself smaller and smaller. "I thought I was going to make him see that he could be a hero."

"You absolute fucking moron," Ildri said, contempt lacing every word.

"What? Why?"

"Nothing. Just go back to your normal life. Go back to

being a *hero*." She whirled back to the work bench, dismissing him.

"Pi—"

"Don't. Call me that," Ildri snapped sharply, slamming her free hand onto the metal table hard enough to jolt everything on it.

"Ild—"

"Just get out of here, Jericho. I don't want to see your face in here again." The anger had ebbed out of her tone, and all that remained was the exhaustion of loss.

"I'll just—" He turned for the door and opened it again. "For what it's worth, I'm sorry."

"Yeah. I know. Me too."

Jericho nodded and shut the door behind him, leaning against the wall beside it heavily. He didn't notice how his fingers trembled until he lifted them to drag down his face.

"Fuck," he rasped softly, his body sagging against the wall.

Ildri's words echoed in his mind the rest of the day. Sol had done this for him, to save him, to protect him, to let him have his life back. Sol knew what being a hero meant to Jericho. How all his life, it'd been all he'd ever wanted, ever striven for. But that didn't make going back to "normal" easy. What even *was* normal now? And how could he go back to it after he'd seen so much?

When he returned home, the phone resting on the charging pad called to him like a siren. It was a beacon of light in the darkness of a Sol-less apartment. Jericho typed in the password, and the messenger app popped up where he'd left it open. Fizz had replied, but when Jericho read the messages, his heart sank.

F 2:36PM: There is nothing next
    Not for you

It's over

Let it go, J

Jericho fumbled to pull the device from the pad and typed in a clumsy reply.

J 7:32PM: What if I can't?

He held his breath, waiting. Would Fizz blow him off just as Ildri had? Was he angry with Jericho too? They both had a right to be. Jericho should have done something to stop Sol. He tried to think of something, anything he could have done to change Sol's mind, to make him see that there was another way. Maybe if he'd been with Sol, the heroes wouldn't have found him. Maybe if he'd been smarter, he'd have come up with a plan, so they didn't have to do things the way Sol had. Maybe if he'd been faster, he'd have been able to keep Sol from drugging him and escaping. Maybe—

Those thoughts were cut short by the soft buzzing of the phone again.

F 7:34PM: You have to

He couldn't though. Jericho knew that now. There was no letting this go, there was no moving on. There was no normal, not after this. Why couldn't Fizz see that?

F 7:35PM: It's what he wants

JERICHO LET OUT A BREATH, his hands clutching more firmly at the device. Fizz was right; Sol had said as much. He wanted Jericho to go back to that world of heroes and villains—of black and white—with this new knowledge. He wanted Jericho to try to help from the inside. He'd sacrificed himself to let that happen. Jericho should honor that sacrifice.

J 7:37PM: I'll try

BUT THE CRUX of the matter was that Jericho didn't want to try. He wanted to find out what they were doing to help Sol, and he wanted in on it. Still, he vowed to try.

●

SO, for the next week, he buried himself in his work, watching file after file come across his desk. They had stopped Pendragon from taking Ilygroth, and it seemed that the crime rate there at least had abated. But in other places, it was growing worse. In the wake of Sol's video, several copy-cats had popped up, claiming to have similar information. Each was investigated and found to be a fraud. The misinformation spread like wildfire, and Jericho wondered if that wasn't part of the plan.

"This can't be right," he muttered to himself, scrubbing a hand through his blond hair. The image of a kappa smiled back up at him from the file of an arson case.

"Talking to yourself again?" Erling sneered.

"No one else will fucking talk to me!" Jericho snapped.

Erling snorted but said nothing else and let Jericho return to his work.

"It just doesn't make sense," he whispered. He saved the file to his tablet, making a note to look at it more closely when he got home that evening.

•

FIZZ ANSWERED on the third ring when Jericho called him later that night, midway through scarfing down another frozen dinner. "What is it, J?"

"What do you know about a kappa named Cale Bowie?" Jericho asked in a rush of relief that Fizz had answered at all. He flopped down onto the couch and studiously ignored the mess still left from his and Sol's binge-watching day. He just didn't have the energy to deal with it.

"I know this might be hard to hear, J," Fizz said, taking a deep breath as if frustrated, "but not all Unseelie know each other."

Jericho huffed, his hand lifting to press at the bridge of his nose where a headache was forming. "Answer the fucking question."

"Haven't heard of him. Why?"

Leaning forward, Jericho set down the bowl containing his cardboard dinner so he could rest his elbows on his knees. "He was brought in a couple of days ago for arson."

"Well, that makes no bloody sense." Fizz was frowning; Jericho could hear it in his voice. "Kappa are afraid of fire."

"I know!" Jericho smiled a little to himself, feeling victorious. Maybe this was enough to get him back in. Maybe now he could find out what they were planning to do about Sol's capture. "How can I send the file to you?"

"I'm already looking it up in the system," Fizz muttered, and Jericho could hear the tapping of a keyboard that was old with time and wear in the background. "The building he burned down was—"

"Yeah. It was an elementary school right next to that new factory that's being built."

"The one with the massive protests. They think it's going to pollute the swamp lands." Fizz hummed thoughtfully. "Certainly makes the story believable."

"Do we have records on what the insurance policy was like for it?" Jericho frowned, putting Fizz on speaker so he could flip through the file on his tablet.

Fizz sighed, and Jericho heard him fall still on the other end of the line. "Let this go, J."

"I'm sorry. What?" Jericho sat up straighter. "This is clearly some kind of bullshi—"

"Oh, it's definitely being orchestrated by the same people who were helping Pendragon," Fizz agreed without even letting Jericho finish. "But that's not why I want you to let this go. Let us handle it. You've done enough by bringing it to us. We can do the rest."

"What are you going to do?"

"Don't worry ab—"

"No. I want to know. With Sol locked up, what are you guys going to do?"

"We're going to do what we've been doing. We're going to make it right."

"How?"

"Like I said, J, let it go. You aren't part of this organization anymore. You never really were. It'd be better for you if you just let this drop." Fizz sounded tired. Why did everyone sound so tired all of a sudden? Fizz. Ildri. Jericho even heard it in himself. As if when Sol had been taken in, the life had been sucked out of them all. Maybe it had.

"I . . . I . . . I don't think I can, Fizz. I've been trying. For fucking days. But I can't . . . I can't get it out of my head."

"Damn it. All right. Let me see what Pickle has to say about this. I'm not going to make any decisions on your status with us until I've talked it out with the rest of them. Till then, just don't do anything drastic, okay?"

"Okay."

The line went dead a moment later, and Jericho found himself staring down at the phone sitting beside him on the cushions.

•

THE REST of the week slunk by in a crawl. Jericho didn't hear anything from Fizz, and Ildri avoided him at all costs. His apartment began to feel more and more like a prison cell than anything else. It was the following Monday before another case of that ilk came across his desk. This time it was a ghoul who had attacked someone in broad daylight.

"They're nocturnal," Jericho tried to argue to Erling, who'd brought the poor girl in. "They can't even go out in the sunlight. It burns their skin!"

"We caught her cowering in an alley right near the scene, and witnesses say it was her," Erling growled, shaking the girl's arm hard enough to rattle her teeth.

"But it couldn't have been her! Look at her, she's dead on her fucking feet. She probably left the bar too late last night and then went to hide in the alley to keep away from the sun." It was true: the girl's gray lids were heavy over her eyes, drifting closed every so often as she fell asleep standing up, even when Erling's grip on her arm tightened to nearly bruising. "There's no way she would have had the energy, much less the strength, to mug someone. And did you find anything on her? If she did it, where is the woman's purse?"

Erling passed the girl off to a K.N.I.G.H.T. with a curt, "Take her down to interrogation room 413. I'll be down shortly to get a confession out of her."

"A *false* confession!"

Erling rounded on Jericho next, thick finger jabbing into Jericho's sternum hard enough to leave a mark. "Look here, you traitorous little shit. I don't care what kind of brainwashing that banshee pulled on you, but you will not interfere in hero procedure so long as you're here. If you get in my way again, I'll be sure you're sharing a cell with your little friend. Are we clear?"

Jericho's jaw clenched hard enough to make his teeth ache. "Crystal."

A sharp nod, then Erling turned to head down to the interrogation rooms.

"I'll just have to figure this shit out myself," Jericho muttered under his breath.

Erling returned an hour later with a signed confession, and that was that. Jericho sent the file to himself, and when he got home, he called Fizz.

"J," Fizz answered, sounding more exhausted than he had the last time.

"There is a ghoul named Ciarra Baq in custody for a mugging in broad daylight in Ilygroth. She was brought in under duress and hardly able to stand, then coerced—I'm sure—into signing a confession. It looks like they haven't given up the idea of a stranglehold on Ilygroth yet." Jericho let the words rush out of him in a steady whoosh.

Silence reigned on the other side of the line for a few long moments before Fizz let out a breath. "Send me the file. I'll see what I can do. Who was the hero in charge?"

"Rutherford Erling," Jericho answered without any hesitation. "And honestly, I want to investigate him. Something is off with him. If I could just have spoken to her th—"

"No." Fizz's tone was hard. "You do nothing. You do no investigating, no talking to witnesses. Nothing. You just bring information to me. That is your role here, and that is the end of it. Dusk wanted you to have a normal life. Go have a normal life. Go on dates. Be a hero. Do all the things you always wanted to."

"But I can—"

"No. This is what you can do."

"And what if I want to do more?!" Jericho's voice broke mid-shout.

A long silence followed. "Is that your final word on the matter?"

"Yes," Jericho forced past the choking emotion in his throat.

"Don't call me again."

"What?"

"This is it. This is the end of your participation in our organization. Do not call this number again." Fizz's voice had gone cold, resolute.

Then he hung up.

Jericho stared down at the phone for a long moment, taking a deep, calming breath.

Could he let this go? Could he go back to how things were before?

No.

He dialed, but the line just rang over and over. When it clicked over to voicemail, Jericho hung up and tried again.

And again.

And again.

Until finally, a robotic voice told him, "We're sorry. The number you have dialed is no longer in service."

"Fuck!" Jericho threw the phone across the room. It cracked against the wall, leaving a dent behind, before clattering to the floor. "Damn it!" His shaking fingers went through his hair, twisting and tugging hard enough to leave sharp pinpricks of pain along his scalp. Then he felt the heat of tears burn at the corners of his eyes. They left hot trails down his cheeks. He had no doubt that even if he did go down to the food pantry, Fizz would bar the way. If they were even still operating out of the same building at all. That was it, he thought, his last connection to Sol. It was gone. There was nothing left.

"Fuck," the word came out in a hoarse rasp. His eyes landed on the table still cluttered with their snack leftovers. The remote was nowhere to be seen, lost under the trash. "TV, on," he muttered in a voice that sounded hollow. "Play Dusk's video."

A spinning wheel appeared on the screen as the computer searched, and then there was that freckled face again. Eyes bright and cheeks slightly flushed. Jericho let his body fall to the side, drawing his knees to his chest and pulling his hood up over his head.

"The world changes now, or else . . . "

Jericho let the video play all the way through, his eyes glassy and reflecting the light.

"Repeat," he told the system, and it played it again from the beginning.

"The world changes now, or else . . . "

"Repeat," he said again when it was done. And a third time. And a fourth. And a fifth. Until the sound of Sol's voice was so ingrained into his memory, he was sure he'd never forget it.

CHAPTER TWENTY-ONE

Jericho must have fallen asleep to Sol's voice, because when he woke, the television was blank, and the time on his phone read 6:14AM. Jericho ran a hand over his face, looking blearily around the still half-dark apartment.

"TV, play Dusk's video again."

The spinning wheel reappeared, silence dragging on and on as Jericho waited for it to load. But after a few grueling seconds, it returned an error.

"TV, repeat."

More spinning. Another error.

"Fuck," he muttered, searching for the remote. His hands were frantic as he shifted the trash on the coffee table, dumping melted and curdled ice cream onto the floor in his search, and came up empty. Next, he ripped the couch cushions off the sofa, and when he finally found it, he left them on the floor, sitting instead on the frame. After some furious typing and searching, he could find no sign of Dusk's video anywhere. It was as if it had been erased from Mythikos' network entirely. He even went as far as to pull up the news-cast which had played it a few days ago, but there was nothing. All traces were gone. The silence closed in on Jericho. Suffocating him and forcing hot tears down his cheeks again.

"I'll just . . . I'll go see him," he breathed, hands shaking, nodding to himself. It sounded absurdly simple when he said it that way.

And that thought carried Jericho through her morning routine until she was standing before an extra-large K.N.I.G.H.T. and wiping sweaty palms on her leggings.

"What can I help you with, Jericho?" it asked, eyes blinking at her as its processors tried to understand what she was doing there.

"I'm here to see Soliel Tsuki."

Only the whirring of fans followed as the robot processed her words. Jericho raised her brows, wondering if the robot wasn't going to answer at all. Maybe it'd just let her pass . . . She moved toward the door to the holding cells, intending to continue on her way—until a shiny metal arm shot out, blocking her path. "All access to prisoner Tsuki is restricted."

"Why?" Jericho's eyes narrowed.

"The prisoner is under quarantine."

"Excuse me?" The wolf snarled angrily in her belly, snapping its jaws, green eyes flashing for a moment as fear gripped her insides. "Quarantine for what?" There were only so many reasons why a prisoner would be on quarantine, and Jericho liked none of them. Soliel could be hurt, or sick, or he'd gotten himself into trouble somehow.

"All access to prisoner Tsuki is restricted," the android repeated mechanically. "The prisoner is under quarantine."

"I got that, but what the fuck for?" Jericho asked through clenched teeth, screwing her eyes shut in an attempt to maintain what little patience she had left.

"All access to the priso—"

"I fucking heard you the first two times, you moronic bucket of bolts! *Why* is he in quarantine?!" Jericho shouted, grabbing ahold of the cold metal arm still keeping her from Sol.

"All access to—"

There was no thinking, only rage. It gripped Jericho in its fist, and before she could think better of it, her arms shifted to the powerful limbs of the wolf. Razor sharp claws ripped at the front of the bot, exposing a chest full of wires and hardware. And then an arm was wrapped tightly around Jericho's neck, applying enough pressure to pull her back but not enough to cut off her airways.

"Get ahold of yourself, J," an all too familiar voice murmured against her ear, and Jericho stilled. "That's it, calm down," Ildri soothed, her hand gripping Jericho's shoulder. Jericho took one long breath, then another, and by the time Ildri released her, her arms had returned to their human state.

Jericho's chest was still moving in harsh pants, but already the robot was putting itself back together. Turning wide eyes on Ildri, Jericho lifted her brows in confusion.

"Come with me," was all Ildri said by way of answer, then she turned to head toward the bank of elevators. Jericho climbed in beside her, and they headed down to Ildri's lab.

"What are we—"

Ildri shook her head. "We'll talk once we're in my workshop."

Those words bled into a pregnant silence that made Jericho uneasy. When they arrived, the door to Ildri's workspace shut behind them with the soft whoosh of pressurized air, and Ildri did a quick once-over with some device she'd pulled from her pocket before nodding, seeming pleased with herself.

"Okay, what the fuck was that?" Jericho frowned as Ildri pocketed the device again.

"Had to check for bugs." Ildri moved to drop onto one of the stools along her work bench.

"Bugs?"

"This whole building is kind of one big bug, to be honest. The hold wasn't originally intended to be that way, but as the years wear on, the council has become more and more suspicious of its heroes."

"Right. Of course. That makes perfect sense." Jericho nodded sarcastically. "What the fuck are you on about, Ildri?"

Ildri narrowed her eyes on Jericho, looking incredulous. "I'm on about the fact that this is the only room in the hold where we won't be overheard, you dunce."

Jericho blinked at Ildri for a moment, then shook her head, deciding it was better not to ask. They didn't have time for a history lesson. "You know what's going on with Sol."

"I know what's going on with Sol," Ildri agreed.

"So why the fuck is he in quarantine?"

Ildri looked her over for a moment, and Jericho noticed that Ildri's eyes looked somehow redder and puffier than they had the last time she'd seen her. She also noticed that Ildri seemed to be inspecting her for similar signs of distress. "I need you to promise me you're not going to do something crazy, J."

Jericho frowned, her fists clenching in her jacket pockets. It was bad then. "I'm not going to make promises I can't keep. You know that."

"I do. But I need you to try to restrain yourself this time."

Inhaling deeply, Jericho forced her hands to relax, then nodded. "I'll do my best."

Ildri waited a moment, her own hands twitching in her lap as if trying to clutch at strands she couldn't quite reach. Then she nodded to herself, lips settling into a hard line. "Dusk is scheduled for surgery."

"Surgery? What kind of surgery? Did someone hurt him?

What's wrong? Is he sick? You let me at whoever hurt him, and I'll—"

"Not . . . " Ildri swallowed. "Not that kind of surgery. They want to ensure that he won't be using his Voice on anyone, so they're going to remove his vocal cords."

Jericho's stomach did a sick lurch, threatening to throw up the bowl of cereal she'd had for breakfast. "When?"

"In a couple of days."

"Then . . . Then they'll release him, right?" Jericho's voice rose an octave, though whether it was in hope or fear, she wasn't sure at this point. If they were going to go through that trouble, then maybe they were planning to set Sol free. They just wanted to neutralize him first. But no . . . that didn't make sense. The true danger of a villain like Dusk wasn't in his ability as a banshee, it was his mind. He knew too much and was too damn smart.

"I don't know," Ildri breathed, her shoulders sagging. "They haven't made a ruling yet. They're not letting him stand trial until this is done."

"Then . . . he won't be able to testify for himself," Jericho croaked. "His testimony could be warped."

"He won't. But they really don't care about that. So long as they get the information they need to sweep this whole thing with Pendragon under the rug. He'll probably get a shortened sentence for testifying against Pendragon, but—"

"But by then they'll already have taken his voice from him." Jericho's throat felt raw, the words rasping from her harshly.

"It's not ideal. But I think this is the best solution we could have hoped for," Ildri whispered. "Adelia would be happy to know he won't spend his life in prison, and he could continue with her mi—"

"That's not good enough!" Jericho's hands tore from her

pockets to straighten at her sides, anger writhing inside of her.

"What?"

"I said, that's not good enough." Jericho spun and left the workspace, ignoring calls from Ildri to stop and listen. She didn't stop walking once she had left Ildri's space. No. She grabbed her things from the bullpen and walked out of the hold entirely. And she kept walking. Her steps ate up the blocks between her apartment and the hold, then the stairs— because she couldn't be bothered to wait for the elevator— and then the hall. Jericho was standing in the middle of her apartment before she'd even really processed the decision to go home.

Her feet were rooted to the spot just behind the couch. It felt emptier than she remembered it ever having been—this stupid apartment with the over-stuffed couch Sol had chosen for them—even when there hadn't been furniture to fill it. Merlin, it wasn't even the apartment, Jericho realized belatedly, it was her whole life. There was no one to bicker with while cooking, so she'd gone back to her freezer meals. There were no late-night meetings with annoying foxes and sharp-toothed redcaps. No more harebrained schemes to change the world. Sol had given this back—her old life—and they had both foolishly believed it was what she'd wanted all along.

It wasn't.

Jericho's whole existence—the life she'd been working for since she was sixteen—it was wrong. She had been wrong. And that's why it was so easy to make the choice—if there had ever really been a choice in the first place—to give up everything and save *her* Sol.

"The end of an era," she whispered to the cold, vacant room, eyes skimming over the trash that had been left on the floor as she'd dug through it to find the remote just a handful of hours before.

The turning of a page, she imagined Sol would add, because he always did have to have the last word—the cheeky little shit.

And then Jericho nodded once to herself and headed for her room.

It took less than half an hour to pack everything she deemed necessary into a duffle. Then she was snatching the long katana blades from a vault in the wall, pulling a hood over her head, and leaving her phone on the island in the middle of the kitchen. The second order of business would be finding Fizz, and Maz, and anyone else she could gather around herself to help. The next? Get Sol the fuck out of the hold before they could tear a piece of him out that Jericho would never be able to replace.

But the first? The first order of business had been sending a text to her mother.

Colette 5:47PM: I'm going off on a business trip

This number won't be available where I'm going, but I'll be in touch

I love you

And for the first time in a long time, she thought she actually meant it.

CHAPTER TWENTY-TWO

FINDING FIZZ HAD BEEN EASY ENOUGH. JERICHO HAD BEEN worried that he'd have closed down the soup kitchen but hoped that even with everything going on, the redcap wouldn't have it in him. Which meant that Jericho was able to walk through the front door and into the jam-packed cafeteria where Fizz was spooning out healthy portions of vegetables without any trouble. The door swung behind her, knocking against the frame lightly, and Fizz looked up from his work. A scowl tugged at the man's lips, and his eyes narrowed on Jericho in question.

Jericho just shrugged, then moved through the bustling room to the back wall lined in tables of food.

"How can I help?" she asked, setting down her duffle and nudging it beneath the table with her toe.

Fizz grunted but didn't argue. "You can man the potatoes again."

Jericho moved to her station and got to work. Her own belly growled in protest, but it was ignored in favor of feeding the slowly shrinking line.

With the whole room fed, Fizz moved to Jericho's side.

"Make yourself a plate and then get your ass back to my office," he muttered on his way to the hall.

Silence enveloped Jericho when the door swung shut behind her. She adjusted the strap of her duffle over her shoulder, walking toward the office where she'd first looked over the files Fizz had been collecting. It felt like it'd been ages ago, but it hadn't been more than a few weeks, had it?

"You've got a lot of balls coming down here." Fizz sighed, slumping down into the chair behind his desk, piled with papers and binders stuffed full of case files.

"I was hungry."

Fizz looked up from where he was trying to reorganize a stack of papers to glare at Jericho. His eyes narrowed dangerously, and if Jericho had been a lesser woman, she might have felt nervous. She was not a lesser woman. "Of course you were."

Jericho set her plate down on a binder and carefully moved a stack of empty folders from a chair to settle into it. "Has Pickle been in touch?"

"I know about Dusk," was Fizz's only answer. The tiredness Jericho had heard over the phone seeped into his shoulders to make them sag as he leaned back in his chair again.

"Then you know we have to do something about it," Jericho insisted, her hands clenching around the plate of untouched food. "We have to get him out of there."

Fizz's hands lifted to rub circles into his temples. "That's not really an option at this point. We were given specific orders from Dusk not to attempt a rescue mission. He was worried about the position it would put you in."

"And what position would it put me in?"

"He thought it would force you to turn on the heroes, he didn't want that. He wanted—"

"Too late for that," Jericho said, leaning forward in her

chair to brace herself on her knees. "I walked out today, and I'm not going back there. I can't."

"What?" Fizz asked weakly, looking up from his lap. "You have to go back."

"I don't *have* to do anything. I can't do any good there, not any real good. You don't need me feeding you information, not with Pickle embedded there. I'll be more beneficial to you on the outside." Panic gripped Jericho's heart, making her feel for the first time like she wasn't just arguing a point but actively pleading for her life. Maybe she was. Maybe there was no life for her outside of Sol and his organization. Maybe if she walked out of there tonight and went back to the Alliance, it would be all over for her. She'd be nothing more than a shell of the person she'd been before. She didn't plan on finding out.

Fizz's eyes flicked over her, his brow bunched in thought. "How?"

"What do you mean, *how?*"

"I mean, how will you be beneficial to us on the outside? State your case. Tell me why we should bring you into the fold and risk our lives for whatever fucked-up plan you've got in your head." Fizz pressed his fingertips together and lifted them to his lips, almost as if in prayer.

"Am I on trial now?"

"Sure. If you want to think of it that way." Fizz continued to sit there, examining Jericho with those sharp eyes.

"I'm strong."

"We have fighters," Fizz said carelessly.

"I'm smart."

"We have a mastermind. Three, actually."

"I have good instincts."

"So does Maz."

Jericho growled, frustration seeping into her shoulders and making them rigid. "I know the inner workings of the—"

"That's what we have Pickle for," Fizz cut her off. "Why do we need *you* specifically? What do you bring to the table?" Fizz insisted, a small smile tugging at the corners of his lips as if he knew a secret Jericho didn't. Fuck it, there were probably plenty of secrets Fizz knew that Jericho could never hope to discover. The man was a vault, and he was far smarter than he let on. He'd have made one hell of a councilman if he weren't Unseelie. "Why *you*, Colette Jericho?"

Jericho breathed—inhaling deeply through her nose and then exhaling through her lips. "I love him." Jericho hadn't been able to put words to her feelings for Sol outside of "please don't go" and "we're a team" before, but there it was. Plain and simple. "I'll do anything to protect him. He's the hero Mythikos needs, not me."

"And what are you?"

"I'm just the hero he needs," Jericho finished, her heart clenching at the words. It was true. All she could hope to do for Mythikos was save Sol. And she planned to do that, with or without Fizz's help.

This seemed to convince Fizz, who nodded in agreement. "All right then, we need to get the crew together."

"Did Pickle say how long we have?"

"Forty-eight hours." Fizz pulled a phone from his pocket and began typing away at it. "You should eat and get some rest. This is going to be a long couple of days."

"I can't rest." She'd tried. She'd tried so hard. She was tired, but no amount of exhaustion seemed to help her sleep.

"You have to. You look like shit, and we're going to need everyone at their best if we're attacking the Alliance. Go down the hall. Second door on your left, you'll find a room with cots. We haven't been an active homeless shelter for a few years, but we keep them in case the weather turns and the shelter a few blocks over is full." Fizz stood from his desk. "The others won't be able to meet with us till morning anyway, so you should get some sleep."

"But—"

Fizz moved to her, resting a hand on Jericho's shoulder and giving it a gentle squeeze. "Look, if you're going to fight for his life, we need you fighting fit. You won't be any good to anyone sleep deprived. Go. Sleep. I'll come get you when the others arrive."

Jericho nodded wordlessly and rose from her chair. Once in the empty room, she wolfed down the now cold food and curled up on her side on the cot. It was easier to fall asleep than she'd have thought it would be in that room surrounded by empty beds and deafening silence. Maybe it was the tension that had leaked from her body because they finally —*finally*—had a plan. She slept soundly for the first time in days.

●

WHEN SHE AWOKE, it was to the gentle shaking of her shoulder from someone crouching beside her. Green eyes opened to meet the luminescent golden ones of a young chimera boy, his thin horns casting heavy shadows onto Jericho's face in the harsh overhead light.

"Mister Jericho, sir," the boy stuttered through trembling lips.

"Miss," Jericho corrected gently.

"Miss Jericho, ma'am," the boy nodded. "Mister Fizz says it's time."

Jericho nodded, sitting up abruptly enough to scare the boy and send him reeling onto his backside. "Sorry," Jericho grunted. She pressed her boots to the floor to stand.

"It's—" The boy swallowed hard. He pushed himself to his hooves and dusted off the back of his pants. "It's all right.

Mister Fizz and the others are in the rec room. I'll take you there."

"Thanks." Jericho gestured and followed when the boy whirled around to head back out into the hall. "What's your name, kid?"

"Not important."

"Sure it is." Jericho frowned.

"Mister Fizz says I shouldn't tell strangers my name," he whispered, hands fidgeting at the end of his too-long belt.

"Right," Jericho grunted. "Mister Fizz is super smart."

"He is!" The boy beamed up at her, bright as the sun, showing off a row of pointed teeth. "Mister Fizz says that you're a hero."

Jericho shrugged, running a hand through tangled blond hair to try to brush out the worst of the knots. She'd need to braid it to get it out of her fucking face for later. "Used to be."

"Used to be?" The boy's smile faltered. "What are you now?"

"I don't really know anymore," Jericho whispered, more to herself than to the child beside her.

The boy opened his mouth as if to say something else but was cut off by the sound of shouting from a room at the end of the corridor.

"He can't be trusted!" It sounded like Maz was shrieking at the top of her lungs.

"You need to calm down, Maz." Ildri's voice sounded tinny, like it was coming through a speaker instead of directly from the room itself.

"I will not calm down. That wolf is—"

"Is what?" Jericho asked, pushing the door open to greet the others. In spite of the small organization that Sol had introduced her to, this room was full. There were at least twenty-five people crowded around a tablet someone had propped in a chair so Ildri could face everyone in the room from where she sat behind her screen in a dark room some-where. Was this even all of them? How large was Sol's group?

"A traitor," Maz growled, bearing sharp fangs.

"Is that so?" Jericho tilted her head, her expression impassive. Maz wasn't the only one looking at her with obvious distrust, but she did her best to shake it off. These were Sol's people. If she wanted to save Sol, she'd work with them. And getting into a shouting match with Maz wasn't going win her any brownie points. Jericho had to stay calm.

"Even Dusk didn't trust the wolf. *He's* why Dusk is in the mess he's in right now. Why should we trust him to help us?" She hissed, still displaying a truly impressive amount of fang for a woman of such small stature.

"Her," Jericho corrected calmly.

"Whatever."

"I trust her," a soft, sleepy voice insisted. The crowd parted to let a girl with gray skin shuffle through toward Jericho. "If it weren't for her, I'd still be in the hold." The ghoul smiled at Jericho, showing off a row of yellow teeth.

"Ciarra?" Jericho asked, her eyes flicking toward Fizz, who nodded with a warm smile. "How did you get her out?"

"Pendragon isn't the only one who has friends in high places." Fizz tapped the side of his nose with a wink.

Ciarra smiled more, pressing a fist to Jericho's shoulder to knock against it lightly. "Thanks."

"You're welcome." Jericho's voice felt a little choked and hoarse, so she cleared her throat.

"Enough of the dramatics," Ildri said from the tablet, sounding very much like a schoolteacher trying to wrangle a class of wayward kindergartners. "We don't have time to get sentimental. You said you had more information, Ciarra?"

Ciarra nodded, turning to look at the screen-bound Ildri, her arms wrapping around her middle. "I overheard some of the guards while they were escorting me out. They don't plan to let Dusk make it to the hospital at all."

Those words were sandpaper, rubbing Jericho's throat raw. "What?"

"The plan is to kill him in transit and make it look like he tried to escape," Ciarra continued. "That way, he'll never have time to testify against Pendragon, and they can get the councilman off on a technicality."

"And then they'll just pretend the video never happened," Maz seethed, her body trembling with rage.

"They've already removed all traces of it," someone that Jericho couldn't see supplied from farther back in the group. "They'll just cover it up, or ignore it and move on."

"Will that work?"

"It's what I would do," the person answered. "In PR, sometimes the best response is to pretend nothing happened. People have short memories."

Jericho was still focused on what Ciarra had said, the words repeating in her head on loop. *The plan is to kill him in transit. Kill him in transit. Kill him.* An ache had settled into her chest the night Sol left, but hearing those words echoing over and over, that ache turned into a sharp point of pain, like a knife slipping in past her armor. Merlin, it hurt. She felt it squeezing at her lungs, threatening to cut off her air entirely.

"What's the plan?" someone else asked, and every set of eyes in the room turned to Jericho expectantly.

"What?" Jericho squawked, drawn out of her spiraling thoughts by the words.

"Fizz says you showed up on our doorstep like some kind of avenging angel. Don't tell me you came here without a plan!" Maz's tone was frustrated, and heat had begun to cling to her cheeks in an ugly, blotchy way that could only be from slowly simmering fury.

"Oh. I—" Jericho started, swallowing roughly.

"You did come here with a plan, didn't you?"

"Of course she did!" the boy at Jericho's side said defensively. "Of course she has a plan."

Maz quirked a brow, her head tilting to the side in question, and for a heartbeat too long, the room was silent, each of them waiting for Jericho and her wonderful plan.

With a deep inhale through her nose, Jericho closed her eyes and thought quickly. She opened her eyes on the exhale and smiled. "They're already planning to make the transfer as chaotic as possible so it'll look like he escaped, right?"

A collective nod passed through the group.

"They probably plan to let him out of the vehicle to make it look like he was actually running. That will be our best chance." Jericho nodded to herself, a grin creeping up her face. She hadn't come with a plan, but one was quickly forming. This could work. "We can use their own plan against them and strike when they're least expecting it."

"Right before they pull the trigger," Fizz agreed, a sharp smile lighting his own face.

"Exactly. Their guard will be down." Jericho felt a near hysterical chuckle rise up her throat. "It'll be easy."

"Shouldn't take more than a handful of people to execute an extraction," Ciarra supplied.

"We just need to track the vehicle's progress." Jericho nodded, turning to Ildri. "Do you think you can do that?"

"We'll need to be able to hear inside too," Ildri added, already typing furiously on a keyboard. "So we know when they'll strike."

"I can map out the route they'll use. I've done a couple of those transports." A lightness had settled into Jericho's chest. This was it. They were going to get Sol back.

"Can you hack into the comm lines?" Maz asked, already

moving to dig through a pile of papers on a table near the wall.

"I won't even have to hack into them." Ildri snorted. "I already have access to those lines. Patching it through to your comms will be the tricky part."

"And you can do that?" Jericho's tone was perhaps a little too eager, her hands trembling, for the first time in weeks, from excitement instead of anger or fear.

Ildri laughed, throwing her head back. "Does a centaur shit in the woods?"

"Hey!" someone grumbled.

"Sorry, Phil." Ildri was still snorting back a chuckle though. "The answer is yes, I can. You still have the set of comms I gave you for our last mission, Fizz?"

Fizz nodded.

"Good. I'll get that set up. J, you draw out the map. Let's get moving, people. His transfer to the hospital is scheduled in less than forty-eight hours, and we don't have all sorts of time to dilly around." Ildri was all business now, her fingers flying over the unseen keyboard as she worked, eyes focused.

"Once I've got it drawn out, we should send a group out to scout the route and see where they might pull off to make their move." Jericho took a map and marker from Maz. She uncapped the marker with her teeth and began tracing the route with practiced ease. "We should set up people at those spots, just in case we lose the comms," she mumbled around the cap in her mouth.

"I need a team of two to scout the route. Who's up for a walk?" Fizz turned to the gathered group.

Hands shot up all over the room, and Fizz was left to pick those he thought would be most proficient at assessing the path and finding what they needed.

Jericho held the map up so Ildri could see it. "Get this sent to their phones and make it so they can drop pins on the places they think we need people set up."

Ildri nodded. A map appeared on the screen to replace her face, then a thick red line traced the route Jericho had sketched out from the hold to the hospital. "Is that right?"

"Perfect." Jericho nodded.

"Sent." There was a soft chime from the phones of the team Fizz was prepping.

"What should they be looking for?" Fizz asked, calling Jericho over to their little trio. The two who had volunteered were a pair of imps with red skin stretched over the wings fluttering behind them. Their eyes were sharp with intelligence, and Jericho felt herself smiling.

"They'll want places that are private and that won't echo the sound out onto the streets to passersby. Alleys are good, but not all alleys will be suitable, especially those with exits to businesses or more than one way out to the main road. Look for something with a dead end, and if it abuts an abandoned building, that's all the better. You got it?"

They nodded, then left without a word.

"In the meantime, we're going to need a team of at least four to take down the transport van. Do we have a vehicle that can follow them without being suspicious?" Jericho turned back to the room as a whole.

"I drive an ice cream truck," a young woman spoke up. "We could use that."

"And that won't be suspicious following them?" Maz asked, her tone sarcastic.

"I drive that route all the time." She shrugged. "The place where I park the truck is a few streets down from the hold, and it's not unusual for me to take the truck by the hospital to give ice cream to the kids."

"That's perfect then." Jericho's shoulders relaxed a little. "I just need a team."

Hands shot up again all around the room, and Jericho felt herself growing eager for the fight ahead. This would work. They would save Sol. And she didn't have to do it alone.

"Anyone who I don't choose to ride with me will need to break off into teams of two to stake out the potential pull-off places. I hope you're all ready for this."

•

IN THE END, the team she'd chosen consisted of herself, Maz, a wraith named Rachel, and a kelpie that went by Dominic. Fizz led them back to a room deep within the building, and the light flickered on to reveal rows of weaponry.

"Great Merlin," Jericho hissed, her eyes flicking over the small armory. "We aren't going to fucking war, Fizz."

"Not yet." Fizz shook his head, and they turned to watch as the small group examined the glass cases on the walls to select what they wanted for the mission. "Nothing you've never trained with before," Fizz chided, cutting Maz a knowing look.

"Where the fuck did you get all of this? I thought Unseelie weren't allowed to own weapons." Jericho's fingers ran slowly over the cool glass of a case containing a row of well-polished daggers.

"I'm a hobbyist," Fizz answered with a secretive smile.

"Right. Hobbyist." Jericho lifted the heavy lid of the case. Her fingers ran reverently over the hilt of a short blade. It'd be the perfect size to tuck into her boot, just in case, so she snatched it up.

"Well. I don't own any ammunition," Fizz said in his defense. "That's the rule: as a hobbyist, I can own and maintain them, but I can't own ammunition. So. No guns." He cut Maz another look as she spun a revolver on her finger like a cowgirl from the Wild West. With a sheepish grin, she put it back in its case.

"I should have just brought my own." Maz sulked a little, her fingers still tracing the smooth handle of the gun before Fizz moved to snap the lid shut nearly on her hands. She shot him a glare, snarling.

"No guns. We're more likely to hurt each other if we have guns," Jericho said. She stuck the dagger down into her boot to the hilt, nodding to herself. "Besides, last time you used a gun, you shot me."

"It was only a graze, you big baby."

"Jericho's right," Fizz cut in, silencing any further arguments. "We can't take the chance that you'll accidentally hurt yourself or someone on your team."

"I'm a trained marksman," Maz grumbled under her breath. "That's why Dusk brought me on."

Fizz eyed her, and she deflated, crossing her arms over her chest with a little pout.

"What time is the transfer?" Rachel asked, breaking the tension between the trio.

"They're going right after lunch." Fizz turned back to watch the others choose their weapons. "Ildri thinks they chose that time because the traffic will be light."

"Less witnesses." Dominic nodded in agreement.

"Right, so we've got—" Jericho reached to pull her phone from her pocket to check the time, then huffed a little when she remembered that she'd left it in her apartment. "What time is it?"

"Two o'clock," Rachel supplied.

"Nine hours, give or take." Jericho nodded her thanks. "Everyone should get some rest in the meantime. It's been a long day of planning, and I don't need any of us too tired to fight."

The group nodded and disbanded to go to the room lined

with cots. Before Jericho could follow them, Fizz took her wrist.

"Let's get you a new phone," he said softly.

"What?" Jericho frowned.

"If you all get separated, I want you to have another mode of contact in case the comms go out. I'm not taking any chances with anyone else from our organization," Fizz explained, but Jericho could hear what he wasn't saying too: *I don't want to lose anyone else.* He led the way to another room much like Dusk's lab, full of tables and electronics. He pulled a phone from one of the tables and held it out to Jericho.

"What? So now you're worried about if I'll make it back or not?" Jericho teased, tucking the device into her back pocket.

"You're one of the team, of course I am. Go get some sleep."

Jericho swallowed around a lump in her throat, blinking back the burning of tears in her eyes, and turned on her heel before Fizz could see what those words had done to her.

CHAPTER TWENTY-THREE

SLEEP ELUDED JERICHO. SHE DRIFTED IN AND OUT OF ITS WARM embrace, glaring at the dark wall of the shelter as she listened to Rachel snore loudly on a cot behind her. Everyone around her seemed to be sleeping, but she wondered how many of them were just lying still with their eyes blinking into the darkness like her. Maybe all of them— except Rachel—or maybe none of them. She wasn't sure, and she was too afraid to ask lest she wake someone. So instead, she let herself drift in and out of memories of the last few weeks. Of the warmth Sol had brought back into her life. Squeezing her eyes shut, she forced herself to see Sol smiling, expression open and happy, not hard as it'd been in the video.

She must have drifted off to that image finally because what felt like seconds later, the lights were being turned on, and everyone was grumbling awake. Jericho sat up on her cot, stretching, and then stuffed her feet into her boots again.

"Where's the rendezvous point?" Jericho asked, shoving a comm into her ear and strapping the katana to her back while the others around her finished getting ready.

"Pickle will give that to you after the fact," Fizz answered. "We don't want it falling into the wrong hands. If your comm is out, she'll send it to the phone. If your phone is out . . . "

"Then you're out of fucking luck." Maz laughed, slinging her arm over Jericho's shoulders in a mockery of a friendly embrace. "And wouldn't that just be a shame?"

"Maz." Fizz shot her a warning glare.

"We want everyone back safe." Maz said the words like she was reciting a rule set by a school principal. "Yeah, I know. Even the traitor." She rolled her eyes and gave Jericho a hard shove. "Come on, let's get this shit over with."

"Remind me why I picked her to go with me?" Jericho mumbled to Fizz, who just offered her a shrug in response.

"We'll need to take the bus to the lot where I park the truck." Rachel yawned into the back of her hand. How she could still be tired, Jericho didn't know. Jericho was wired. The hum of what they were about to do buzzed under her skin like electricity, muscles jolting and jerking as they readied for action.

"What about the teams along the way?" Jericho led them down the hall with Fizz at her side.

"They're already in place. They've been out for an hour. We didn't want to take the chance that they wouldn't be ready." Fizz scrolled through his phone, humming thoughtfully.

Jericho nodded. "Does Pickle already have us tapped in?"

"She does. She's just waiting until you're in the truck to turn it on. We're about an hour out from takeoff, so you should get moving." Fizz smiled at them with his sharp teeth and moved to give them each a tight hug. "Good luck, all of you."

"We don't need luck," Jericho and Maz snorted at the same time. They both turned to glare at one another, and Fizz choked out a loud laugh.

"You're adorable. All right, go get our boy back." He clapped them on the shoulder, then shoved them out the door.

The air outside was already stiff with humidity, and Jericho gritted her teeth at the trickle of sweat crawling down her back.

"Wish we could just take a cab," Dominic groaned. His black hair was dripping, but whether it was from the sweat of hiking to the bus stop or just due to his kelpie nature, Jericho couldn't tell.

"We can't take the chance of being traced," Maz said, tone surprisingly reasonable.

They fell into a small huddle as they waited for the bus. It arrived a few minutes later, and they loaded up, all sitting in separate seats in an attempt to distance themselves from what was about to happen. The minutes dragged and sped in fits and starts as the bus made its stops before finally pulling up a block from the lot where the truck was. Then they were loaded into the back. Cold bit at Jericho's sweat-soaked neck, but she didn't say anything.

Rachel typed in the address for the hospital, and the truck got to work.

"You'll need to put it on manual for the getaway." Maz leaned cross-legged against a freezer full of ice cream bars.

Rachel let out a soft eep, her hands gripping the useless steering wheel hard enough to turn her knuckles white.

"Don't worry." Jericho kept her voice low and soothing, smelling the panic coming off the wraith in waves. "I know how to drive."

Rachel nodded mutely, relaxing into her seat.

The black transport van came into view just as they pulled out onto the main road, and Ildri's voice drifted into their ears. "All right, folks, here we go. I'm patching you through to their comms now. You'll be able to hear them, but they won't be able to hear you. *I* will be able to hear you though, so if anything goes wrong and you need an out, I'm here for you."

"Thanks, Pickle." Relief settled into Dominic's shoulders.

"Any time, kiddo," Ildri chirped, and then there was a soft crackling as she patched through the comms of the men in the van.

"I can't believe I drew the short straw on this," a voice whined into their ears. "These are new shoes, and now they're going to get all—"

The voice was cut off by the soft thump of a skin hitting skin, and Jericho could only assume one of his comrades had smacked him.

"Shut up, you idiot," someone hissed, probably the person who'd hit him.

"What? Like he doesn't know. You know, don't you?" the first voice asked, directing the question at someone else in the van.

"That you're going to kill me?" Sol's voice—distant because he wasn't on the comm system, but Jericho would know it anywhere—responded with a note of idle boredom. "I'm not stupid."

"See, he kn—"

"For the record though," Sol interrupted, and Jericho could hear the smirk in his tone. "Those shoes are fucking ugly as sin, and it'd be my pleasure to ruin them with my blood."

"Why, you little—!" The man's shouts were followed by the sounds of a struggle. Jericho held her breath, half afraid that they'd be too late by the time the idiots decided to pull over.

"No, Elijah. Not yet," the calmer man hissed again. "You'll get your chance. But it's got to look like an escape attempt. If you beat the living shit out of him right here in the van, it'll look suspicious."

"Yeah, Elijah. Down boy," Sol snarked. "Don't want to ruin Pendragon's efforts to make himself look good again."

"I'm going to fuck you up so bad," Elijah threatened.

"I look forward to it, sweetheart."

Jericho gritted her teeth, gnawing on the tender skin on the inside of her cheek hard enough to make it bleed. "Don't instigate shit, you fucking idiot."

"He'll be okay, J. He's got this," Ildri soothed through her earpiece.

"Does he know we're coming?" Rachel asked.

"No. But I'm sure he expects something." Ildri sounded more cheerful than she probably should have, but it eased something in Jericho. If Ildri thought this was all going to be all right, then it would be.

"He knows I wouldn't let it end like this," Jericho whispered, wiping sweaty palms on her jeans.

"Exactly."

The harsh sound of skin on skin drew their attention back to the conversation coming from the van.

"Is that the best you got? My grandma hits harder than that." Sol cackled.

"You Unseelie piece of shit," Elijah rasped through what sounded like clenched teeth. "Keep talking."

"Why? Are we almost to my stop? I can't imagine it's much farther. The hospital is, what? Five miles from the hold? We're about three from it, I'd say, though without windows, it's obviously tough to tell. That makes us about two miles from the hospital, right? So yeah, murder time, she comes." His tone was light, playful. Like he was purposefully trying to rile them up. Maybe he was. Maybe he thought if he did, then they'd be easier to take down. That they'd make a mistake. "And you lovely gentlemen. All, what, five of you?"

"Five," Jericho repeated, lips curling back into a feral smile that was all sharp canines. Sol was giving them information, even if he couldn't be sure they were coming. Even if he didn't know they could hear. He was planning. *Sneaky bastard*, Jericho thought fondly.

"Is it just going to be me and Elijah duking it out, man-to-man?"

"Up ahead. Take this right," another voice said.

"What? This isn't the designated spot. I'd have to take manual con—" another argued.

"Just do it," the voice ordered.

The van in front of them swerved down a side street, and Jericho leaped forward, leaning over Rachel to jerk the wheel from her hands. "We've got to get back to them. Pickle, give me a route."

"Won't it look suspic—" Dominic started to argue.

"Pickle! A route!" Jericho shut Dominic up with a wave of her hand, already in control of the vehicle and speeding through traffic to try to find a turn that would take them back.

"Working on it." Jericho could hear Ildri's fingers flying furiously over the keyboard. "I need to change some lights to get you there quicker."

"Faster, Pickle! We don't have any people at that spot!" Maz shouted, leaning against Jericho's back as she looked out the front window at the traffic steadily backing up.

"Get out of the van," Elijah growled through the comms.

"How about I don't and say I didn't?" Sol laughed softly, but Jericho could hear a touch of fear in it now. "If I don't get out of the van and run, then you don't have an excuse to attack me, right? Isn't that how it works?"

"Get out of the van, or we'll make you get out of the van," someone else said.

"You know, there are five of you and one of me. This is

going to look suspicious any way you slice it, boys. It's going to be pretty clear this was a hit." Sol was stalling. Jericho could hear panic creeping into his voice. He knew something was wrong. He knew that they were coming for him, and this sudden detour had put a wrench in things. There was a muffled thump, and Jericho heard Sol grunt in pain. "Fuck. Okay. Okay. I'm getting out."

"Pickle! Faster!" Terror gripped Jericho, and she was two seconds away from turning around and heading back the wrong way down the street.

"Okay, got it. Take the next right. They're inside of an abandoned warehouse two blocks back. I've got a route coming your way. Check the nav." Ildri's voice was breathless, but she was still typing hard on her keyboard. The route appeared a moment later on the little screen on the dash. "And . . . there, all green from here to there."

Jericho swerved down the street, slamming Maz into Rachel, but no one complained.

"So, how are we gonna do this, boys? Are we going to make it look like a fight? Shouldn't you uncuff me if that's how we're playing it?" Sol's voice had risen another octave, and where the mania had been false before, Jericho could hear hysteria now. Fear had gripped him, and Jericho felt it too. What if they were too late?

"The fuck we're going to give you a fighting chance," Elijah snorted.

"No. Actually, that's a good idea," a new voice said, one Jericho recognized all too well. Erling. "We can say he got out of his restraints." The lie was smooth. A moment later, Jericho heard the soft clank of iron hitting the ground as Sol was unchained. "And then he took control of the vehicle before bringing us here. Held Fennella at gunpoint. Sadly, he shot Fennella before climbing out of the van."

A crack sounded through the comms, and Jericho's hands

clenched tighter around the wheel in her grip. Cold seeped into her very bones. Erling had lost his fucking mind, and he had Dusk right where he wanted him.

"You just—! You just killed her!" Sol let out a soft sob.

"No. *You* killed her," Erling corrected, still eerily calm. "But then, Elijah here got the gun away from you." Jericho heard it skitter across the cement.

"Pickle, how far?" Jericho hissed.

"It's right up ahead." Ildri's voice sounded panicked. "You have to get there, J. Oh, Merlin. You have to get there."

"I'm not going to let anything happen to him, Ildri," Jericho promised.

"You . . . You don't make promises you can't keep." Ildri stumbled over the words.

"No. I don't."

"Sadly, you stabbed him," Erling continued.

"Wh—" Elijah started, but the sound was cut off by a pained yell.

"You're hurting your own men!" Sol whimpered.

"No. *You* are. You've been hurting everyone, Dusk. Your mother. Jericho."

Sol inhaled sharply, a choked sound. Jericho could hear the tears cutting off his airway.

"Here, this is yours," Erling said calmly.

"It's . . . I don't use knives."

"Well, you better start. Because I've got one too, and if you don't come at me, I'm going to kill you right here, right now." Erling laughed.

"What's the best way in?" Jericho asked, slamming the ice cream truck to a stop outside of the building.

"There's a side entrance, it should be unlocked. If not, you may have to force it. It's not on an electrical grid." Ildri's voice had gone rushed in Jericho's ears. Like she felt if she didn't get the words out quick enough, she'd be the one killing Sol.

"No problem." Jericho leaped from the vehicle, not bothering to see if anyone followed her. She heard them behind her, feet slapping hard on the pavement. Sol and Erling had gone eerily quiet, but she tried not to think about that. The side door was at the front of a dingy alley. Jericho clutched the knob and pushed. It didn't open.

Erling laughed again, high and cold, the sound hissing through a clenched jaw. "You got me once, and maybe you'll even be able to take me down. But will you be able to take down the rest of us?" There was the slam of one body against another, followed by something clattering against the cement, then a soft yelp. "I've got you now."

Jericho slammed her shoulder into the door, but it didn't budge. She tried again, feeling the force bruise her skin and the muscle beneath. And then a heart-stopping scream shot through the comms, loud enough to leave all of their ears ringing. Something snapped within Jericho, and the wolf roared to life, slamming its body against the door. The shift had been instantaneous; she hadn't even noticed it happening until the lock on the other side clattered to the ground loudly. Her katana fell into the alley behind her. Jericho growled loud and low in her throat, the blond fur along her hackles rising in fury. The door banged against the wall, loud enough to stop everyone in their tracks for one suffocating moment.

There in the center of the wide-open room was the van, two bodies bleeding out, and Erling on top of Sol, a knife gripped in his hand, trailing blood down Sol's throat.

"You'll never scream again," Erling hissed through his teeth as he dragged the point of the blade down the front of Sol's neck, scraping over the soft tissue beneath. "Don't move, Jericho, or I'll finish the job!"

"Let him go," Jericho rumbled, pacing forward.

Sol hissed as the point of the knife was driven farther into his throat, enough to draw a gush of crimson. The other two guards were just watching with morbid fascination, their weapons forgotten at their sides.

"Lettie," Sol gurgled, sounding like he was choking on the words, and the air, and the blood staining his shirt. The sound forced the point further into his skin.

"Get the others. Erling is mine," Jericho hissed to the team behind her. Not bothering to look for their confirmation, Jericho lunged for Erling, dragging him off of Sol, who whimpered in pain. "I thought you were one of the good ones." She slammed the griffin onto the ground.

"My sentiments exactly," Erling laughed. He lashed out with the blade, slashing at Jericho's furry cheek. "But you just couldn't keep it in your pants, could you?"

Jericho snarled, jaws snapping as she went for Erling's throat, only to be blocked by an arm. Her teeth dug into the skin hard enough to snap the bone, and Erling screamed.

"Jericho, we gotta go!" Dominic shouted over the fight. "Dusk is—"

Jericho turned to see what Dusk was and found more red —too much red—staining the front of Sol's shirt, turning the bright orange into a burnt crimson color that made her insides feel like ice.

"Sol," she whined.

Erling took his opening and slammed the knife into Jericho's gut. Pain bloomed red and hot; Jericho whimpered. Her eyes jerked back to the man beneath her, and with a snarl, she slammed her fur covered head into Erling's. A crack of skull on cement, wet and final, filled the near-silent warehouse. Blood quickly began to pool beneath them, Jericho's and Erling's mixing together.

"We have to go," Jericho rasped through the pain, pushing herself to her paws.

Maz and Rachel, who had dispatched the other guards, were lifting Sol between them as he pressed one hand to his still-bleeding throat. It wasn't doing much to stem the flow, and they left small puddles in their wake as they hobbled for the door.

"We're going to get you back to the healer, she'll get you all stitched up," Rachel said soothingly.

Jericho wobbled, fighting the pain to follow them. Dominic looked between the two women and Jericho, and then started toward her.

"No. Leave her," Maz ordered over her shoulder. "Dusk is our priority. If she can't get back on her own, that's her problem."

Jericho whimpered, the wolf shifting away to leave a shivering human in its wake. She reached down to grasp the dagger and pulled it from her stomach with a soft hiss. She squeezed her eyes shut to keep from looking at the gap where it'd cut through her shirt and into her stomach.

"Maz, she's a part of the team." Dominic was still making his way over to Jericho.

"She's not a part of my team!" Maz hissed.

"You'll leave her here to d—" the argument was cut off by the sound of one of the guards groaning.

"You piece of shit," Elijah snarled. His hands shook as he lifted the gun Erling had dropped. He pointed it and fired before any of them could stop him. Jericho roared, the wolf taking hold briefly as she stumbled, then leaped in front of the bullet, letting it bury itself into her flank instead of Sol's back. Then she whirled on the man, adrenaline doing what she couldn't alone, and with one slash of sharp claws, ended his life.

The threat dispatched, the shift faded again, leaving

Jericho trembling as her eyes looked down at the new and growing red patch on her jean-clad hip.

"Fuuuuuck." She forced herself to her feet again.

"Pick her up," Maz ordered softly. "We've got to get back to the rendezvous point. Pickle, we need all green and a medic waiting for us."

"Aye, aye." Ildri's voice sounded strained through the comms, harsh, like she was barely repressing a scream. But Jericho didn't have time to worry about that. Her vision was going fuzzy around the edges. "I'll patch you over to Otto. He can help assess the wounded and give enough first aid to keep them conscious."

Conscious. Jericho didn't think she wanted to be that anymore.

Dominic moved to Jericho's uninjured side, lifting her arm over his broad shoulders and helping her to the door.

"Come on, J." Dominic kept his voice soft and soothing. "Let's get you patched up."

Jericho grunted her agreement.

CHAPTER TWENTY-FOUR

THE TRIP BACK TO THE TRUCK WAS COLORED IN MORE PAIN than Jericho had ever experienced in her life.

She ground her teeth as the truck hummed along.

"What have we got?" the man Jericho assumed was Otto asked.

"Dusk has a thin laceration from sternum to chin. It wasn't too bad until the knife was torn away, making the bottom of it much deeper. He's lost a lot of blood." Maz's voice was calm, probably calmer than Jericho had ever heard it. But Jericho didn't really have the mental capacity to fully appreciate that. "It's a pretty clean cut. Jericho has a gunshot wound on her right hip and a deep knife wound in her stomach. Do you think he hit any organs, Jericho?"

"Fuck if I know. Not exactly going to go poking around to find out!" Jericho pressed the heel of her hand to the wound, hoping to stem the flow of blood.

"Hmmm," Otto hummed almost indifferently. Jericho didn't think she liked this fucker very much. "How far out are you?"

"Five minutes if they don't hit any reds," Ildri supplied.

"Five minutes?!" Jericho tried to shout, but it came out a little strangled. She sat up, but the pain and the blood loss quickly made her think better of that, and she lay back down on the blessedly cold floor of the ice cream truck. Merlin, she was hot. Why was she so hot?

"We're going to Ilygroth, it's a bit of a hike," Rachel said, her hands gripping the wheel even harder, as if she could make the truck move faster by sheer force of will. She couldn't. Self-driving cars had speed caps on them. Even if she did take manual control, the vehicle wouldn't go above a certain speed.

"Isn't there any place closer?" Jericho croaked.

"Look, I'm doing the best that—"

"Arguing isn't helping." Maz growled, her hands shaking as she held a towel she'd found in the back of the truck to Sol's neck. It was turning red in her hands. "What can I do to stop the bleeding?"

"Sit him up," Otto said. "Keep applying pressure. How much is he losing?"

"I don't know! I don't have a fucking measuring cup here to check."

Otto huffed, and Jericho thought the sound was almost affectionate. "What kind of fae do you have with you?"

"What? How is that fucking relevant?" Jericho asked, her hands clutching the wound on her torso harder. No one had given her a towel, so either it was the only one they had, or Sol was worse off than she was. Considering where he was bleeding from, it was probably the latter.

"Some fae have natural healing agents in their DNA," Otto responded calmly. "What do you have with you?"

"Wraith, kelpie, banshee, werewolf, and kitsune, obviously," Maz said with a hint of a scoff.

"Oh! You have a werewolf! That's perfect!" Jericho thought she heard Otto clap in his excitement. "You just need to have them bite Dusk. That'll help begin the healing process and should slow the bleeding."

"You want me to bite him." Jericho groaned, squeezing her eyes shut when the truck turned a corner and the movement made her stomach twist with nausea.

"Sorry," Rachel whispered.

"That's a stupid idea. It could turn him." Dominic sounded like he was feeling a little sick himself. Who would have thought? A kelpie that didn't like the sight of blood.

"A werewolf can't turn another fae. They can only turn humans. Everyone knows that." Maz forced Sol up to lean against one of the freezers. "I swear, what the fuck do they teach in fae physiology these days?"

"Right?" Jericho muttered her agreement.

"Just help her get her ass over here," Maz snapped

"Where do I need to bite him?" Jericho moved with the help of Dominic toward Sol's limp form.

"As close to the affected area as possible. The neck would probably be the best." Otto's tone had gone clinical. "Is Dusk awake?"

"No. He's been out since we got him into the truck." Maz took hold of Jericho's collar and hauled her a little closer, then readjusted the towel to give Jericho room to work. "I think it's shock."

"That's probably for the best. The pain from the saliva might send his heart into arrest if he were awake."

"What?!" Jericho shouted, wondering how anyone could be so calm when talking about something like that. "I don't want to give him a heart attack!"

"Didn't you hear him, you idiot? If he's already knocked out, he won't even notice. He'll be fine. Just hurry the fuck up." Maz's fingers were stained with blood from Sol's neck now, and Jericho wondered hazily if she'd ever get them clean again, or if Maz's nails would forever be tinted pink. She shook herself, and Dominic helped her sit up.

"Still three minutes out," Rachel called an update.

"He won't make it if you don't," Otto said reasonably.

"No fucking pressure," Jericho hissed under her breath. "You know we're really not supposed to do this when we're not . . ." Jericho let the words drift off, swallowing roughly as she ran her tongue over her blunt human canines. Already, saliva was pooling in her mouth, and soon, the teeth would be sharp like the wolf's. Jericho didn't have time to think about how the wolf seemed to have been wanting this all along and wasn't even fighting this decision. If anything, it was encouraging it, rumbling soft and low in her chest.

"Mated. I know." Otto sighed. "You could bite him somewhere else. Then it wouldn't be a mating bite. But it wouldn't be as effective."

"No. I know." Jericho breathed out. She ran her tongue over her teeth again; they'd grown longer, sharp enough to slice her own tongue, drawing blood. "Irony at its best."

"Huh?" Dominic asked.

"I promised we'd do this one day when we were old enough." Jericho laughed, but the sound was mirthless and pained. "We were going to be partners. In everything." Shaking her head, she took another deep breath, eyes watching the blood continue to darken the towel and coat Maz's fingers. "May as well make it official." She snorted, then ducked her head.

No one said anything. No one asked. But they understood what this meant for Jericho. She was giving up the opportunity to love anyone else. Her wolf would never recognize another person as her mate. There would only ever be Sol. But then—that was it, wasn't it? There only ever *had* been Sol.

Sharp canines cut too easily through the tender skin on

Sol's throat, drawing blood from the new wound in a slow gush that made Jericho feel sick. They retracted a moment later, their work done, and Jericho took a moment to lap slowly at the wound, cleaning it and cutting off the flow of more blood. Then she forced the wolf back down and scooted away. She cleared her throat, ignoring the flush that heated the tips of her ears. Everyone else had looked away, but now their eyes returned to their injured comrades.

"He's going to be fucking livid when he finds out he was asleep for that." Maz shook her head, looking a little amused. Which was . . . fucking weird, given the situation.

"Check the bleeding," Otto ordered.

Maz pulled the towel away and nodded. "It's almost stopped. He should be okay until we get there."

"Good. Because I'm passing the fuck out now." Jericho gritted her teeth and settled onto her back beside Sol's hip.

"Two minutes out," Rachel shouted from the driver's seat. "And you're melting all my ice cream back there!"

Jericho blushed brighter, unsure how she'd lost so much blood and yet could still feel it pooling in her cheeks and neck. "Shut the fuck up. No one asked you."

Everyone laughed, and Jericho joined in, unable to help it.

"How's our other patient?" Otto asked.

"I have a bullet lodged in my fucking hip and a knife wound to my abdomen, but it looks like he missed everything vital. I'm fine, doc, how are you?" Jericho's words slurred as the blood loss began to pull her under. Sol was safe, and she was going to be okay. Nothing else mattered anymore. She felt the wolf curling up and preparing for a contented nap at the knowledge. The pain, which had been like a fire in her gut before, had ebbed to something dull and almost numb now. That probably wasn't good. But the cold floor felt so good on her overheated skin. And it smelled like

Sol here, with his leg right beside her head. Surely a nap wouldn't be so bad.

"Jericho?" she heard someone ask, but the voice was so hazy and far off, she wasn't sure who it was.

"'M okay," she slurred.

"Shit. We're losing her!" someone shouted, panic seeping into their voice. "Rachel, how much longer?"

Jericho didn't hear the answer, and a moment later, everything went dark.

●

WHAT FOLLOWED WAS a blur of pain, too-bright lights, and distorted sounds that Jericho couldn't quite make sense of in her haze. She wanted to fight to stay awake, but every time she tried, the wolf would rumble softly. It would tell her that she'd done well. That she'd saved their mate. That she could rest now. Then she'd be pulled back under.

Whether it was days, hours, or minutes later, Jericho didn't know. But when he woke up, it was to the feeling of a hand carding through his hair, brushing it away from his face.

"There you are," a wrecked voice rumbled softly off to his right. "My Lettie."

Jericho opened his eyes, blinking against the bright light and groaning. But in spite of the pain pounding through his head like dwarves digging for diamonds, he forced himself to look, to see, to drink in Sol sitting there beside his bed. A soft smile was on Sol's face, his freckles standing out even more against the pallor of his normally deep brown skin. A long, tightly wrapped bandage ran the length of his throat, covering what Jericho assumed was a stitched-up knife wound and the already healed werewolf bite. Both would scar.

"You look like shit," Jericho croaked. "Sound like it too."

"You're one to talk," Sol teased, but his voice still had that raspy, ruined sound.

Jericho swallowed, sitting up in the bed, heedless of his stitches. He winced when the skin pulled but refused to let Sol force him back down into the bed. "He fucked up your voice."

Sol shrugged, sadness tinting his smile. "We lost you. Twice. On the table." He swallowed in a way that made the bandage bob.

"How's that relevant?" Jericho asked, all snark, trying to tease the despair out of Sol's dark eyes.

"I thought we were having a contest for who got more messed up in that fight." Sol's lips twitched up into a smile. "If we were, it'd be you."

"Fuck you," Jericho snorted.

"Nah, maybe later. You're still injured."

Jericho laughed, hearty and deep, until it pulled at his stitches and ended in a groan. "Fuck me."

"Again. Later," Sol teased with a soft, reedy chuckle of his own.

They fell into an uncomfortable silence. Sol seemed to be holding something back, and Jericho was biting his lip to keep from apologizing. He wanted to say he was sorry for biting Sol. He wanted to say that it hadn't been his choice. He wanted to explain that it had been their only option. But the truth was, he wasn't sorry, and he'd do it again in a heartbeat. The wolf rumbled low in the back of his mind in agreement.

Sol let out a breath, shaking his head. "I'm not angry with you."

"You should be."

"Why? Because you didn't mean it?" Sol's head had ducked. He was looking down at fidgeting freckled fingers as they played with the end of the clean T-shirt someone had changed him into.

Jericho pressed his lips into a firm line. There was a part of him that wanted to say that he didn't. That he wanted to take it all back and set Sol free, even if he knew he'd always be chained to the other man. He felt anxiety spike through the bond that had been formed by the bite. He hadn't felt it settle into place right away. Maybe because Sol had been unconscious. Or maybe because he'd been delirious from pain himself. He wasn't sure, but he decided it didn't really matter now. What mattered was that the anxiety was not his own; it belonged to Sol.

"If you only did it to save me, I'd understand," Sol was saying, his fingers moving along to the words as he signed them out. He seemed to be having trouble speaking.

"I didn't say that." Jericho reached over to still Sol's trembling fingers and lifted his own to move in motions more confident and smooth than he felt. "I meant it. But I'm sorry it happened the way it did."

Sol looked at him for a long moment, his eyes staring back into Jericho's. Jericho could practically hear the gears turning in his head as he pieced the words together with everything that had happened. Then he nodded. He opened his lips to say something, then he shook his head, perhaps deciding to save his voice, and signed it instead. "I'm sorry it happened that way too. I know you felt pressured to do it, and I wish it could have been . . . " The words trailed off, his fingers stilling as a bright blush stained his freckled cheeks.

"More romantic?" Jericho teased, chuckling softly.

"Yeah," Sol laughed, shaking his head.

"Since when have we ever been romantic?"

"That's fair, I guess." Sol shrugged, his fingers falling still in his lap again. "Do I get to kiss you now?" He croaked out the question.

"I wouldn't suggest it. My mouth tastes like shit."

Sol snorted another laugh, the sound rasping and dry through his ruined vocal cords. But it was nice. It reminded Jericho so much of who and how they'd once been. Who they'd given up being when Jericho had decided to go and be a hero without Sol, and Sol had taken another path. A path that had ultimately converged with his again. Merlin, it was fucked up how life worked sometimes.

"So, what now?" Jericho asked after a moment.

"Hmm?" Sol countered, brows raising as his fingers moved again. "Do you mean, like, what now between us? Or what now with the organization?"

Jericho eyed him blandly. "I know 'what now' between us. You aren't going fucking anywhere again. We're a team, the end. You good with that?"

Sol nodded eagerly.

"Perfect. So, what now with the organization? Team Eventide."

"Well." Sol's smile grew into a smirk, dimpling one cheek and lighting his eyes with that manic expression Jericho had decided he really quite liked—although he wasn't sure when he'd made that decision. "Now, I guess we topple the government of Mythikos."

"After you two idiots are healed," a voice said from the door. They both looked to see Ildri leaning against the frame. Her hair was brushed back into two buns on the top of her head—one blue, one pink—and although there were dark smudges staining the skin under her eyes, she looked more rested than she had in days.

"Right, of course," Sol agreed, a mock-serious expression settling onto his face. "Right after we're healed up."

Jericho frowned, narrowing his gaze on him. "You heard the lady. No plotting until we're both bandage-free."

"But Lettie, I can mastermind without getting myself into any more altercations," Sol whined.

"One: I don't believe that for a fucking second. Two: I don't give a shit. We rest for a while, and then we'll work on our next move." Jericho growled, eyes flashing with the wolf below the surface, pacing in its cage. Sol was his now, and they were going to protect him.

"Fine," Sol huffed, his shoulders sinking, thoroughly cowed into behaving.

"Jeez, if I knew all it would take to get you two to act with some sense was a mating bite, I'd have suggested it weeks ago!" Ildri laughed, bumping her hip against Sol's chair lightly. Sol turned a brilliant shade of red, scowling up at her, but she just laughed again and ruffled his dark hair.

The pair fell into playful bickering, and Jericho closed his eyes, listening. A slow smile twitched at his lips. Sol was safe. Jericho was safe. And in a few days, once they were healed up, they would get back to the fight.

An image flashed through his mind of two little boys, hand in hand, running down the street as they chased fireflies. Sol was in those stupid light-up sneakers that he loved so much. His cheeks were darker from the summer sun, and he'd gained at least five new freckles along his nose—Jericho had counted. But his eyes were the exact same color, lit with that intelligent sparkle that even at seven Jericho knew would change the world.

At some point, Ildri must have left, and when she did, Sol pressed Jericho's hip lightly, urging him to scoot over.

"What?" Jericho asked.

"I'm getting up there with you. I can't sleep in my bed, it's cold," Sol grumbled.

"Oof, fine." Jericho huffed, ignoring the pulling of his wound as he scooted over to the other side of the bed. "Just watch my stitches."

"They're on the other side, don't be a baby," Sol chided.

"You're a baby."

Sol snorted, resting his head on Jericho's shoulder as his arm curled over Jericho's waist, mindful of the injuries on his hip and abdomen. "Your baby."

Jericho choked, face flushing brightly. "Don't say shit like that!"

Sol snickered, pressing a kiss to Jericho's jaw. "Shut up. Sleep. In the morning, we change the world."

"Right. Love you," Jericho grumbled, his arms drawing Sol in tighter.

"I know."

Jericho chuckled softly, squeezing his eyes shut. "Not gonna say it back?"

"Don't have to."

"No, I guess you don't," Jericho mumbled, one hand lifting to rub at the slow warmth spreading through his chest where their bond resided. He didn't need Sol to say it. He could feel it there.

"Are you going to let me bite you next?"

"Yeah, with your blunt-ass banshee teeth. That'll work out great."

Sol sat up, and Jericho peeked one eye open to see the petulant look marring his face. "That seems unfair."

"I'll get a tattoo, how's that? One of those bond sealing ones with the blood and stuff."

Sol wrinkled his nose. "Gross."

"You don't want me to?"

"No, I do! But . . . gross." Sol mimicked gagging, and then he was laughing brightly. The sound filled the room around them, making it warm in a way it wouldn't have been without him.

"Seriously, shut the fuck up and go to sleep. Or you won't be changing shit in the morning." Jericho grunted.

"I hope I won't be changing shit in the morning," Sol mumbled, resting his head back on Jericho's shoulder.

"Cheeky fucker. Always have to have the last word, don't you?"

"Go to sleep, Lettie," Sol chastised, like an asshole.

Jericho huffed out another laugh and shut his eyes again before letting himself drift off to sleep. In the morning, there would be more fighting, and planning, and struggle. But right then, it felt nice just to have Dusk there and to know he was safe.

EPILOGUE

IT WAS FUCKING RAINING—AGAIN! SOL WAS SHIVERING BESIDE her, where they were tucked into the shadow of one of the taller buildings, watching the lights slowly turn off one by one in the office across the way. Jericho lifted her hand to scratch at the still healing skin of the tattooed bite mark on her neck. It had scabbed over a couple of days ago and had been itching like shit ever since.

"Leave it," Sol chided, grabbing her wrist to pull it away. "You'll ruin the lines."

Jericho grumbled, shaking Sol's grip off and pulling him into a tight hug under the overhang they'd decided to camp out beneath. She leaned in to press a kiss to the scarred mark on Sol's neck, and Sol lifted a shoulder to discourage the casual contact.

"Pay attention."

Jericho grunted but pulled back. "Fucking Merlin, don't these people ever go home?"

"They're workaholics." Sol shrugged. "Just like you."

"I am not a workaholic."

"Mhm," Sol hummed in obvious disagreement. His

fingers moved to tap at his jaw. "Pickle, how's it looking in there? We haven't seen anyone come out in a while."

"I don't see any signs of motion. Looks like they all went home, some idiot just left the lights on," Ildri muttered through their earpieces.

"Morons," Jericho growled. "What a waste of fucking energy."

"Well, add that to the list." Sol laughed. "You ready to head in?"

"Let me just give one last sweep," she murmured, lifting her head to sniff the air around them, focusing on the different scents lingering. Then, when the wolf determined it was safe, she nodded. "We're all clear. Let's go." She leaned in to steal a quick kiss before they headed for the ladder that would take their little team down to street level.

THE END

ACKNOWLEDGMENTS

First off, thank you—the reader—for reading this, and hopefully enjoying J and Dusk as much as I did. I really appreciate it, and I hope you'll drop a review on GoodReads to let me know what you think.

For those of you who may feel unsatisfied with the ending (if you're returning readers you should know me well enough by now) this is just the first book of J and Dusk's story. The next will be from Dusk's point of view, and I hope to have it out in 2022. So, keep an eye on my social media for future updates.

Next, I'd like the thank my small hoard of beta-readers. You guys gave some excellent insight, and I really appreciate all of your hard work. And my editor Meg for turning this into a story worth reading.

And last but certainly not least, thank you to my writing community. Particularly, Tiss, Elle, and Jasmine who I have known for near a decade now—without you there would be no Lou. And to my new friends, Candace, Melania, Nancy, Tanya, and Erin for being supportive and awesome.

ABOUT THE AUTHOR

 Born and raised in a small town near the Chesapeake Bay, Lou Wilham grew up on a steady diet of fiction, arts and crafts, and Old Bay. After years of absorbing everything, there was to absorb of fiction, fantasy, and sci-fi she's left with a serious writing/drawing habit that just won't quit. These days, she spends much of her time writing, drawing, and chasing a very short Basset Hound named Sherlock.

When not, daydreaming up new characters to write and draw she can be found crocheting, making cute bookmarks, and binge-watching whatever happens to catch her eye.

Learn more about Lou and her future projects on her website: http://louinprogress.com/ or join her mailing list at: http://subscribepage.com/mailermailer

facebook.com/LouWilham

instagram.com/lou.wilham

MORE BOOKS YOU'LL LOVE

If you enjoyed this story,
please consider leaving a review.

Then check out more books from
Midnight Tide Publishing!

The Rose and the Claw by Nancy O'Toole

A woman on a mission...

Rose Gardner never thought she'd leave the small town of West Ridge. But when her husband dies at war, she must return his arms to his place of birth to set his spirit to rest. After traveling into enemy territory, Rose falls into a trap. Held captive in an enchanted manor, she finds herself face to face with a beast who is equally horrifying and kind. Will she manage to complete her quest or be pulled in by the secrets of the manor?

A man haunted by his past...

Trapped within his own home and in the body of a hideous beast, Kris never wanted to share his prison with another. As much as Rose may draw him in with her beauty and stubborn strength, he knows she must escape before the next full moon. After all, he remembers all too well what happened to the previous caretaker.

The dead won't let him forget the blood on his hands.

Available on
8.4.21

Magical Mutant Nightmare Girl by Erin grammar

Fight like a magical girl in this paperback original contemporary fantasy in which a Harajuku fashionista battles mutants-and social anxiety-by teaming up with an elite group of outcasts. Perfect for those obsessed with the technicolor worlds of *Sailor Moon*, *The Umbrella Academy*, and the Marvel Cinematic Universe. Book One of the Magic Mutants Trilogy.

Holly Roads uses Harajuku fashion to distract herself from tragedy. Her magical girl aesthetic makes her feel beautiful-and it keeps the world at arm's length. She's an island of one, until advice from an amateur psychic expands her universe. A midnight detour ends with her vs. exploding mutants in the heart of San Francisco.

Brush with destiny? Check. Waking up with blue blood, emotions gone haywire, and terrifying strength that starts ripping her wardrobe to shreds? Totally not cute. Hunting monsters with a hot new partner and his unlikely family of mad scientists?

Way more than she bargained for.

Available Now

The P.A.N. by Jenny Hickman

Since her parents were killed, Vivienne has always felt ungrounded, shuffled through the foster care system. Just when liberation finally seems possible—days before her eighteenth birthday—Vivienne is hospitalized with symptoms no one can explain.

The doctors may be puzzled, but Deacon, her mysterious new friend, claims she has an active Nevergene. His far-fetched diagnosis comes with a warning: she is about to become an involuntary test subject for Humanitarian Organization for Order and Knowledge—or HOOK. Vivienne can either escape to Neverland's Kensington

Academy and learn to fly (Did he really just say fly?) or risk sticking around to become a human lab rat. But accepting a place among The PAN means Vivienne must abandon her life and foster family to safeguard their secrets and hide in Neverland's shadows... forever.

Available Now

Emma and the Tudor King by Natalie M

One moment, Emmie is writing her high school history paper; the next, she is lost in 16th century England, where she meets a dreamy Tudor king who vacillates from kissing her to ordering her execution.

Able to travel back to her own time but intensely drawn to King Nick and the mysterious death of his sister, Emmie finds herself solving the murder of a young princess and unraveling court secrets while trying to keep her head on her shoulders, literally.

With everything to lose, Emmie will come to face her biggest battle of all: How to cheat the path of history and keep her irresistible king, or lose him-and her heart-forever.

Available Now

CPSIA information can be obtained
at www.ICGtesting.com
Printed in the USA
BVHW031358250621
610447BV00005B/935